THE
GREAT
FROST

CHRIS SPECK
Copyright © 2021 Chris Speck
Flat City Press
Hull 2021
All rights reserved.

Somewhere in East Yorkshire yet lies the Pearlman's silver. Hidden within this book are three words. Put these into https://what3words.com/ to find it.

ISBN-13: 9781838127350

INTRODUCTION

The Great Frost of 1708-9 was the sharpest winter of the past 500 years. Setting in on the night of Christmas Day, temperatures in England plunged below -10C. Across the country, fish froze in ponds, bird numbers plummeted, and livestock perished in the bitter cold. To make matters worse, the wet summer that followed blighted harvests and created a scarcity of corn. These conditions created an economic downturn in Britain unmatched until the recent COVID-19 pandemic. Contemporary observers looked for explanations in the scientific, the sacred, and the stars. The frigid weather was even more destructive in Europe. Ports choked with ice and the canals of Venice froze. In the ongoing continental war, the campaign of the Duke of Marlborough against Louis XIV pressed on as the people of France faced famine.

The people of the East Riding, the smallest and most agricultural region of the vast county of Yorkshire were particularly susceptible to the Frost. When Daniel Defoe visited in 1720 – around the same time he published Robinson Crusoe, who embarked on his ill-fated voyage from Hull - he remarked that the Riding was 'very thin of towns', and also of people. The economy then was almost wholly dependent on farming, and very little has changed in the intervening centuries. The landscape of the rolling chalk Wolds remains dominated by the great houses of ancestral landowners with the estate villages built to support them. North Burton (or Cherry Burton as it is now known) stands around three miles from Beverley and is a typical Wolds village. With few natural building materials in the county, most of the vernacular houses in North Burton were reconstructed in the later eighteenth and nineteenth centuries. Victorian improvers also restored the church of St. Michael leaving little trace of the former medieval edifice. And whilst the outward face of North Burton changed, older traditions lingered on. As late as the

2

1890s, when the master of a house died their beehives were clothed in mourning to secure their future prosperity. It was believed that if the bees weren't informed of the death, with all due formalities, they would leave.

From folk customs to folk heroes, it was in the East Riding where England's most famous highwaymen was finally captured. In October 1738, Dick Turpin (alias John Palmer, as he was known in Yorkshire) was apprehended at Brough after shooting dead his landlord's cockerel and threatening to do the same to a witness. Poultrycide being a relatively minor crime, Turpin was only committed to the House of Correction at Beverley after refusing to raise a bond for keeping the peace. This raised suspicions, and evidence soon gathered about Turpin's lavish lifestyle supported by an illicit trade in stolen horses across the Humber. As the seriousness of his crimes came to light, he was sent for imprisonment in York, where he was famously betrayed by his penmanship. That city was also the destination of a mythic ride by another highwayman of the previous century. The Yorkshireman John (or sometimes, William) Nevison is said to have galloped 200 miles to York after committing a robbery in Kent. Arriving in the early evening, he secured his alibi by placing a wager on a bowls match in the presence of the Lord Mayor. The jury came to the verdict that Nevison couldn't possibly have been 'at two places so remote on one and the same Day'. Daring feats by these 'civil, obliging robbers' became enduring legends in the nineteenth century as epitomised by William Ainsworth's novel Rookwood, in which Turpin makes the audacious cross-country ride. Disentangling fact from fiction, both Nevison and Turpin ultimately suffered the same fate; they were hanged for their crimes on the Knavesmire in York.

Dr Daniel Reed
Hutton Cranswick
June 20

PROLOGUE

Beverley, East Riding of Yorkshire. March 1709

It's dark and bitter cold. The cartwheels creak as they roll over the cobblestones of Highgate towards The Minster. On a clear day, you can see the great towers from Park Lane, Cottingham and from the hill at Skidby, from Walkington too, but you can't see it from North Burton, that's where Carrick has travelled from. It has not been a long journey, just a few hours to the great church, but the frost and the snow have made it harder than it should have been. It's not supposed to be this cold in March. It's been a bad year so far.

He has brought two horses to pull the simple flat cart where he would normally have used just one, and he's wearing his heaviest winter clothes, two cloaks and a woollen hat, his breath makes steam in the cold night air. Beside him and nestled under one of the cloaks is the heavy-set German hunting dog with thick fur and piercing eyes. It rarely leaves his side, he calls it Bear. It may have had other names previous.

Carrick drives the cart down Highgate and turns left, he draws to a halt and a stable man swaddled in a big cloak steps out to greet him.

"What are you about, Sir?" he says in the darkness. His voice is high-pitched and simple.

"It's Carrick from Burton the North, come on business with The Curate, as asked."

"That was this morning," answers the man.

"I had an errand. I'm here now."

"It's too late, best you turn back to North Burton. The Curate will be in no mood to speak with you now."

"It's already late, and as I am God's servant, I ask you to help me do his work. I am to see him tonight." The stable hand tuts.

"Very well then, bring the horses inside." Carrick gives a

4

wry smile in the darkness. He should have been there this morning like every other rector, at the request of The Curate, but Carrick does not do as he's told. It's much more profitable if he does as he pleases, especially with all this ice. He clicks his tongue and the two horses walk the cart into the stables, the man closes the double doors behind him. Carrick gets down from the trap.

"Looks like you'll be spending the night," says the stable man.

"Aye," whispers Carrick. He has thick black hair with a roughly shaven face and is tall and broad with strong shoulders, like he's too big to be a rector. He looks down on the stable man in front of him.

"Is that your dog?" the man asks.

"Aye," says Carrick, "and you'd be advised not to go near him, or this cart, he'll have your hand off…" Carrick removes his hood to reveal his cold blue eyes, "…or your face." The man steps away. He's heard of this Carrick of North Burton. Someone you should avoid.

The big Rector moves up the ancient steps in the darkness without grace, he dips his head to go through the wooden door and into the grandeur of The Minster itself. The air is cold like it always is, colder than the frosty air outside. Even on a full-summer day, the air here is dead. At the far end of The Minster, there are lamps and voices. The Curate would have already said grace for the evening.

It is just as Carrick planned it.

He walks towards the north end and from the sides of the church, grotesque statues gurn down at him from the darkness, but Carrick does not need to worry about them, he has nothing to fear here, in God's house. His heavy feet clump on the stone and the little dagger strapped to his waist rattles in its scabbard. Just before the chapel at the back, he stops where a lamp lights the old moon face of The Curate. The man closes a big bible on the lectern in front of him and looks up,

5

he has a white beard and faint wisdom in his pale eyes.

"You were meant to attend this morning, Carrick," he says.

"Someone needed me. I came as soon as I could."

"You have missed the help I promised. It has already been given away." Carrick puts on his most pious face.

"We need the fuel as much as anyone." This is true. It has been a year like no other. The frost bit hard on Christmas Day and now, towards the end of March, the hard cold has not gone away. The people of the East Riding can prepare for winter, but they have not known a winter like this before, by now, there should be some respite, they should be out in the fields, but this year has been like nothing in memory. Fish have frozen in ponds, boats on the River Hull are as still as if they were in paintings, icicles have formed on thatched rooves, cracks have appeared in the bricks on the North Bar Gate that guards the entrance to the town, old men who should be alive are buried already, sheep have frozen to death in pastures.

"My parish deserves the coal like any other." The Minster in Beverley has promised coal and fuel for the poorest in the region, and a message was sent to the parishes to collect. Carrick here is late, by design.

"If you had been here this morning, Carrick, I could have helped." The dark-haired man looks down at his boots.

"There was a boy. I needed to attend to him." Carrick should address his elder with more reverence.

"Could you not have had another do your duty in your stead?"

"Not for the duty I had to perform. I am here now. I do the lord's work." The old man scoffs at this.

"I know you, Carrick, God's work is whatever you want it to be. I have told you already, there is no more coal left for you at North Burton. It's all gone."

"There is another matter." The old man takes a breath in through his nose and sighs as he picks up the book.

"Yes?"

"The cold, do you think it is a sign?"

"A sign of what?"

"A new beginning?"

"Speak plainly, Carrick."

"We know that the devil uses fire and heat in the pits of hell. What say you of this frost?"

"I do not know."

"I believe it is a judgement. The cold purifies and cleanses the filth. The insects no longer plague us. The fleas and lice have frozen solid. The stench from the unwashed is gone. What are your thoughts on this?" The old man steps down closer to this big, intense and dark man.

"This is no time for cheap words, Carrick. This is a cold winter. People suffer and die. We do not need to stir up fear. There is no need to call upon evil to explain it, that is the nature of the dark arts, not the scriptures."

"Do you deny it then, that the cold has come to freeze out the worst of us, to make pure that which was once filth?" The old man steps nearer still and his voice turns to a whisper.

"You speak like a fool." Here is advice. The Curate is a man of God but he is a man also, not a zealot. Carrick makes his voice a whisper as well.

"I can spread such ideas wide across Beverley and the East Riding, there are men on the edge of starvation who would follow me. Not just here in Beverley but the villages also, in Kingston Upon Hull too." The Curate moves closer yet to Carrick so his face is only an inch away.

"You do not scare me, boy," he whispers. Carrick pulls his cloak to the side to reveal the handle of the dagger in his belt.

"I should. You know what kind of man I am and I know what kind of man you are. You'll do whatever it takes to keep the peace because peace keeps men safe."

"God will deal with you, Carrick. You'll be punished for the wicked things you have done and will do."

"Better make your decision quickly old man."

"You'll have your coal, Carrick."

"I will have double."

"One and a half times only,"

"Agreed.' The Curate is not the only one who wants to make a profit from this.

They load the coal that night, and in the early morning Carrick rides it out through the North Bar. He has more than a half as much as he should. It's alms for the poor and destitute, for those who cannot heat their hearths and squalid wattle houses.

Carrick will charge more than the going rate for a bag - much more.

CHAPTER ONE

It's bitter. It's been bitter for months. Not the normal frost of winter - this is something else. It should be nearly spring but no sunlight gets through the clouded grey sky. Meg carries her bucket of ice past the row of four cottages to the door on the end. She pauses for a minute to look at the ruined alehouse building opposite, with the roof all covered in snow. The door hangs off its rusted hinges in front of cold darkness inside. It's been closed a while since. Once upon a time, the people of North Burton sat inside The Bay Horse on a white-Sunday drink up or Christmas Day after service, or harvest festival in October. They went there after Meg got married. They went there when Nana's old man died too.

When the snow first came to North Burton in late November there were smiles all round, Little Richie and Archer Farthing spent all day making snowmen and throwing snowballs. Adam Gamble and Julia Farthing went up to Etton hill for some sledging, and there was good cheer for a bit of snow.

Not so now.

Christmas was frozen solid, and in mid-January, Nana said the cold was sure to lift. At the start of February, Mr Pennyman of the estate told, in church one Sunday morning, that the snow was soon to melt away. By the end of February when the ice was still there, nobody had the heart to say anything at all. Carrick, the huge Rector up at St Michael's, warned his congregation that the cold was their fault – it was to clean away their sins.

Now it's March.

Nobody plays snowballs or wants to go sledging. Richie does not want to make snowmen. The ice and cold are just a pain, a dreadful, dangerous pain. Rooves have fallen in under the weight of snowfall, they've dragged sheep frozen to death from fields, one of the small ponies in Mr Pennyman's livery yard died a few nights back, even when you stand right next to a fire you feel cold, even when you're wearing all the clothes you own.

Meg steps inside the last, run-down cottage and closes the door. Inside the tiny front room, in a high-backed wooden chair next to the open fireplace, is an old woman wrapped in blankets and wearing a grey headscarf. Her face is flabby and big, and her cheeks droop from age. This is Nana. She doesn't like to get up. A little boy of about four is breaking pieces of wood with an axe that is too big for him, he is Richie. When one of the serving girls at the Pennyman House had a baby on the cowshed floor and died, Mr Pennyman said that the child should be laid to rest with its mother. Nana wouldn't have that and so, Richie is her boy.

"What has Richie got now?" asks Meg. She means the wood.

"It's that little chest from upstairs," says the old woman. "Better it's on the fire. It's no use up there."

"That was worth something, Nana. Your old man said it came from a pirate ship that plundered the south seas." The old woman wafts her hand in thin air.

"He was full of nonsense that old bugger. He lied about everything, especially to you. He always thought a story would make things better. What a bloody fool." Since her husband died, Nana has revealed a seemingly endless list of the man's faults. Meg sets the bucket away from the fire and takes out handfuls of ice to put into the black pot hanging over the weak flame. "Not too much," snaps Nana. "You have to fill it up slowly." Meg has melted ice before, but this is Nana's house, her husband who she calls her old man, passed many years previous, he wouldn't have lasted long in the cold anyway, not like Nana. She'll see this out, however hard it gets.

Meg takes the axe from the little boy and begins to break wood from the old chest. Her hands are strong and rough from work like any village girl. Richie sits on the bottom of the ladder that leads upward to the shelf that they used to sleep on. They live in one room now. There's no point in going up the ladder – it doesn't have a fire or any fresh straw. On the ground floor, as well as Nana's chair there is a wooden bench against the wall with a carved backrest. They have debated whether to burn it but then there would be nowhere to sit, and Nana was given this as a wedding present by Mr Pennyman elder who died many years before even her old man.

Nana rarely gets up these days owing to the pain in her legs and the boy sleeps curled up on Meg's lap at night. In the day she gathers what food and fuel she can as well as looking after the chickens and big sows up at The Pennyman Estate farm. A month back Granddad Blackwood next door butchered a goat and it fed them for a good long time. Nana is mean with portions. They grind down bones to eat, boil leaves, steal eggs from the Pennyman farm when they can. Meg feeds bits of wood to the flames so they heat the pot. She's lucky. They're all lucky. At least they have a roof over their heads, even if it is thick with snow. A black cat creeps along the side of the room towards Nana and the old woman moves her foot as if to kick at it, but she would never try too hard.

"Bloody Dutch cat," she curses. "Always on the scrounge. The way it looks at you like it knows something." They were given the animal when the alehouse across the road closed for good last year; the landlord's wife was a Walloon woman. Meg thinks the cat is probably deaf, but Nana is convinced that it only reacts to commands in Dutch. "We shouldn't have taken it in," she mutters.

"I need to go and see my mother," says Meg as she chops the wood.

"I'm your mother now. You live under my roof and it's too late in the day, you'll get lost. What if it snows?"

Meg comes from a village two miles from North Burton called Etton. There's an old church there with a squat tower, a few cottages and a blacksmith. It's been some weeks since

Meg visited, and her mother is all alone, of course there are people to look out for her, she's part of the village, but Meg wants to see the woman with her own eyes. Her mother is sometimes called the cunning woman, that's not to mean anything bad, like Meg's grandmother, she can heal. She can set bones and knows when to use wild carrot for breathing problems, she can sew up nasty cuts, make a compress, she can deliver a baby or a piglet, and she can mix pastes and ointments to make things that are poorly well again. She's taught Meg a great deal of what she knows already.

"My mam needs me," says the young woman.

"Me and Richie need you," answers Nana. "You've got responsibilities here, Meg, you married my lad and now you have to make good on your promises. Everyone's struggling can't you see, it's the worst winter anyone has ever known." Nana has a gift for going on and on, and even though Meg wants to leave for a few hours only, listening to the old woman it's as if she is off to the colonies over the sea, never to return. Nana continues now she's got started:

"When my boy gets back from the fighting, you'll see what he brings. We'll buy a pig from Farmer Thorne, the biggest and plumpest of the lot. We'll invite everyone round, The Blackwoods, the Gambles too and even them Farthings. Richie here will have one of the ears and we'll make black pudding, just like we used to do when I was a young lass. You'll see my Meg; you'll see what happens when my boy gets home. You'll see that there's good times here in North Burton. Just wait till my boy gets back, then you'll see."

His name is John. Meg was never in love with him like you hear in silly stories that girls tell, there was no time for that. They were married in the summer and lived in the upstairs platform in the bed that is long gone to the fire. Meg was meant to be pregnant by harvest time but it did not transpire. Maybe it was Meg's fault. Maybe that's why, when her new husband got wind of soldiers needed for the Duke of

Marlborough's army on the continent, he walked to Beverley and caught a black carriage to York to enlist. He would be away six months he said, it's been four summers since. Meg would not be surprised if he never came back. There's nothing much to come back to.

There's a thump on the door.

"If it's that Granddad Blackwood asking for wood, tell him to piss off," says Nana. She does not mean this.

"You can tell him yourself," says Meg. She stands, opens the front door, and the man outside hurries in. It is Miles Blackwood. He is their neighbour, a little man with a big grey moustache, a heavy cloak over his shoulders and a battered top hat. He has red cheeks and dumb eyes with his teeth clenched – like always. Miles Blackwood caught a chill and a fever last winter, and his jaws have been locked shut since then. Meg has tried to help him with what her mother taught her to no avail. He mashes his food up and pushes it through the gap in his back teeth and dribbles when he speaks sometimes. If you didn't know, the state of him might put you on edge, but this is North Burton. This is how people look.

"What's your business?" asks Nana. She can afford to be rude to Miles Blackwood because they know each other so well.

"It's Carrick up at the church, he's got coal." If you could imagine a rat speaking, this is how Miles Blackwood sounds. Through his teeth tight together and his nose. "Alms for the poor it is, all the way from Beverley." Meg steps back and reaches for her heavy cloak.

"How much?" asks Nana.

"It's alms for the poor," replies Miles Blackwood. His teeth are rotten, and he stinks even in the cold.

"Nothing in this world is free, Miles Blackwood. That Carrick is a piece of work if I've ever seen one. If there's a profit to be had, he'll achieve it. Meg, come here." She steps towards the old woman while Nana struggles at the side of her

13

chair and reaches under her bum. Meg can see the fat blade of a carving knife and a little leather money pouch, Nana opens this and pulls out a coin. A penny. "Take this, Meg. Get us as much as you can." Nana presses the money into her palm and Miles Blackwood stands looking at the old woman in his daft way. He doesn't mean anything by it.

"If you ever even thought about stealing this money Miles Blackwood, I would cut you open from your neck to your belly button." Nana means it. She could probably do it too if she got herself angry enough.

"I'll be as quick as I can," says Meg. "Richie, keep the fire going." The lad nods.

Outside, Meg follows Miles Blackwood down the line of four little cottages on the village street of frozen over mud. The houses can be described thus: Nana Jackson's is at the far end next door to The Blackwoods, two men who are as stupid as they are strong, then the Farthings – horse people and newcomers from Essex and finally, The Gambles, Adam Gamble and his bedridden father and mother. Opposite is the pub, The Bay Horse with its roof caved in from the first big snow in November, the low windows are dark. Like most buildings in North Burton, apart from the Pennyman House and the church opposite, they look like a strong gust of wind could blow them down at any moment.

Waiting outside the last house is Adam Gamble with his thin face and clever eyes. He's twelve, but easily smarter than anyone in North Burton already. Adam is too young to be the sexton up at St Michael's, but his father is too old to do it now, so it's young Adam who digs the graves, rings the bells and sweeps the floor. The three of them make their way along the main street of North Burton, past the frozen up well pump and the large duck pond to the hill. The huge Pennyman House is on the left with a big iron fence in front between red brick walls. It's as grand as the rest of the houses are shabby.

When there's a summer fair, Mr Pennyman opens the gardens up to the rest of the village. It's a magical place for a woman like Meg, with a lake, a little stream and hanging oriental lanterns. Behind that, is the livery yard and the farm, acres of fields and a wood next to the north drain. The three of them keep on towards St Michael's. Meg wraps her heavy cloak over her nose and her green eyes show in the cold.

"What about the Farthings?" she asks. "Did you tell them too?" Adam Gamble nods.

"They said they'd rather go alone. Typical Farthing," he adds. Meg does not say anything. It's much easier if everyone is your friend.

At the bottom of more steps, Meg stops and narrows her eyes at the door of the Norman church up above. She has seen the grandeur of The Minster in Beverley and it makes St Michael's look small, but here, against the winter sky and the three-week-old ice crunching under their feet, even the cold church seems inviting. The window of one end glows orange from a fire within. There's a bark and growl and the side door of the church opens to reveal a figure dressed in black with a floppy hat of the same colour. It's Carrick. Next to him and without a leash is the German hunting dog. Its fur is dark and thick, the animal's ears are back and it's snarling already as the three workers make their way up to him. Carrick grins as he sees the figures.

"I saw you coming, my children. What is it you heard?" He has a powerful voice and is a good singer. If you didn't know better, you might think you could trust him. The Gamble lad speaks up:

"Alms for the poor. We heard you had coal?" Carrick's head cocks in sadness as he tuts. As the sexton's son, Adam should really have been given a bag already, a perk of his job, but Carrick is not like that.

"I did have. It's all gone. Mr Pennyman took some and Farmer Thorne, more has gone to the parish at Etton and I have a few bags for myself."

"It's alms for the poor," says Adam. That means it should go to those without any money, not Farmer Thorne or The Pennyman House or Carrick and his nasty eyed dog. Meg hangs back with the cloak over her face, she knows that charity is the guilt of the rich. To give, you should not understand what money is, or how you come by it. There'll be no charity from Carrick - he knows too much about the world.

"I would gladly give you what I have," he booms, "but as I say, I have none left." Meg steps forward with the penny in her palm. She's no trader but neither is she a fool.

"We have money, Rector. I wonder if I could trade for as much coal as that would allow." Meg speaks earnest across at him. Carrick grins and shows his yellow teeth under his clean-shaven face. You should never trust a man without a beard, Meg's father used to say, it means he has too much time on his hands and thinks too much of himself to boot.

"It would be a half-penny a bag." Too high a price. It is a fine balance she has to achieve. She can't be seen to be too clever or too pushy, that will make Carrick notice her. She doesn't want to be noticed – she just wants the coal. Meg prepares herself to speak again but Miles Blackwood cuts in:

"We have a full penny," he says with his jaw set tight in a grimace and his daft, battered top hat. He says the obvious like a dim wit. Meg wishes she could slap him.

"A penny?" says Carrick as he steps forward, intrigued. "Where would you get a penny?"

"From Miss Charlotte Pennyman, last Christmas Eve, a gift. We all got one." says the Gamble lad, Adam. It's not beyond the truth, Miss Charlotte has an easy ear for those less fortunate than herself. Adam Gamble is quick and sharp. He did not know that Meg has a penny in her rough hands, but he does now.

"A penny would get you a whole bag," says Carrick.

"I thought you said there was none left?" It's Adam

16

Gamble again – he must be careful not to be too clever also.

"As if you really had a penny," huffs The Rector.

"We do," says Blackwood with his head on an angle. "The lass has a penny – give it up to The Rector, Meg." The two figures of Blackwood and Adam separate to reveal Meg behind. She stands taller than both of them and lets the scarf fall from her face. Carrick holds out his big hand, palm up, the fingers are strong and dirty.

"Let's have it then, if you want that bag of coal." She bows her head as she approaches and stretches out her hand with the coin between finger and thumb. She lets it fall into Carrick's palm and prays that Adam Gamble will not work out that a penny should fetch them two bags according to Carrick's first figure. She glances at the boy and he gives a kind of clever grin, with a sharp look in his eye like he has pulled one over on Carrick, even though it is the other way round several times over. Meg does not care, as long as they get something to heat the houses. What does money matter if you are frozen to death?

With a swoosh of his black cloak, Carrick turns and makes towards the side door of St. Michael's church. He calls over his shoulder to the three wretches:

"The last of the coal is over there," he motions over to the cart he drove to Beverley the day before. A light line of ice and snow has gathered on top of the three bags of coal that are stacked at the back. Adam Gamble steps forward but Carrick's grizzly hunting dog, Bear, growls through its long white canines with its ears back. Carrick gives a click and the dog follows him, under the back wheels of the cart is a long metal cage, he opens the door and the dog goes inside as he closes the catch. Looking out from behind the bars, the big dog's eyes are wild and orange.

"Bear here will bark if anyone comes near and I'm not around." Carrick makes it sound like this is a good thing. He's not been in North Burton long, perhaps a little less than two years. Already there are whispers about him, that he doesn't know the scriptures properly, that Mr Pennyman does not like his grotesque sermons, and that he treats those that work for him badly. Adam Gamble's father Nicholas can testify to this although he would not. Carrick was a hard taskmaster and cruel with it, no job was ever done quite to his standard. It broke the old man. Now Carrick is doing the same to his son Adam.

Blackwood walks to the cart and pulls one of the bags onto his shoulders. His legs give way and he staggers at the weight, Meg steps forward to take the load off him and onto her own shoulder. Adam notices a few stray lumps of coal under the bags, he quickly slips them in his pockets. He's a good, smart lad but he needs help with his counting. Meg makes off down the steps with the heavy bag on her right shoulder and her legs taking the strain.

Somehow, it's always Meg's job, whatever job that may be.

"You were meant to get two bags," says Nana. Her jowly face is red. "A penny should have fetched two bags at least, maybe three. In my day, a penny would have got you the whole bastard cart." It's not like Nana to swear, at least not in company. Meg hangs her head. Adam Gamble has gone home but Miles Blackwood stands next to her in the tiny room. The bag of coal is against the wall. "Damn it, Meg. If I could have gone there myself, I would have grabbed that bloody Carrick by his ears and boxed him into next week." Nana's flabby fist swings in the air in front of her. "It's not like I couldn't do it neither. Walkington Show, it was, 1685." Not this again. "I was picked for the wrestling I was, and I bested those big Walkington lads as well, and I've outlived them." This is a familiar story. Thankfully, Nana has been brief. Richie squats in the corner with his black hair over his blue eyes, he has a blanket across his shoulders and somehow, Dutchy the cat has managed to get in to snuggle next to him. Nana is not really angry, this is just one of her occasional storms, but it's dampened very much by the fact that they have a full bag of coal that will heat the house for a few days. The old woman looks down at her knees and then back up at the two of them. Miles Blackwood produces a lump of coal from his pocket and his teeth are still clenched together in his dumb lockjaw. He tries to grin. Nana gives him a scowl.

"I want you to split the bag and divide it up, Meg. Half for us and a half for the Blackwoods here. There's no point in having a nice warm house if your neighbour freezes. I couldn't stand it." Meg begins on the bag and Blackwood produces a sack from one of his pockets, she carefully fills it with the black gold.

"And make sure there's some for them Gambles," she adds.

That's Nana all over.

She's as mean as they come. Nasty as the raw wind from over the Wolds. Bitter as rhubarb. Like a wasp sting, and then, when it really matters, she's the only one who cares at all.

When Blackwood has gone, Meg makes the fire and they don't build it too big – that would be foolish, but they get it going just enough to warm their faces. Meg boils up water in the pot and they drink it from their wooden cups while Nana tells a story of the fair that used to come to Walkington. She tells Richie about the things you can see there – great bears and jugglers in bright costumes and tall Nubian men with dark beards, dwarves and giant lads from Europe, colourful birds from the New World and as much bright sunshine as you could handle, so your skin turns as brown and as smooth as a fresh mahogany conker. There's an easiness to the house tonight, with the warmth from the fire on their faces. If Nana is in a good mood, then everybody is.

Richie falls asleep on Meg's knee and wakes when there's a dull thud at the wooden door. Nana looks up. It's late. Meg swaps places with Richie and goes to answer it. He has not come far. It's Granddad Blackwood from next door and his face is dirty. He doesn't take off his tatty cap as he steps inside and Meg shuts the door behind him.

"Nana," he nods in greeting.

"What the bloody hell do you want, this time of night?" They call him Granddad Blackwood even though he is the father of Miles Blackwood. He looks old and has lost most of his teeth. From under his jacket, he pulls out a square of cloth and passes it to Meg who gives it to Nana. Then he puts his hand on the door, nods at the women and steps back outside into the cold.

Nana opens the material – it's food. A rabbit's leg. She knows how to cook it right and they boil it slowly in the water above the fire. The smell is sweet in the little room and it wakes Richie. He moves over to the fire and watches the piece of bone rattle in the pot. Nana cuts the leg into threes with her sharp knife when it's done, and they drink the water it boiled in like tea.

That's how it works in North Burton.

Nana won't see the Blackwoods freeze and they won't see her starve. If it wasn't like that, they'd all be dead; every one of them.

They let the fire burn down as the night sets in proper. It begins to snow outside and sucks all the warmth and air from the darkness. Meg peers through the tiny gaps in the window shutters and she can see nothing but black. It's March. It should not be like this. There should be a nip of cold, but not driving snow. She has heard Miss Charlotte up at the Pennyman house say it is The Great Frost. That's what they call it in York and London and in the cities on the continent far away.

The fire is just embers in the hearth and Nana lightly snores under the blanket wrapped over her shoulders. Meg is awake still, with Richie on her chest. He's warm but he can wriggle sometimes. She thinks about her husband, John, somewhere off in the world, perhaps he's warm, perhaps he's happy, or both. They have not had any news all this time. It's not like John knew how to write in any case.

There is a single light thump on the wooden door and a weight falls against it outside so the latch takes the pressure. Meg looks up and there's another single thump. It is eerie, this sound in the darkness of the still winter night. She glances at Nana asleep across from her and moves Richie to the side. The noise has not woken them, it was too soft to be rousing. She moves to the door in the darkness and thinks to whisper through, but she's got a feeling that she might know who is behind. It could be him, the man she married, it could be John. For a moment, she does not want to open the door, she does not know how she feels about him and the words of her thin mother back in Etton over the hill ring in her ears. "I never loved your father, Meg, that's not what marriage is about."

She swallows and opens up.

A tall figure staggers through and she catches him before he falls. He is wrapped in a heavy cloak and with a black scarf over his nose and mouth so that just his eyes show under his battered and snow-covered tricorn hat. Meg stumbles backwards as he drops. Like his thumps on the door, even in this movement there seems to be grace, as if he does not want to make too much noise. As soon as he is inside on the floor, Meg closes the door gently and looks at the figure laid out in the darkness, who, miraculously has not made a single sound. She squats down in the darkness and the cold, her hand goes to the back of his neck and his face. He turns slightly and she can sense he is in pain. The eyes she can only just make out wince in agony.

"John," she whispers. "Is that you?"

The mere mention of her son's name is enough to wake Nana though she will sleep through a strange bang on the door. Meg leans closer and gets a sense of the visitor by his size and the black hair spilling out of his hat. This is a taller man than John. There's a different energy to him also. Nana calls out in the darkness like she is in a dream:

"John, oh John, you've come back. I knew you would. I told her, I said to Meg every day that you'd come home to your Nana." Meg pulls the visitor up, and with his help sets him sitting against the wall. Nana fiddles with a candle in the embers of the fire and a single flame lights up the darkness, Meg takes it from the old woman and holds it over the figure's face as he pulls down his scarf.

"That's not John," barks Nana. Meg sees the beginnings of a beard on the man's smooth skin and his eyes flash in worry. She smells a rich and heavy aroma on him and lowers the candle to where the dark man holds his hand over the left of his stomach. Oily black blood runs through his fingers.

"He's hurt," whispers Meg.

"Toss him out into the snow," orders Nana. Richie wakes and pulls a blanket over his head when he sees the man. Dutchy has not heard a thing, but at the sight of someone she doesn't know, she clambers off into the roof. "Take him by his ear and chuck him out the door, Meg. Hurt or not, this isn't a poorhouse, if he's been shot then it's his own bloody fault." Meg looks at the old woman and narrows her eyes, even in the flickering darkness, Nana can sense the disapproval in her daughter-in-law. Her jowly face quickly recalculates. "Check through his pockets before you do, there might be a piece of bread or a lump of cheese."

There's a click in the darkness next to him, and the candlelight catches the shiny metal of the pistol he holds gently in his right hand. Meg has never seen one like this before and her eyes examine the details, the silver flintlock and the long, dark metal barrel inlaid in wood. It's beautiful. The man does not point it at anyone, rather, uncocks the flintlock with his thumb and then, slow with pain, passes it to Meg. She takes the handle and the smooth mahogany is heavy in her hands, it's warm.

"He means us no harm, Nana," she whispers. The old woman struggles for her carving knife under her big arse, just in case. The man finds it difficult to speak.

"The wound will not kill me," his voice is a rasp, his accent familiar somehow. Meg leans into him to listen. "Hide me here and I will pay you well," he says, "when I am able." Nana brings out the knife though she is far away. It's more to make a better show than anything else. She looks him up and down. The dull leather boots, the fingerless gloves, the black scarf that was over his face.

"You're a robber," she says.

"Aye," he whispers, "but when they have more than they need, who is to say I'm in the wrong." This is common sense from those that steal and is repeated in the pirate ports of the Caribbean all the way to the inns of York. Nana frowns. This robber has a point already. "I hid a pouch some hours before on the road upon the hill. There are enough silver crowns in there to feed you for a year. I promise half of them to you if I am alive to retrieve them."

"You said your wound wouldn't kill you," says Nana.

"Not right away," he answers.

"Who did you rob?" The man struggles to take a breath.

"A coach on the road to York."

"How many of you?"

"Just I."

"You're lying. Robbers work in threes, they always have." Nana does not know this to be true for sure, but she heard it said and sung in the highwayman song they sometimes do when there's a big drink up.

"Just I," he whispers. "I jumped the driver and took his pouch and I would have taken more but he was too quick. He dealt me a blow to my stomach here with his knife. They left me for dead in the snow. Like you, he must have thought there were more of me."

"You've got his pouch?"

"Aye. There must be twenty guineas in there." Richie wrinkles his nose. It doesn't make any sense to him how much it's worth. Dutchy, the black cat, looks down on The Robber from her rafter with worried wide eyes.

"How much is a guinea, Nana?" he asks. Nana says that if you don't ask you don't find out.

"A guinea's 21 shillings," she answers. Richie still does not really know how much that is. "20 shillings makes a pound." Richie knows that a pound is a lot of money. Meg makes two pounds for a whole year of work at the Pennyman House.

"Pass me the pistol, Meg." Nana takes the heavy gun in her fat hand and inspects it. The mechanism has been oiled and it smells of black powder. Unlike Meg, Nana has seen one of these before – it's worth something, perhaps more than a few crowns if you know who to sell it to.

"Show me his boots, Meg." The blonde woman lights up the Robber's shoes. His feet are big and the leather is scuffed but without holes. Meg holds the candle back up to his face. His eyes are bleak and he cannot hold his head up straight.

"Can you hear me, Robber?" Nana asks.

"Aye," he whispers as the strength drains from him.

"If you live, we'll have the guineas and the silver you stole. If you die, we'll have your pistol and your boots. Have you got anything else?" The Robber nods to his chest pocket. Meg feels inside and draws out a small brown glass bottle with a cork in the top. "Pass it over here," says Nana. Almost as soon as she has it in her fat fingers, the cork is out and she empties the lot into her mouth. Her throat gulps and she returns her face to the man on the floor with the stab wound in his stomach. "Brandy," she whispers. Nana spits in her right hand and holds it out to the man to seal the deal. He tries to move but cannot, so Meg feels for his right hand and holds it up in front of Nana for her to grab.

They shake on it.

Meg catches the limp hand as it falls and the man's head slumps into his neck. He's out cold.

There's silence in the candlelight as the three of them look at each other. Little Richie from under his blanket, Nana with a slight brandy grin, Meg knelt on the floor in front of The Robber. Duchy senses the trouble has passed and drops to the back of the bench, her eyes are still wide in the darkness. It must be the middle of the night and somehow, they have made a deal with a robber straight out of nowhere. Meg holds up the candle to the man's face with his eyes closed. She glances at Nana.

"Don't look at me like that," she says to Meg. "It's opportunity. You know how it works. You find a rabbit caught in a thorn bush and you eat it up. That's how it is." Meg is not judgmental, she knows this. Nana feels like she has to justify everything she does, probably more for her own benefit. "That's what it is living in the country. You don't know what it's like when things get difficult," continues Nana. Meg feels the neck of The Robber and for the pulse that will tell her how weak he really is. He is already cold.

"If he is a highwayman, and any Pennyman finds him here, we'll be hung with him," says Meg. There's no anger in her voice. It's just the truth. Nana fidgets in her chair.

"We'll tell them he did something unnatural to us, or that he threatened to." Meg looks at the man.

"What happens when he dies?" she asks. "Where will we put the body? You know what it's like here. Everyone knows everything about everyone." Meg has the steel of reason on her side. Nana hasn't thought it through.

"It was you that wanted to help him," she snaps. "It was you that let the bugger in." Meg doesn't need to be told that it's her fault because it's always her fault. She stands and goes to the side of The Robber, puts her hands under his armpits and begins to drag him to the foot of the ladder.

"What are you doing with him?" asks Nana.

"I'm taking him up. I'll lay him next to the chimney breast for the warmth. Tomorrow I'll check the wound when it's light." Nana grunts.

"Don't think you're getting any help from me," she huffs.

Meg manages to get him onto her shoulders and then climbs the first rung of the ladder, she has carried pigs before like this, but with a prone body, it's not the same. Though he's tall, The Robber doesn't weigh as much as you might imagine. She dreads to think what the movement might do to the wound on his stomach, but she has no choice.

When she gets him up top, she sets him on his side around the chimney breast like she said, with his hat as a pillow and his black cloak over him like a blanket. Richie lights her way with a candle and Dutchy walks in front and around them with her tail up like she's something important. Meg tucks The Robber in and looks down at his smooth face, he might be thirty or even forty. He has crow lines at the side of both eyes. She looks under his top lip at his teeth and they are white and well kept. He takes care of himself, this highwayman. Meg feels his head and he is cold.

If he's still alive in the morning it will be a miracle.

When Meg gets downstairs, Nana is already snoring. She sits on the bench by the wall and little Richie clambers onto her knee as she sits down. He's cold and afraid. Dutchy appears on the bench and squeezes up next to the lad.

"Nothing for you to be worrying about, Richie, me boy." She rubs his little head as he rests it on her chest. "Nothing for you to fret on," she whispers. "You know your old Nana, she always gets it right in the end."

CHAPTER TWO

It's first light, only just grey. Dutchy lays on her stomach at the back of the little room, her green eyes fix on a tiny mouse hole in the corner and her shoulders are up. She is ready to pounce. The long winter has been easy for the black cat, the cold forces dormice inside and they will take bigger risks to get at the crumbs that Nana drops from the side of her high-backed wooden chair.

Meg moves Richie from her knee on the bench, covers him with a blanket and reaches under to her cloth bag. Just like her mother showed her, this is where she keeps herbs and a knife, twine and patches of cloth, moss - things you might need to heal or help. Clutching it in one hand, she creeps up the ladder to The Robber.

On the last rung, she can smell him, sweat mixed with the rich aroma of blood. The floorboards creak under her weight. It's still dark upstairs but there's light peeping between the gaps in the thatched roof where ice has fallen through, she moves over him and his face is pale, but not white. Gently, she rolls him onto his back using his shoulder. Now she can see him. There's a heavy black cloak that covers his chest and Meg undoes the clasp at his neck. Below, is a quality dark blue blouse that stretches across his big body and down to his hip. She glances to the boots that Nana was so impressed with and sees that they are well made, scuffed but also clean. He is well dressed. There's a brown leather strap across his chest too with an empty sheath where a rapier might have fit and next to that, the holster where the pistol sits yet. There's an expensive-looking knife tucked into his belt.

Meg's fingers go to the wound at his left side, just above the hip where the material is sticky. There's no way to pull the cloth of his shirt away because it is tucked in tight to his belt. She goes to her bag, removes her knife then cuts a hole in the material, careful, like the cloth is his flesh, then pulls it back to reveal the injury. The wound is a large hole and has ripped some with movement. Dried blood is caked around the edges but it's open. Meg will need to sew it up if he is ever to get better. Back in Etton, her mother showed her how to stitch cuts on horse's legs and cows, she showed her what leaves would numb the pain and how to make sure the flesh knits back together. Meg has set bones and pierced boils but she's never sewn up a wound as big as this before, and never on a man.

Downstairs, Meg makes the fire and blows the flames back into action. On a metal spoon, she boils her big sewing needle and some hemp twine. Nana stirs behind.

"What are you doing?" asks the old woman.

"It's your Robber," says Meg. "I'm sewing him up. He's got a stab hole the size of Granddad Blackwood's gob."

"He's not my Robber, he's yours if he belongs to anyone. You let him in," Nana wipes the sleep from her wrinkled face. "We might as well let him die anyway, Meg. You can say he broke in and I stabbed him." Meg looks at Nana's grey, drooping eyes. They both know this is not any sort of a plan, and that Nana doesn't believe it anyway. It would be impossible for her to mean everything she said. Meg stands up with the needle and the twine in her finger and thumb.

"Best we fix him and he walks out of here on his own two feet. Then I don't give a toss where he dies."

"After we get our money," adds Nana. Meg stops.

"Maybe I could go up to the house, find Danny Reed and we could tell him what happened." Danny Reed is Mr Pennyman's coachman and just recently, a constable of the peace, meaning it's he who makes sure the folks of North Burton follow the laws. He's new to the village and has a lax attitude that has allowed him to gain friends. "We could say he knocked on the door and we let him stay for Christian charity." Meg has been brought up to believe it's always best to be honest. Nana shakes her head, she knows better.

"It wouldn't go well, Meg. We'd get pulled into it somehow. People like us are easy for Mr Pennyman to blame. Think about the future. They'd be nobody in North Burton would trust us again. Poor folk deal with poor folk. That's the way it is."

"Have you seen what he's wearing? His socks alone are probably worth a guinea," says Meg.

"He's poor, just like we are."

"How can you be sure?"

"I can just tell. Don't you think, if he were someone with brass, he'd have gone up to the Pennyman House or Farmer Thorne's place? Oh no. He came to the first run down poor cottage he saw – here."

Meg goes back up the ladder and to The Robber laid prone next to the chimney breast. At the wound, she kneels, takes the needle, and threads it in the grey light. The face of The Robber is calm, it's a good job he's unconscious, otherwise, this would sting. Meg does not waver as she goes at the stitching, it's best to just get started with such a task and the needle complains against the flesh and muscle of his stomach. She works quickly and uses the diamond shape stitch that her mother taught her, keeping the twine tight. It takes time and patience to do a good job. Richie has clambered up, and stands behind her, looking at the neat line in The Robber's stomach that she is sewing together. Dutchy has been watching too, her stomach to the floorboards and her shoulders hunched with her triangle ears pointing up straight. She can smell The Robber too but unusually for her, she's not afraid.

"Will he live?" asks the little lad.

"Aye, if you pray for him." Meg knows that praying won't do any good at all.

"I will," says Richie. He stands the same height as Meg though she is kneeling and his big eyes look like they are about to cry. The boy has a good heart:

"Will he turn into a ghost if he dies here?" he asks.

"Not with your Nana around. He wouldn't dare." Richie nods in solid agreement with this. Meg wipes the wound down with a rag she brought from her bag.

"I'll be right behind you," she says as she looks over her shoulder. This means that he should go back down the ladder – Meg has learned this kind of doublespeak from Mr Pennyman. You say one thing but you mean another. Richie loiters for a moment and she shoos him down - there's a little bit of the procedure she doesn't want the boy to see. When he's gone, Meg spits on her fingers and rubs the saliva into the cut she's just stitched up. For good luck.

She looks up to The Robber's pale face as she puts his cloak back around him, now the wound is covered, she smells faint perfume, Meg can't tell if it's expensive, all she knows is that it's nice. She looks at his face with the eyes closed and his jet-black hair, his strong jaw and the beginnings of his beard. Perhaps she looks at him a little too long. Meg gently rolls him on his side against the chimney. She's been close to her husband before, a few times, but there was never any sense of wonderment, not like there is for this man. She frowns as she examines her feelings and puts her hand on his forehead, he is cold but not at all dead, and somehow, she can sense him thinking. There's something about him, she remembers the way he held the door as he fell into the cottage, as if he did not want her to take his full weight, the polite way he spoke despite his pain, the respect that he showed as he bled out onto his legs. Meg likes this. She likes him. Back in Etton, she has seen big men with toothache yelling and weeping in pain. She likes the way this Robber is dressed too, they are not frivolous clothes like Mr Pennyman would wear, but hardwearing and understated for a life of work, clothes that will not let you down when you need them. Perhaps he's a gentleman, perhaps he's a gentleman thief. Meg sits back and light bleeds in through the gaps in the roof. There are no gentlemen robbers, she reasons, there are no gentlemen. Perhaps he is like Nana says, dirt poor just as the rest of the working folk of North Burton.

Meg builds the fire with some of the coal but not too much. She sets ice to boil that Richie has collected. Nana watches her work.

"Don't build it too big," she nags. Meg carries on as she was. Nana is a bully. "What about our Robber? Will he live?"

"I don't think he will," she answers. "I think he'll die from the cold as well as the wound." Nana rubs her chin with one of her big pink hands, she has had a chance to think this through a little, they were foolish to take the man in. The best thing would be for him to get better.

"We can't have him die here."

"You've changed your tune," answers Meg.

"I can change my mind as often as I like in my house," says the grey-haired old woman. "I need him out of here, Meg, if anyone finds him, us with no man in the house, then…" She swallows. "I dread to think." Although Nana is tolerated in North Burton, in other places she may not be. Without a man of the house, technically, the property belongs to the Estate. She bleats on about being a widow and having rights to the house but she's on thin ice, a hundred years ago she might have had a leg to stand on but it's 1709, women don't have the right to own anything. With her son away or maybe worse, she is vulnerable and while no one will bother them during this cold spell, they will surely ask where the man of the house is when, and if, the cold eases.

"I need to see my mother," says Meg as she looks into the flames of the little fire and then up to Nana. "She'll be able to give me something to help him, one way or another."

"You mean she'll give you poison?"

"Aye, in case we need it, or something that could make him better." Nana sits back and her weight makes the chair creak.

"I don't like it, Meg. We're your family now, you know that. You promised to look after us when you said them vows in St. Michael's just up the road. You can't go running back to your mother at the first sign of trouble." Nana is unfair to say this.

"It's for you that I go. If we can get him better then we could have that silver he talked about." Nana shakes her head, she has thought about this.

"He's a robber, Meg. He won't make good on his word even if he survives, even if there is any hidden silver, we'll be getting none of it. We just want him out before anyone sees that he's here."

"When it's fully light, I'll walk up the hill. I'll be back before noon."

"What about them sows?" Meg collects eggs from the hen house and feeds them, she sweeps out the pig muck too and beds the fat lady sows down on fresh straw.

"It will keep till this afternoon, as long as I'm back."

"What about the porridge?" asks Nana. "I can't get down to that pot to make it, what with my bad legs and knees. You know that, Meg." Her voice has taken on a gravelly whine that rattles round the house.

"Little Richie can do you some porridge. I'll have to leave early so I can get back." Nana's face turns into a grimace and her ugly, flabby cheeks redden as if she is going to cry. "He's got to learn Nana and we have to fix the problem before it fixes us." This is one that Meg has heard Nana use before. "If they find him here, then we'll be for it. Grandad Blackwood shan't be able to do a thing to help us, and don't think Carrick up at the church will do you any favours." Nana is now beginning to see that Meg is right. This girl's mother is known to be a healer. Best let her get on with it.

"You will be back before noon then, won't you, Meg? Little Richie gets awful worried when you're not here." Meg has already said she would be. The lad looks up at her with his big blue eyes.

"I will," says Meg. She begins to do up the buttons on her petticoat and bends to pull up her socks. She already has her boots on - it's too cold to take them off.

"Don't forget that hairpin," says Nana. Meg nods. At the side of the fireplace in a wooden box along with woollen hats and odd gloves is a long and thick hair pin. Meg fishes it out and shows it to Nana. "That's the one." It's a good four inches long with a big metal ball at one end. Nana likes Meg to wear it if she's going anywhere because you never really know what sort of people you'll meet. She gathers her blonde hair up behind her head and deftly fits the pin into place holding it all together. She wraps her brown scarf over her head and ties it under her chin, then picks up her cloak from the back of the door and wraps it round her. For a moment she thinks about The Robber upstairs near the chimney breast, his cloak is twice as thick as hers, that would make a much better shield against the wind. She thinks on. She will see people on the green lanes to Etton and they will wonder where a farm girl from North Burton came upon such a cloak, and it will cause tongues to wag, as they do. Meg thinks better of it. She pauses at the door and looks at Nana and Richie.

"I'll be back as soon as I can," she says.

"You said it'd be noon," says Nana.

Meg is free.

The air is crisp and clean in the morning and the sky is stone grey. She goes at a good pace with her hood over her headscarf. It is cold, sharp and dead as her boots crunch on the iced grass. It's no good walking on the mud paths they usually use, these are frozen and slippery. Up ahead is the Thorne Farmhouse, the red bricks of the big cowshed and the livery yard stables behind the main building. The roof has a fresh covering of snow from the night before. Meg makes her way up the slight hill.

At the field to the side of the house, walking behind a

wooden fence is Farmer Thorne himself with his red cheeks. He has hold of a great brown bay who he is leading back up to the stables. He sees Meg and stops. Farmer Throne is a personable man, if a little loud, and he likes to chat.

"When's this going to end then, our Meg?" he shouts as he sees her. He means the weather.

"I dunno," she calls back as she walks towards him. Meg has been a milking girl for Farmer Thorne before and he's not a bad man at all. He keeps his animals well and those that work for him too. There's always a glass of ale on him at Christmas.

"Where are you off to, lass?" he asks.

"I'm to see my mam in Etton, Mr Thorne, I haven't seen her in a month or more."

"Aye well, just you be careful, there's a storm coming in this afternoon." Now Meg has got closer, she can see that the big brown bay is struggling to get away from Farmer Thorne's grip on its reins. A smaller man might be pulled to one side. "Jamie here is having one of his turns, he always does before a storm. I'm putting him inside. I'm getting them all in." The bay is Farmer Thorne's finest gelding and as fast as they come, sleek, silk brown with a proud lean face and fourteen hands high. Meg would give a week's hard graft to ride him.

"Afternoon you say?" asks Meg. She knows Jamie has been proved right before. Animals have a sense of the world that humans don't. Granddad Blackwood's old ratting dog could see ghosts, Miss Charlotte up at the Manor house has a parakeet that squawks when someone in the village is going to die, Rector Carrick has that big dog, Bear, that can hear anyone coming. When their own black cat, Dutchy, sits with her back to the fire, Nana says that something bad is going to happen, and it sometimes does. There is sense in listening to Farmer Thorne on this one.

"I'd say it'll come late afternoon, Jamie hasn't started with the kicking yet. You'd best be quick as you can, our Meg, you wouldn't want to get caught out."

"Thank you, Farmer Thorne," she says as she hurrie
past him. She'll be as quick as she can anyway, with that
Robber breathing his last next to the chimney breast.

Etton is not far away. About two miles. There are no really
big hills this side of The Wolds and she'll make good time if
she doesn't bump into anyone who wants a chat. The sky is
still a stone grey as she picks her way up the frozen track.
While she's out, she might as well make use of her time, and
her eyes dart across the hedgerows that line the lane, looking
for something that could be of some use, berries, mushrooms,
wood that they can burn or anything they can use.

As she gets to the top of the hill looking down on Etton,
Meg realises that the green lane has been foraged already by
keener eyes than hers, perhaps many times over. The wind
picks up. She wraps her cloak around her and keeps the same
steady pace down towards the village she once called home.
There's an Inn opposite the junction, The Light Dragoon, it's
a whitewashed building of black timbers and a bowed roof
with the light glowing from within. Meg turns right and it does
not take her long to get to the little church set back from the
road on a hill. She walks past the headstones in the fresh snow
and crunches across the grass to a tiny cottage behind with
pale grey walls and a wet thatched roof that looks like it is
about to fall in.

There's no need for her to knock. This is where Meg comes
from. This is where her mother is. She lifts the latch and the
black door creaks open as she steps inside the tiny room.
There's an odd smell from within that she has never noticed
before, and the air is still and perhaps colder than the wind
outside. Something is wrong. Meg pulls back her headscarf as
she walks further into the little cottage. A weak fire burns at
the foot of a wooden chair and in it, sits a thin figure huddled
up in a blanket, her chin on her chest. She's so small there's
nothing to her. Meg kneels and takes the woman's hand.

"Mother," she has never seen the old woman like this. The head looks up, and in the flickering light, Meg can see that her face is skeletal and her cheeks sunken into the side of her mouth. This is where the smell is coming from. Meg's mother was always a thin, little woman, but she had a sparkle and a wry wit, leathery skin and strong hands from a life of work. There was mischief in her so that she used to tell Meg she had kissed Granddad Blackwood at harvest festival a few years back, she could wrestle teenage lads and swore when you least expected it. There was spirit in her, spirit that has dribbled away since the month previous when Meg walked the same four-mile round trip in the cold.

"What's happened?" The old woman's grip is ice with thin, paper frail nails and veins that creep up the back of her hands.

"I've been hanging on for you, Meg." Her voice is just a whisper but there is still a sense of the wild in it. Here is the woman who taught Meg to deliver baby ewes in spring, which mushroom you could eat in late October, how to sew pockets into a petticoat. Tears begin in Meg's eyes.

"Don't do that, lass," rasps the woman. "I haven't got time, there's things you have to do and know."

"We'll build the fire, Mam, get you warm. I'll make you something to eat and we'll rub your ointment on your chest, see if we can bring out the cold." Meg knows the game as she speaks, she must copy the old woman and make light of her overly dramatic talk, she can bring her back from this, if anyone can.

"There's no time for that, Meg, no time at all." The old woman's voice is hoarse and suddenly loud. "I just need you to hold my hand and listen. That's all you need to do, that's all you've ever needed to do. I've told you everything I know and it's your job to send it on down the line to the next lass." Meg's mother is calm but stern, like the time they had to rescue Mrs Connor rather than her baby on the kitchen table, or when she had to put little Andy Piper out of his misery after he'd come off a pony and bashed his head into a drystone wall. If there's a nasty job to be done, you best get it over with quick. Meg takes a deep breath to calm herself as the woman begins to speak.

"At my feet there's a packet, Meg. I need it to get to someone. Out at Dalton, in the Coaching Inn, there's a lass who needs it for the pain she's got. You'll take it to her, as soon as I'm gone. Tell her who you are and you'll get your reward. There's my medicine bag there as well, take it with you, add it to your own, I'll not be needing it again."

"Mam, save your strength."

"Just listen," whispers the old woman and her voice is tender, young even, in the darkness of the falling down cottage with a wonky table behind her and clothes strewn on the floor. "Hold my hand, Meg, just hold my hand and I'll tell it to you just like my mam told it me." Meg squeezes the bones of her mother's fingers in tenderness and leans in, to listen to the whispers. "There's a line of us that goes right back to the start of the world itself, my Meg, a great chain of us, and each one linked to the next by love and blood and birth. If you ever think that you might be alone in this world, you best shake your head, because I'll be following you wherever you go, just like my mam is now and my grandma and her grandma too, right the way back to the old times. You're going to need someone to love. All the young lasses talk about someone to love them, but all that you need to keep you steady is someone to give your heart to, it could be a child, or God or even a man, or your work, you just need a thing to devote yourself to. It will already be close, whatever or whoever it is. You were the one I chose to love and care for, it kept me steady, it did. You've been a good one my Meg, a good one, kind and clever and with your ears open, brave too." The old woman licks her cracked lips with her dry tongue.

"I'll get you a drink, Mam." Her mother's fingers squeeze to stop Meg from pulling away.

"When I'm gone lass, it won't be time to listen anymore, it'll be time to tell and do. It'll be time for you to do the telling, just like you've done the listening so far. If you need us, Meg, all you have to do is call, you'll remember that won't you, my lass? Call on us and we'll send help, your mothers and your grandmothers, we're all here, behind you. Just call for us and we'll come. You'll know when the time is right. Say you will."

"I'll remember," she whispers.

"Tell it me back." This is her mother's way of making sure that you heard her right. Meg's eyes fill with tears. "Tell it me back, lass."

"I'm to find someone to love."

"Aye, and…"

"I'm to stop listening."

"Not that, start telling what you know and what you think. You're not a child anymore, Meg. What else?"

"That's it?"

"What else?" the frail old woman grasps her daughter's hand tight. Meg knows what to say but it feels foolish to. "Go on."

"I'm to call upon you, if I need your help." The grip relaxes and her hand goes limp. There's no final gasp and no groan but she knows that her mother is gone. The old woman's chest is still, and whatever flame that burned in her has flickered out. The front door creaks and there's the noise of a person coming:

"Who's here?" It's the rough call of Mrs Allan the church sexton's wife. "I've not been gone a few minutes. Who's this who's just bloody walked in." Meg stands and turns and Mrs Allan recognises her straight away in the darkness. The woman's tone changes. "She's been waiting for you, Meg. I sent word a week ago, I thought you'd have come sooner."

"I didn't know."

"She's not got long left, she wants to see you."

"She's seen me," whispers Meg. "I've seen her." Mrs Allan

stands blinking into the darkness of the battered cottage. She's smaller than Meg and has big blue eyes with short blonde hair.

"Is that it then? Is it over? Has she gone?"

Meg nods.

Mrs Allan half stumbles forward, beginning to blub at the same time as she and Meg embrace. She has stooped strong shoulders and Meg rests her face on the woman's neck as she feels her own chest heave in sorrow. It's Mrs Allan who breaks the hold first, wiping the tears from her eyes.

"You'll have to stay with me the night, Meg, Just while we get things ready for the funeral."

"She left me an errand, Mrs Allan," her voice is earnest. Meg has all but forgotten the dying Robber who lays in the upstairs room of her house in North Burton and the Nana and little Richie who she is meant to be looking after. Mrs Allan rubs her nose with the back of her hand.

"You mean take the package for the Inn keeper's daughter over in Dalton? She's been wittering on about it for weeks. Meg, there's a storm coming. You can see it yourself. If you get caught in it, you'll die." This is a bit dramatic.

"She asked me to do it. I want to. I need to."

"Nonsense. You've had a shock. We all have. Come up to the house and we'll have a nip of Mr Allan's brandy. I know where he keeps it." As the woman is speaking, Meg is already working out what she will do. It must be ten o'clock in the morning and it's only two miles or so to Dalton, she can run her mother's errand and be back in North Burton before the storm hits proper. In the meantime, she'll have to figure out what to do with their Robber, either get him back to health or out the door feet first. She's not sure yet which would be best. Whatever happens, she has to make the decisions on her own, isn't that what her mother told her? She has to learn to speak.

CHAPTER THREE

Mrs Allan delays Meg by crying some more and telling her that her mother, Ann, was 'the loveliest woman' she had ever known. Mrs Allan is full of praise for most people. She is to make preparations for the funeral and Meg will return to North Burton after she has run her mother's errand and delivered the package to the sick daughter. Mrs Allan will set the funeral and they will send word.

It does not seem real to Meg.

She walks the hard mud lane out of Etton, past run-down cottages and sheds stooped with rot and age as she looks for patches of grass where she won't slip. Then, on either side of her, there are fields that should be busy with folk at this time of year but are just blankets of white snow. The hedgerows have been picked clean of anything useful but Meg cannot help but look, it's as her mam trained her, and Nana too for that matter. She will make good time if she keeps this pace and she tries to put thoughts of her mother from her mind. She has lived away from her some four years now and she knows the woman was old, she lived longer than most and knew more than all. Meg worries and hopes that she learned everything from her.

At the end of the cart track, there's a junction, straight on to join the York road or right up the hill to Dalton. She begins up the hill, on the left side is a thick forest that they call Dalton Park. It belongs to Lord Hotham and stretches for a good many acres to his great mansion three miles away. The Lord is real wealth, gentry even, with links to royalty, he makes Mr Pennyman look like a shopkeeper. Dalton Park is overrun and wild and kept that way. Inside there are deer and rabbit, wild pigeon and every kind of flower you could imagine. It's where Meg's mother, Ann, found her herbs on moonlit nights. It's where those with a taste for danger come to poach. Meg feels a light sweat under her headscarf as she reaches the top of the hill and looks across the flat landscape in front of her. The wind has picked up and whips across the fields of white that are level and open, pure, clean and still, with the horizon a straight line on all sides. She huddles herself in her cloak and shuffles on.

Meg takes in a sharp breath when she notices the figure on a horse blocking the green lane in front. He is dressed in black atop a dappled grey mount with a wide hat, the bitter wind makes his cloak flap behind but other than this, he is completely still. Meg glances at him, only briefly, and keeps the same pace, she doesn't want this man to think that she is afraid. As she gets closer, she can see there's a bright feather tied to his hat and he has a thin moustache with an angular face. He has black boots to his knees that shine and the cloak is tight to his shoulders. The tack on the horse glistens with golden designs on the bridle and its mane is combed in a tight plait. Here is someone who looks after themself. It's not the sort of person Meg expects to see on the road to Dalton, in a winter that has lasted longer than a winter has ever lasted before. He watches her approach and she does not alter her speed or course. It takes a minute for her to reach him.

"Well met," he calls when she is twenty yards or so away. He has been waiting for her. Meg feels happier she still has the hairpin Nana made her wear, she loosens the headscarf so that if she needs to get at the weapon, she can.

"Well met, kind Sir." It's a figure of speech.

"Kind Miss, can I take a moment of your time?" He has a clear well-spoken voice but the accent is not familiar. He's from working people but not from the East Riding, somehow.

"I am in a hurry, Sir, I have medicine for a sick lady not far away up the road." She can see, now she is really up close, that this man is not as well turned out as it appears. The boots are cracked although they have been polished and the cloak tatty, the grey dappled horse is filthy and underfed with shifty, frightened eyes.

"I promise it will not take a moment. I will be able to pay." This man on his horse is blocking Meg's path anyway between the two dry stone walls. It doesn't look like she has much of a choice.

"Please make it quick Sir, there's a storm coming in." The man looks up at the sky briefly and then grins. It's not the kind of grin that Meg is used to, and she cannot work out his intentions.

"I'm looking for a dear friend of mine. He's injured and without bothering you with a long story, I need to find him to save his life, something unfortunate has happened to him. It would have been sometime yesterday." The man grins once more. His teeth are clean and straight but pale yellow. Meg is not afraid of him. Perhaps she should be.

"I know how it works in the country," he continues. "News spreads quickly. Have you heard of an injured man? He would be tall, handsome you might say. He has a flintlock pistol similar to the one I have right here." The man on the horse pulls open one side of his cloak to reveal the fat handle of a pistol tucked into a belt. Meg's mouth dries up. Her feet go cold. Perhaps she may need the pin after all.

She briefly glances at the man's face, Meg doesn't want to give him the wrong idea. She calculates. This could be the solution she is looking for, a way to get The Robber out of their house, but then, she gets the sense from this man, that the less she has to do with him, the better, like a dog you know will bite you if you get too close. She must play this with caution.

"I have not heard of any such man," says Meg. She looks down at the frozen hard ground and her breath makes steam in the air. "You might try the rector up at North Burton, Carrick. He hears everything." Meg tries to make her voice more afraid than it is, but not enough so this man may believe she is lying. If he does visit Carrick of North Burton, this odd horseman may find himself swinging from the gallows, for the rector is no friend to anyone, that's why Meg has given his name.

The man reaches into his satchel and the side of his horse and pulls out something wrapped in cloth, he tosses it to Meg and, instinctively, she catches it in both hands.

"I told you I'd pay," says the man. Meg unwraps the first layer and sees a white and hard cheese peeping out at her. There's not much, but she gives this man an honest grin, wishing that she had not given him the name of Carrick at North Burton.

"Thank you, kind Sir," she says and means it. "There is a storm coming, it would be best you were off the road and somewhere warm."

"My colleague and I are in the woods just here." The man points into Dalton Park behind him and the thick dark trees. Meg has heard of men tried at the quarter session at Beverley and then sent up to the castle at York for poaching within its wide boundary.

"You'll not be safe in there," says Meg and wishes she hadn't. She needs to get to Dalton and be back in North Burton before the sky breaks. She remembers the wild eyes of Jamie, the bay horse, and the words of Farmer Thorne. The man smiles down on her knowingly.

"We're men who are used to such situations, Miss. I may have a flintlock at my hip, and a hat made by Atkinson's of York, but I am more the same as you are than the lords and ladies who live in these big houses and farms, those that keep a whole forest for themselves."

"Are you a robber?" she asks.

"Not to folk such as you, Miss," he answers. "If you hear anything of our friend, please, come this way again and let us know. We will reward you and it will be substantially more than a lump of cheese." Meg nods and keeps her own counsel with closed lips. There are already too many variables for her to help this man, maybe her robber is already dead. Perhaps

43

he was attacked by these men and doubtless, they are looking for the money that he hid somewhere. It must be worth more than a few guineas, much more.

"I will, kind Sir," says Meg. He pulls the reins and the horse moves for her to go by the side. She gets a whiff of his rich perfume as she passes. It's sweet and flowery.

"Who shall I tell my Nana gave me this cheese?" she calls over her shoulder.

"If you've a mind to, tell her Dandy Jim passed it you, out the goodness of his heart. There's more if you can help me find my friend." Meg nods and hurries on. She can feel Dandy Jim's eyes on her back as she walks away up the track towards Dalton with the wind in her face.

Dalton is slightly larger than North Burton, there is a lord here with a bigger house and many more acres, so they need more workers, more servants and more animals too. Meg walks up the main street past rows of cottages similar to her own in various forms of repair or disrepair. This is the East Riding of Yorkshire, the ground here is chalk, if you want stone for bricks you have to bring it from miles away and that is beyond the likes of Meg or the poorest workers of the Dalton Estate. She turns right into West End road, the entrance to the great house and the way is frozen over and slippery. At the end of the lane, is the white building that is the Pipe and Pot Inn. Granddad Blackwood says it's over a hundred years old and that when he was a boy, they used to have bare-knuckled fights in the garden behind. Nana warns never to go near it, inns and pubs have characters just like people do, some are friendly and warm and others cold as the icy wind. The Pipe and Pot here sits on the entrance to an important country house and as such, people without good breeding aren't welcome here. Good breeding is just another way of saying rich. Meg stands a few feet from the front door and looks at the smooth thatched roof covered in snow

44

around the chimney, smoke draws a thin line into the grey sky. This is how a house should look.

She knocks on the front door and steps back in respect. Unlike The Bay Horse in North Burton, The Pipe and Pot is very much in operation. She can see the long bar through one of the windows. Meg should not just walk into a pub, especially not a pub of wealth such as this one.

The door opens and a girl with a white apron and hat appears, she is younger than Meg and has a clean look about her that says she deals with those of money.

"Yes?" she snaps.

"I have a package for Miss Rice. I've come from Etton to deliver it on behalf of my mother." The woman frowns before she steps back and lets Meg into the hall of the pub. The heat makes her ears burn instantly, there's the smell of food from over the bar and the kitchens and the sweet aroma of beer brewing somewhere with notes of whiskey. Her dirty boots sink into the doormat she stands on and Meg feels out of place. Like a blemish on smooth skin.

She pulls off her headscarf and looks into the empty front room, two men stand near the door but at the bar. One leans on his elbows over a drink and the other, with his sleeves rolled up, is facing Meg. He grins. He's handsome. His shirt is open a few buttons down his chest and he has a small mutton chop beard. They are close enough to talk to.

"Where've you come from?" he says.

"Etton," she answers.

"You do know there's a storm coming, young lass?" Meg smiles. She's not been called a young lass very many times in the last few years.

"Aye, I'll be home before it sets in." He looks her up and down and raises his eyebrow as if to flirt. Nobody would do this in North Burton where they know Meg.

"There was a robbery, you know, on the York Road a night back," he says. "Do you not worry, travelling on your own, lass?" He has a half smirk. Meg has seen this look before. She examines him again, sees the well-made shoes with a shiny buckle, the tights and the expensive material of his white shirt. He means her harm. This is why Nana says the Pipe and Pot is a bad place. It's here where rich men can do as they wish because they have a purse full of guineas, if he were to look at Meg the same way in the alehouse at North Burton, Nana would split him in half with a barbed comment about his mother, and if it came to it, she'd break his nose as well. Meg understands how to defend herself. First with words.

"Thank you for your worry, kind Sir, but I've got my mother's big pin to hold my hair up. Anyone comes near me in the wrong way, Sir, and they won't be fathering any children. It's about five inches long and so sharp." The man leaning on the bar but facing away laughs and he turns, elbowing his friend in the ribs in gest.

"Lasses who work the fields are not whores. You try your silver talk on the girls round here, and they'll gut you." The man is broader and older. He smiles out of kindness at Meg.

The serving girl arrives back and beckons her to follow. They go past the bar and through the building and the smell of the kitchen makes Meg's insides growl as her boots clap on the polished oak boards. At a door, the girl knocks twice, opens it and bids Meg to step inside, then backs away, leaving her standing alone in a long, ornate and clean smelling room that might as well be in a dream. The pale walls are bathed in lamplight from the ceiling, and a fire roars at one end next to two dark, red leather armchairs. The floor is polished wood and the air smells of flowers. A woman sits in one of the chairs and she is so thin that she takes up half of the seat, Meg looks her over. This must be Miss Rice. She sits up straight like she's got a stick down her back.

"You have a package for me?" asks the woman.

"Yes, from my mother, Ann. She wanted me to give it you." Miss Rice has a thin gaunt face with high cheekbones and her hair neatly combed and swept to the side, there's a faraway look in her eyes. Meg reaches into her cloak and removes the packet that brought her here, she walks over, passes it to Miss. Rice and feels more out of place. The woman hardly turns as she takes the package in her porcelain hands. Meg can't place her age but she is not young.

"Please, have a seat," says the woman. Her voice is strained.

"I have to get back," says Meg.

"Just a few moments, please."

Meg nods and sits, uneasy on the red leather of the armchair.

"Your mother is a good woman to send this to me," says Miss Rice. "Can I get you a drink for your journey? Some tea?" Meg shakes her head.

"I have to be back in North Burton before the storm hits, Miss. I have my Nana and little boy to look after." Miss Rice smiles and Meg can see that it is only a movement of her facial muscles, there is nothing behind it at all. The lady is not unpleasant. It just seems like every action is difficult for her.

"How is your mother? You will send her my regards, won't you?" Meg looks down at the floor and then up into the lady's brown eyes.

"I'm afraid she passed on."

"Oh," at this, Miss Rice seems to display genuine emotion with a frown and then gives a deep breath. She places her hands on the packet, tied with a willow chord in her lap that Meg has just passed her. "Do you know what this is?"

"For your pain," says Meg. The woman nods.

"It's for the relief of it. Do you know what are inside?"

"Mushrooms," says Meg. "Mushrooms that grow on open ground near the forests in October. They have a pointed cap and gills. Mother said they can make you see all sorts of unnatural things, tree faeries and goblins in the darkness. They're not for normal folk." Miss Rice nods.

"They are dangerous but powerful. Your mother taught me how to use them and yes - there are things that are unseen all around us, but I would take their chattering over the pain. With your mother gone, how will I acquire these?"

"I can get them for you," says Meg, "but only in the autumn. Do you have enough?"

"I do not use them all the time. Your mother showed me how to breathe and move so that it does not hurt so much day to day. Sometimes the agony stops me from getting up or from lifting one arm from the bedcovers, this is when I need to take them. So, I may not need them at all if I am lucky."

"What is your sickness, Miss?

"Too much black bile. Every nerve in my arms and legs dance in pain. It makes my head swim. I can hear the serving girls and my brother complaining about me. My father says it's a punishment, and not for my sins, but for his."

"Do you think it is so?" asks Meg. The woman manages a light and knowing smile.

"I thought so for a long time as well, but not anymore. A creature from the woods explained in a way that I cannot explain to you. Not everything grows in the way it should. Some of us are born weak and some are strong but God loves each as much as the other." There is a touch of madness in her eyes.

Meg looks at the shiny floorboards and the roaring fireplace, at the lamps with oil that will shine through the night, she thinks about the serving girl who will bring this thin woman her meals and keep her warm. Meg does not feel envy like she ought to. Unlike the cottage in North Burton, there is not a scrap of humour here, not an ounce of love either. Meg looks through the window to the sky outside, she needs to be on the road. The sense of being in the wrong place also makes her feel uneasy.

"I need to get home, before the storm, so, thank you, Miss Rice," says Meg, although she has nothing to thank this lady for. It is she who made the journey out to Dalton and she who risks being trapped by the weather. The woman takes a stick from beside her chair and uses it to begin to stand.

"There's no need, Miss. I can see myself out."

"You are like your mother," says the Innkeeper's daughter. She gets to her feet with some difficulty and on frail legs, steps to a wooden cabinet against the wall. She pulls open one door and then the other to reveal shelves. She beckons Meg over.

"Take what you want," she says. Inside there are perhaps twenty bottles of liquor and half a dozen of perfume. There are little wooden stands with rings and necklaces hanging from them, a silver bangle and other trinkets that shine. Meg looks at the woman incredulous. "The package you bring is worth all of this to me. So, take what you want."

Another soul, richer and less hungry may wonder at the opportunity, but not Meg, she steps forward to examine what she can take. The perfume is of no use, as are the rings and jewellery, anyone she tries to sell them to will think them stolen. She looks for the biggest liquor bottle with the most in it and picks it up.

"Is this ok?" she asks.

"Of course. Put it away and we'll go out through the kitchen and the back. Next time you come, use the rear entrance then you won't have to go through any of the drinkers in the front room."

Miss Rice is slow, but proud to lead, as Meg follows her out the door and down a corridor to the kitchen. There's a big burly man kneading bread and a white-haired woman at the oven. They look at Miss Rice with worry.

"Fetch out one of the chickens from the pantry, Mrs Hawes," she commands. "You'll wrap it up for this lass here. I've given her a bottle of brandy as well, just in case you think she's pilfered it." The woman makes her way over to the pantry without question. Miss Rice turns.

"What was your name again, young Miss?" she asks.

"I'm Meg," she says.

"The Pipe and Pot is always open to you and yours, Meg."

"Thank you, Miss Rice."

One of the good things about a well-made dress is that you can carry just about anything inside it. Meg has the chicken in a string bag over her shoulder, and the bottle of apple brandy that Miss Rice said her father had sent up from London, in one of her front pockets. Meg has thought about having a swig already but she knows there's too much ground to cover and, just as she gets outside Dalton and begins down the steady slope, the first flurry of snow falls. This is not so much of a problem because the going is fairly good on foot but the wind whips up from the Wolds in the north and sends an icy backdraft down on her. The snow thickens, and before she's got to the hill where she saw Dandy Jim, Meg is in a place that she does not want to be in. The snow begins to lay heavy on the ground, great clumps of it stick to her feet and she peers upwards to a sky that is blank white and thick with cold. It will take her more hours than there are left in the day just to get back to Etton in this, but she pushes on. She has promised.

As Meg gets over the brow of the hill, she sees Dandy Jim atop his horse once more. He has his head down and his face covered in a scarf, his collars are up and the quality hat made by Atkinson's of York is pulled low over his eyes. He beckons and calls, she can hear him, faraway and muffled by the snow that fills the sky. It takes a few minutes for Meg to reach him and she has the feeling that he has been waiting for her.

"I'll take you as far as I can," he calls with just his eyes showing.

Meg has no choice.

She clambers up on the drystone wall, then onto the dappled cob behind him, and the horse takes the strain of two. She can tell already that Dandy Jim is a rider, his feet point upwards at forty-five degrees and he holds the reins thumbs forwards and without slack. There is no time for Meg to get comfy and she wraps her arms around his waist to find he is thinner than she would have imagined. He clicks his tongue and gives a kick and they are off into the driving snow.

He makes good time this Dandy Jim. He seems to know yet where the path is under all the snow and in the black grey of the blizzard. He does not worry that the horse might find some hole or root that would throw them off and rides well, like a gentleman might, light with the whip and careful with his commands, without any of the shouting or anger of a rider like Farmer Thorne. Meg directs him over the fields and south so that they do not need to pass through Etton at all, and within an hour they are to the west of North Burton. If the day were clear, they would be able to see the top of St Michael's in the distance but they are still a long way out.

Meg calls to Dandy Jim to stop and she gets off. It is still snowing heavily and there is perhaps only half an hour left of the day, Meg knows her way from here. It is still a trek but she will make it and, with the bad weather and where he has dropped her, hopefully, nobody will have seen them together.

"I thank you, kind Sir," she calls upwards to him. This time, the kind Sir is genuine. He turns the horse round and tips his hat. Meg reaches into the folds of her dress, to the bottle of apple brandy, and passes it up to him. Dandy Jim pulls his face scarf down with one finger and she can see he is grinning.

"You're a fine lass," he says. Meg smiles. Dandy Jim's complement is honest. "You'll walk from here. A man like me isn't welcome everywhere. Keep your ear to the ground for my friend, will you? A body doesn't just go missing, someone would have seen him." Dandy Jim pulls out the cork with his right hand and empties a good glug into his mouth before he replaces it and tosses the bottle back down to Meg.

"I'll be on the hill where we first met. We'll see you before you see us." He uses his heels to get the horse moving and, within a minute he is gone into the pale, driving snow.

It's perhaps six o'clock at night when Meg finally gets back to the end cottage at North Burton, she is black with fatigue and wet through. She tries the door but the catch is on the other side, she thumps with the fat of her fist on the door.

"Nana, it's me, it's Meg." She can hear wood scraping across the floor inside and then the catch springs loose. She opens the door slowly because she knows that little Richie will be on his tiptoes on a stool at the other side. He grins when he sees her and she shuts the door behind and rests on it with the flat of her back. In the thin light from the fire, she can see Nana looking up at her with her beady eyes.

"Where have you been?" snaps the old woman. "Richie and me have had to do everything ourselves today, and at my age, it isn't right. Don't you think I spent all my years, all my best years, looking after other people, your husband for one and his father, and now all I expect is a bit of help from time to time." Meg cannot concentrate on the words as she peels off her cloak, hangs it up and then undoes the petticoat. Her hands have taken on a bluish colour and her face is red. She pulls her dress down and steps out of the freezing, wet rags to stand in just her undergarments. Nana continues.

"You, bloody gallivanting off to see your mam, it's not Mothering Sunday you know. I let you do it out of Christian kindness, I did. I let you go." Nana sniffs the air coming from her freezing daughter-in-law. "Have you been drinking?" she asks. This makes her nostrils flare and her chest inflates. "I said to John, I said to him you were the wrong sort, I told him, I knew I'd be right as well, you going off drinking all day." During the rant, Meg sets the string bag on the bench and Richie undoes it to reveal the back end of a chicken.

This has a profound effect on Nana and she stops talking. The jowls of her face look in disbelief at it, plucked and ready to be cooked. Meg goes back to her dress and pulls the apple brandy from the pocket, she passes the freezing bottle to Nana and the old woman beams to show a gap where one of her front teeth has fallen out. Meg wraps a blanket around her shoulders and stands as close as she can to the fire while she shivers, waiting for Nana to say something. Brandy and a chicken to cook. Meg has even forgotten about the cheese. It's like Christmas, but it's better than Christmas.

"I'm sorry, Meg," says Nana. "I didn't mean them things. You know what I'm like."

"Just have your drink," she answers without emotion. "I'll show Richie here how to boil a chicken. How's The Robber?"

"Well I can't get up that ladder with my legs like they are, you know that. I want to, I really want to, Meg, but at my age, well, I try my best, I do." Nana is beginning to rant again when all Meg needs is the facts. She stands and makes her way to the ladder on bare feet.

Meg hopes, in some way that he is dead. Everything could be avoided if this is the case. She can say he forced himself in at gunpoint and they tried to help him and then he died. She'll go and tell Danny Reed, the constable, what happened this very night, and he'll tell the family at the Pennyman House and all this will be over. Dandy Jim will find out what's happened to his friend from some gossip soon enough, and they'll leave North Burton alone. All will be well, just as long as The Robber is dead, just as long as his skin is cold and his chest is still. Meg squats down over the body that is motionless on its side near the chimney breast in the darkness. Her hands go to his neck and she sighs.

He's still warm.

CHAPTER FOUR

After a few swigs of brandy, Nana decides to show Richie how to cook the bird. If anyone in the East Riding knows how to do it properly and get the most out of a chicken, it's Nana. The chef up at Dalton has already stripped the feathers and removed the guts so it's just for Nana to cut it up and drop it in the pot. Meg comes down the ladder with her blanket wrapped around her shoulders, she looks morose.

"Meg, get this bottle off me, will you?" says Nana. "I'll end up drinking the lot in one go." Meg takes the apple brandy bottle from her, there's not more than half the bottle left and the old girl is giddy with being drunk. Meg sits down on the bench against the wall while Nana giggles. They have about an hour of entertainment before the old woman either passes out or turns nasty. Richie watches the chicken bubble in the pot on the fire and his eyes blink up at Nana.

"Do you want a story?" she asks. He beams up at her with his straight teeth. "I'll tell you about The Walkington Show, back in the day…"

"Can we have a different one?" says Meg. It's not normal for her to speak her mind but they have all heard Nana's wrestling story hundreds of times, the one where she gets her legs round the strongest man's neck and wins the competition. Nana can hardly refuse, Meg has delivered chicken and brandy, the old woman hasn't even asked where they came from.

"A scary one," says Richie. Nana sits back and begins.

"Do you know of the curse of the stone at Rudston?" she asks the lad. He shakes his head and already, there is a little fear in his eyes. Meg sits forward, she does not know this one. Nana must be drunk.

"North of here is a hilltop and the village of Rudston and there, in the east of the churchyard is a standing stone as wide as five men together and stretching into the sky more than twenty feet. Why, it must weigh more than fifty big cart horses."

"What's it there for?" asks Richie.

"That's just it, nobody knows. It was there when my granddad was a tiny lad like you and when his granddad was little too – they say it comes from the ancient times before we had black powder to put in guns and thatched roofs to keep our houses warm." Nana leans forwards and her lined face drains of all emotion. "There's a curse on that stone," she whispers. This makes Richie's big blue eyes widen and his chin wobble in fear. "On the side of it, about ten foot up, there's a dragon print, clear as day you can see it, the pad of its great foot and three holes where its sharp talons marked the stone. Why, it would have been a terrible beast, Richie, and so big and strong to press its claws into hard stone."

"Will the dragon return Nana?" The old woman shakes her head.

"Oh no, the curse is worse than that. Near to the stone, there's a chalk stream they call Winterborne that rises from under the ground. There are some years when the Winterborne floods and, if the waters touch the shadow of that great standing stone, then a terrible year is to be had by all. It's why they call them the Waters of Woe. It flooded in 1660 when they put King Charles back on the throne and in 1664 before the great plague, the waters touched the shadow when James the Second got back the crown as well." Richie knows that these two kings are bad but he would rather hear about dragons. Nana senses she is losing him and drops her voice to just a whisper. "If you should ever go out to that hill there, Richie, to that standing stone with a dragon's footprint on the side, promise me you'll never touch it, lad. It will be terrible if you do." Nana's face is cold and hard, the lines look deep and her jowls sag as she shows her teeth.

"What will happen to me, Nana?"

"You'll feel barbs in your skin and your face will tighten

and start to shrivel." The old woman, quick as a rabbit down a hole, flicks her fingers at Richie's face and a few drops of water fly off and hit him. He yelps and falls backwards as Nana howls in laughter. Richie gets back up and his face is red.

"It's just Nana playing a daft game," says Meg. Richie comes to her. She wraps her arms around him and sits him on her knee. "Is there really a stone with a dragon's footprint?"

"Oh aye," answers Nana. "Neither of you two ought to touch it either, not unless you want something terrible to happen." Nana leans down and takes a deep sniff of the chicken as it cooks. Dutchy can smell the soup as well, she licks one of her black paws and rubs it down over her nose.

"How is The Robber, Meg?" she asks.

"He's alive."

"Good."

"How's that good?"

"I've been thinking. If he died the first night then we could have got away with it but it's been too long now. If he dies, they'll smell a rat. That Carrick up at the church, he'll say we did something ungodly. He hates people like us, look how he treats young Adam Gamble."

"So what do we do?"

"You'll have to fix him up. You'll have to put him back on his feet. What did you get from your mother?" Meg swallows.

Her mother. It's almost as if what happened this morning is unreal, or at least from a few weeks past. Back in Etton, she wonders if Mrs Allan and the rector there have removed the old woman's frail body from the house yet, and when the funeral will be, and how she will get to go if there are problems with their Robber or more snow.

"How was your mother Meg?" asks Nana. The blonde girl's head dips. Her brow frowns. "What is it?"

"She's gone."

"She's gone where?"

"Where people go when they die." Nana looks confused.

"Mrs Allan said she sent word a few weeks back that my mother was sick, and I was to come straight away. We didn't hear anything, did we?" Nana's face becomes serious for a moment, all trace of the brandy is gone.

"Someone came round, one of them little boys from a farm over there. It would have been a week back before all this heavy snow. He said to give you the message that your mam was ill. Well, I thought he was just messing round. You know, what some of them boys do, they like to play tricks on old ladies like me, so, I just forgot about it, kind of. Did you see her?"

"Aye. I did. Just before she passed. If I could have got there sooner, maybe I could have done something for her." She looks up at Nana's eyes crossed together slightly with London Apple Brandy. The old woman has remorse in her eyes for a split second, then comes out fighting.

"Now don't you go blaming me because you weren't here to get a message or it slipped my mind." Her tone is not as confrontational as it could be, but Nana feels defensive for she knows she has done wrong. "It's always about you, Meg, isn't it? It's always about what you want, you wanted to see your mother, you wanted to help The Robber." Meg looks at the old woman with her eyes rolling around her head. "Don't you look at me like that," she curses.

"I'll look at you any damn way I want," whispers Meg. There is iron in her voice. "Never you mention my mother again." It's not the first time Meg has had to warn the old woman off, but it's the first one since this great frost began for real at Christmas. Sometimes she can't help herself. Nana's face goes a kind of pink colour in the darkness of the fire, and then she bursts into huffing tears.

This is almost worse than the shouting.

The sobbing lasts for a good ten minutes. It upsets Richie to see his Nana like this and he tries to comfort her. The drink will have added to it, and Richie gives her a long, tight cuddle

57

to calm her down before they can eat the boiled chicken. At least they get a bit of peace from her warbling while they do so. Meg feels some of her strength returning as she chews on the gristle and she regrets speaking out of line to Nana, even though she hardly raised her voice. They eat the chicken slowly from their wooden bowls and Meg ladles out some of the water it cooked in to another.

"What are you doing with that?" asks Nana. It won't take long for her to get back to her normal, bossy self.

"If we're going to fix our Robber," says Meg, "then we'll need to feed him." Nana scowls.

"Will he need it all? We just need him to walk out of here and then he can fall dead in a ditch."

"He'll need all of it." Meg stands and walks to the ladder. "I'm sorry I spoke to you like that," she says over her shoulder. Nana considers this apology.

"Sometimes you have to stand up for yourself. You were right to, I wish more people would. Your mother's gone, you've a right to speak out of turn." Nana has bursts of clarity and good judgement that wriggle out of her mouth sometimes. She might be a selfish, nagging old woman but she is Meg's selfish, nagging old woman. Little Richie looks up from his finished bowl and does a burp.

"Not in my house, Richard Jackson," yells Nana.

Upstairs, Meg sets the candle holder down on the floor beside The Robber, and the light dances over the uneven bricks of the chimney breast. She rolls him onto his back and begins to unbutton his shirt, the wound will need to be examined in detail, despite the poor light. Meg carefully removes the dressings that she put there the day before and inspects the stab wound she sewed up. It looks clean, but she does not touch it, if it is going to get infected then it will come later, she just has to make sure that it has not come open. She takes the brandy bottle and pours just a little bit onto the line of stitches, if The Robber were awake this would burn. Meg opens her mother's cloth bag and there are ten or so little compartments with roots and leaves. She rummages inside and sees the same dried mushrooms that she passed to the Innkeeper's daughter. She had not thought of this, but they will help him. Meg breaks up the dried mushrooms and adds them to the bowl of chicken broth with bits of mint leaf, then stirs it with a wooden stick. As she watches the ingredients dissolve, she gathers saliva in her mouth and spits into it. She's seen her mother do it before, it's to have Meg's good humour in his stomach, he'll need that if he is going to get better. She leaves it to dissolve more and redresses The Robber, then, with difficulty, she sits him up with his back on the chimney breast. He's not heavy, just long and tall. His head lolls to the side and Meg stuffs his tricorn hat between his neck and his shoulder as a kind of pillow, the mouth sags.

"Now, Robber, this is how it is going to work. I'm going to talk and you are going to listen, do you understand?" The body is motionless against the wall. Meg gets on her knees and pulls open his mouth then moves his tongue, she fiddles for the flap of skin that covers his oesophagus and presses down to open it with one finger. With the other hand, she dunks the wooden spoon into the broth, brings it up to his mouth and pours it in. She saw her mother do it once for the elderly school master out at Lockington. The little old woman had made the same potion as Meg has, without the mushrooms, but including the spit. The master didn't live, but Meg likes to think that wasn't anything to do with her mother.

She spoons the broth in as quick as she can, but it's a slow job and she stops after a few tries. The Robber goes back to his breathing. She can still smell a little of the perfume on him.

"Listen here then, Robber," she begins. Meg knows from her mother that talking is as good a cure as anything, for anyone, and it's easy to make. "Let me tell you where you are. This here is North Burton, in the said direction from Bishop

Burton and home to The Pennyman Estate in the manor house opposite the church. Mr Pennyman, under whose roof we now sit, employs workers to tend his fields and look after his animals.

"I feed the Pennyman hens every morning and make sure the flock of them is in good stead, as well the pigs, all seven of them. At times, it's also in my employ to milk the cows, sow the fields, cut the hay, stack the hay, weed the yard and brush the horses down – but only on very rare occasions. In the next house along are the Blackwoods, two lads of less than average intelligence but more than capable, they are, of keeping the barns and stables nice and clean and patched up. They cut the wood for Mr Pennyman's fire and keep his garden trim and proper. In the next house along are the Farthings, horse folk, from Essex down south somewhere. They see to the horses that Miss Charlotte rides when she has a fancy to. That Hannah Farthing is a bitch, she looks at the rest of us like we're something on the bottom of her boot. Mr Farthing is as nasty as a nettle sting, they see everything and they love to tell Mr Pennyman if they've noticed a dead hen in my flock or a hole in the barn roof where the rain can get in. They've got two children, the little lad Archer is grand but the big one, Julia, is practically as bad as her bloody mother." Meg doesn't normally use foul words but, there's nobody listening and the words are not for The Robber to take meaning from, more to comfort him. She can say whatever she likes:

"Miss Charlotte is Pennyman's daughter, her mother took sick a few years back and passed on. She was a good woman and Miss Charlotte is too. I mean, she doesn't work and never gets her hands dirty, she's waited on by two girls who dress her every morning and when she wants to go riding, she has a whole livery yard to pick from, but she's not cruel, just unworldly somehow."

"Last of the houses here has the Gambles in it. Him and her as old as the hills and past it by a long way, their lad, Adam, works as the sexton for Carrick up at the church – he's as sharp as a razor and grafts strong. The rector who lives across the road in the cottage by the church, he's Carrick, came here two years back, and as horrible and selfish as any man I've ever seen before, big hands and a big barrel chest, he has, with deep-set eyes and one thick eyebrow. Talk is that Pennyman is afraid of him, and that he was sent to North Burton to get him away from somewhere else, with no wife and no family and just that big hunting dog he calls Bear, he's not the kind of man we like round here. Not us working folk. We look out for each other, apart from The Farthings. Meg stops her whispering for a moment and sits back on her feet. She looks at the gun tucked in The Robber's belt.

"I bet you could fire a bullet right through Carrick's skull if you had a mind too. He's a worse robber than you are, we know that coal he has comes from The Minster in Beverley and we know it's free, but Carrick thinks he's allowed to sell it to Farmer Thorne and to us." She wonders whether she should tell the man that she met his colleague, Dandy Jim, out on the open road. Something else happened to her, and Meg leans forwards so her face is close to The Robber:

"I watched my mother die this day," she says. "I held her hand as she went and, you know, it didn't feel wrong. She wanted to go. I wonder why I haven't cried. Nana says you cry at a funeral because that's what you're supposed to do. Maybe I'll weep then." She looks into his impassive face. She has already revealed more to him than she has to anyone else, and it makes her feel better. "Do your best to get well as fast as you can, Robber, and then be on your way. It would be good if you could pass us some of those guineas you say you have, but just as long as you leave, it's okay with me."

Meg puts the spoon back in the broth. She's got more than half of it down his gullet and he hasn't coughed once. At his chest she listens for a moment, just to make sure it's clear and then, with difficulty, she lays him down on his side again, his

61

body bent around the chimney breast, on the bare floorboards with his hat as a pillow and his cloak over him like a blanket. Meg runs her hand through his black hair, it's much thicker than her husband's was and whimsically, she reaches down into the top pocket of his shirt. There's a scrap of leather folded in half and she pulls it out. Inside is a piece of curly blonde hair. She smiles and puts it back.

"Is this from your lover, Robber?" she mocks. "Just as soon as you get better, you'll forget all about her." Meg thinks on, "unless the hair is from your child, in which case your love for them will be renewed. If you do wake from this, you ought to remember that it's me you have to thank for it, me, Meg the one from the last cottage, the one who feeds the chickens at the Pennyman Manor and the one who knows how to heal. I learned from my mother, but now she's gone. They'll all come to me and like her, I'll help."

Meg looks down on this tall man who lays on his side. It seems strange to be talking to him in these whispers while Nana and little Richie are asleep downstairs. She knows it will help him heal, but just as much as we need to listen, a body needs to be listened to. In all truth, there's not a soul in North Burton who would give Meg a pretty minute of conversation. Nana and little Richie are duty-bound to listen to her, they do not do it because they want to. Meg found it difficult to talk to John when he was here, so, she did what she always does, she listens while they go on and on, encouraging them to speak more by a nod of the head or a question, so that their noise becomes the only sounds and the character of Meg is engulfed by it. Maybe that's why no one notices her. There's a French story that Nana tells about a poor girl who collects ash and looks after her ugly sisters and her stepmother - she could be Meg, only Meg has hands that are strong and ugly from work, her hair is matted and her arms are thick and her legs powerful, nothing like a pretty girl in a story should be, nothing like Miss Charlotte Pennyman up at the manor house. Meg looks down on The Robber with his eyes closed and his black hair, the stubble of his beard growing thick and the slight whiff of perfume cutting through the stink of his blood. He could be a prince in the blink of an eye.

Maybe that's what Meg will make of him. She is going to tell him everything, while he is there and captured. She's going to tell him everything she would never tell anyone else.

What does it matter anyhow? He's not listening and he just needs the words to get better, just the sound of her voice.

What would it hurt?

CHAPTER FIVE

It's morning. Early. Meg leaves the cottage with little Richie making the fire while Nana wakes up. She has work to attend to. She opens the creaky door to the world outside, light snow has fallen and has just recently stopped. The sky is grey and North Burton has an eerie silence to it. There's no birdsong and not another soul seems to be awake. She wraps her cloak around her and strides down the street with the snow coming up to her ankles, it takes her a few moments to pass the row of four cottages. The village pump is frozen solid and looks like it's been twisted by the cold, no one has touched it for many months. The weeping willow just after is petrified. Meg remembers summer days sat under the shade of the drooping branches. Granddad Blackwood will probably cut it down for firewood soon enough.

Meg has duties up at the manor house farm that she neglected yesterday, hopefully, nobody will have noticed because of the storm. She goes past the frozen-over pond and up the hill to the church where she heads left, into the drive of the great Pennyman House, through the unlocked gates and to the livery yard where the faces of horses look out at her from their stalls. The Farthings are beginning their morning work of mucking them out, feeding them and brushing the beasts down, but on a day like today, there'll be no riding. With snow this deep you could catch a horse's leg on something nasty and not everyone is as foolhardy as Dandy Jim who Meg rode with the day previous. She sees Julia Farthing with a pitchfork inside a stall and a white horse tied up outside. They are valuable animals, some go to the races at Beverley or York, and Mr Pennyman has two stallions who those in the business will pay well to put their mares to. The Farthing girl sees Meg and stops.

"Morning," she calls without expression. In the social order of the farm, Meg who deals with the chickens and the pigs is far lower in rank. She would never be allowed to touch the expensive horses - let alone ride them. She continues on towards the pig shed and past Mr Farthing who is shovelling snow to make a path, probably so he can move his barrow.

"Morning Meg," he calls. He's more polite than his daughter but there's still an air of disdain. This farm girl is well beneath the skill of Mr Farthing in particular, and it's not really fitting that he even lives near here, or any of the other workers. Meg gives him a big, daft smile like she does. Smiles don't cost anything, and they prevent all sorts of things, including suspicion.

She arrives at the chicken pen, at one end there's a shelter, and a handful of gaunt-looking birds scratch about on the snow. There used to be a whole flock not three months ago, but some have been eaten and others shrivelled away in sickness. At this time of year, the cockerel should have been at them and they should be sat on eggs that will hatch, but, this is not a normal year. As soon as Meg steps through the door the cockerel comes at her, his beak out, she steps out the way and gives him a light kick. He's protective and Meg is glad of this. She finds a dozen eggs that must be from yesterday and puts them in her basket, they are heavy and frozen solid. At the water barrel, she smashes through the ice.

There are now seven pigs in the sty, a month or so back, one of the younger ones died in the night and by the time Meg had got to it the others had eaten most of her backside. It's warm inside here and Meg counts them up then breaks the ice on their water trough with a stick. She hears voices from the livery yard behind and goes outside to see what's happening. Standing in front of a horse stall is Miss Charlotte from the house. As always, she is the picture of beauty, with clean clothes and delicate smooth features, today she's wearing a pale riding dress and a blue frock coat with gloves. Her black hair is in a tidy bun and she is discussing something with Mr Farthing. They appear to disagree, Meg walks forward so she can hear what they are saying to each other.

"I have promised to see him, Mr Farthing and see him I will, so if you'd be so kind, please could you ready up Ruby?" Miss Charlotte always sounds polite, even when she is giving a direct order.

"If you please, Miss, riding out to Beverley today would not be wise, because of the snow. Think about the animal as well as your own safety, a break could cost a horse its life." Mr Farthing is speaking sense.

"I'm well aware of that Mr Farthing, this is why I've chosen Ruby as the horse I'll ride." Ruby is an eighteen-year-old grey cob with a long straggly face. She's a proper nag and the type of animal you'd put your fat uncle on because she won't throw him.

"Even so Miss Charlotte, have you checked this with your father? And Ruby is perhaps not the best horse to take." Mr Farthing is behaving above his position. Perhaps he sees himself as higher than the rank and file of the farm labourers, perhaps he's just arrogant; either way, he would not dare to question Mr Pennyman. Miss Charlotte however is not a fighter though she knows he's spoken out of turn.

"Please ready Ruby's saddle, Mr Farthing," the tall man nods and disappears off to the tack room in one of the low buildings. Miss Charlotte turns just quick enough to see Meg, she gives a wide, genuine smile. Because she is the top of the tree, the lady can afford to be honestly friendly with someone like Meg at the bottom. They are two extremes. She beckons and Meg is duty bound to take a few steps towards the livery yard.

"I have work to do, Miss," calls Meg. Miss Charlotte strides forward towards with the same friendly grin.

"How are you all keeping in the cottages, Meg?" she asks. "Do you have everything you need?" The young woman continues forward. She is earnest with charity.

"Yes, my lady, we have everything."

Meg cannot say how it really is.

"That's good. We are struggling up at the house. Everything is frozen stiff. I had to thaw this jacket out by the fire this morning. I bet the cottages are nice and snug and warm."

"Yes, they are, Miss Charlotte." The woman looks at Meg the way she might look at a pony that has got covered in mud, with a mixture of genuine pity and mawkish appreciation. "Are you going to Beverley, my lady?"

"Yes. I promised to meet the magistrate by letter some weeks back, and I do not intend to let him down, snow or no snow, when a Pennyman gives her word, she keeps it." Mr Farthing appears with the saddle and tack with quick steps, his daughter walks in front, opens the door to Ruby's stall and he goes in. There's a look of mild disdain on his face. Miss Charlotte moves back towards the livery yard.

"I'd be careful of Ruby, my lady," says Meg. "She's been a biter these last few weeks and no one has been on her for a while." If it had been anyone else, Meg would have put this more plainly. Some horses can be a right pain in the arse.

"Thank you, Meg," she says graciously.

"I'm sorry, my lady. I didn't mean anything by it."

"I know. It's appreciated, Meg. Not everyone has my best interests in mind." Miss Charlotte is probably referring to her father. Not that Meg would know. She watches Miss Charlotte go down to the livery yard and test the tack that Mr Farthing has strapped onto Ruby. Meg can see the horse's ears go back a few times as Miss Charlotte tightens the straps, she may have been riding a long time, but the young woman does not know animals. Unlike people, they will usually warn you before they do something out of character. Ruby bobs her head up and down a few times.

"She's not been ridden for a while," says Mr Farthing. There's a note of concern in his voice as Miss Charlotte puts her foot in the stirrup and hauls herself up into the saddle. She knows horses, but, at the same time she doesn't know horses. Miss Charlotte has never had to clean out a stall, clip or wash a horse down, she's never had to turn them out or catch one in the field, she's never been kicked or squashed up against a stable wall, she doesn't know how difficult they can be. Meg sees the problem as well as Mr Farthing, and his daughter too. Ruby is the worst horse to choose today, she's old and ratty and the young lady may not have enough force to control her. As soon as she gets into the saddle, Miss Charlotte gives Mr Farthing a smile as if to say all is well, and then it unfolds. Ruby jumps forwards with her hind legs together and lifts her head which gives Miss Charlotte far too much rein, if she'd been on more horses like this, she'd know how unpredictable they can be and she'd pull to the left, but as it is, Ruby lurches forward into a run. Up the hill she canters towards Meg and the pig shed at a sharp speed that the old horse does not look capable of doing. Shouts of whoa erupt from Mr Farthing and his mean eyed daughter instantly, but it is Meg who is nearest to Miss Charlotte, who has to act quickly, she can see the frightened eyes of the horse as it canters up the hill towards her. Miss Charlotte pulls frantically on the bridle but as any horse rider will tell you – you don't control a horse, the bridle is only to communicate, a horse controls itself. So, if Ruby wants to bolt off towards the open field because she is angry and frightened, then there is not a thing that Miss Charlotte, who is perhaps a fifth of the size of the animal, can do about it, however hard she yells and pulls on the reins.

Meg makes a dash, and in a few steps to the right, she is in front of the big grey cob with her arms held up to try to stop the horse, but she does not want to panic the animal any more than it already is.

"Miss Charlotte, give me your hand!" she yells. As the beast picks up speed, the young lady unhooks her left foot from the stirrup and reaches out to Meg next to her, her big blue eyes are wide in terror and she falls from the horse. Meg is not a particularly stout woman, but she has been working since she was able to stand so there is iron in her grip and her muscles. Miss Charlotte falls onto her and they both crash into the snow. The grey cob runs on and bounds over the hedge into the field where it continues for another thirty seconds before some hole or stone covered by the snow trips it, and the animal tumbles down a few hundred yards away. Miss Charlotte gets up and brushes down her frock coat, her tight hair has come loose and she has split her lip but she looks okay. More shocked than injured.

"Are you hurt, my lady?" asks Meg as she too stands. If Miss Charlotte had been on Ruby when she fell, it could be much worse than a split lip. Mr Farthing begins up the hill with a real look of concern. If anything has happened to Miss Charlotte, it may be his fault.

There's a loud shout from the livery yard.

"Mr Farthing!" The yell is too loud to have any real gravitas to it and they all know who is shouting as they turn their heads. It's Mr Pennyman who walks through the yard wearing a brown knee-length coat, white knee socks and a grey wig fixed to his little head. Ridiculous attire for a livery yard. He's followed by a smaller man with a bright red double buttoned jacket, cocked navy hat with a feather and a big ginger moustache, a military man. This is Captain Salter.

"Come down here at once and explain what's going on, Mr Farthing, and all of you." Mr Pennyman inherited the house from his father and has never been in the military, his farm is run by the workers and his financial matters taken care of by Treanor and Nephew lawyers of Newbegin Beverley although he would not admit this. In this respect, he has never really had to work alongside people, he just gives orders and there is an unspoken sense on the estate, that it would be much better if Mr Pennyman just let them get on with their jobs and didn't go poking his nose in. Mr Farthing hangs his head in respect.

"We've had a problem with one of the horses, Sir, she

bolted off into the field." Mr Pennyman sees the bloodied lips of his daughter.

"Just what the hell is going on?"

"Ruby bolted father. I was riding out to see the magistrate as I promised. She just took off and if it weren't for Meg here, I think I would have done myself some damage."

"Ride out to Beverley in this covering of snow? Have you lost what little sense God gave you, woman?" Mr Pennyman is not usually cruel. Perhaps he's trying to impress the ginger army captain behind him who watches the discussion through narrow eyes covered by the peak of his navy cocked hat.

"I made an appointment, father and I wished to honour it."

"Whereas that is commendable, Charlotte, did Mr Farthing not offer you caution on attempting such a journey in these conditions?"

"Yes, he did. I think, perhaps I acted a little foolishly." Mr Pennyman flares his nostrils. Someone has to be to blame for this and it can't be his daughter.

"You fell from the horse, you say?"

"Meg helped me, she pulled me from her, otherwise I may have gone off into the field with Ruby, she may have fallen on me." Miss Charlotte smiles back at the girl who saved her. Meg looks at her battered boots covered in dusty snow and the hemline of her skirt splattered with muck. She would rather just disappear altogether than be noticed, especially by these people. Any contact at all with Mr Pennyman is to be avoided, especially since she has a robber recovering in this man's property less than half a mile away.

"She pulled you from the horse?" repeats Mr Pennyman with a raised voice.

"No," corrects Miss. Charlotte, "she caught my hand as I jumped."

"Mr Farthing, could you appraise the situation for us? From a man's perspective." The tall horseman looks down on

70

his employer with understanding. There has to be someone to blame for this, and it can't be Miss Charlotte, it can't be the horse, Ruby, who even now is getting to her feet in the field behind. The blame could fall on someone who matters so little as to be of no consequence.

"It did look like she yanked her a little hard," says Mr Farthing. This is a bare-faced lie. Meg looks up at him. She'll remember that.

There's silence for a few moments as Mr Pennyman considers his next action.

"Step forward please Meg," he says. Mr Pennyman knows everyone who works for him. There aren't too many of them. "I realise that you acted with my daughter's interest and I thank you for that, but I cannot allow anyone to lay their hands on my family. Do you understand?" Meg does not look up at him because this may be disrespectful. "Please put your head up, child," says Mr Pennyman. Meg brings her eyes to meet his.

Yesterday she lost her mother, she does not know why she thinks of the old woman now or why her eyes fill up with tears. She's not going to beg. Mr Pennyman will do whatever he is going to do anyway and there is no law to stop him, Meg belongs to him, her house, the pittance she makes, the air she breathes – it all belongs to him. Mr Pennyman drops his right shoulder and whips his hand into Meg's face striking her cheek with a slap that knocks her sideways so she falls to her knees. It is unnecessarily harsh and even Mr Farthing is shocked at the violence. Mr Pennyman steps back as Meg gets up and puts her hand to her mouth.

"That's an end to it," he says as if he has concluded a great wrongdoing like King Solomon or a court judge. "Mr Farthing, I expect Ruby returned to her stable and Miss Charlotte, there will be no riding to Beverley for you. I'll send Mr Reed out. Back to work the lot of you. You as well, Meg." She does not look up at him and turns to go back to the pig shed and the chickens. In two minutes' walk, Meg is where she should be, she opens the flimsy wattle door and steps inside as it closes behind her. The little group in the livery yard disperse and Miss Charlotte follows her father and the Captain back towards the house.

With the pigs in front, Meg rests her back on the closed door. She feels the tears hot and wet down her face, but silent. They are not for the blow that Mr Pennyman gave her - if he had bothered to learn how to fight he would have broken her cheek, even Adam Gamble could have landed a better shot. The tears are for her mother, fresh and wet. She can still hear Mr Farthing's loud voice in the yard behind as he bellows orders at his daughter.

Meg thinks of the man she met the day before, Dandy Jim, and of The Robber with his belly full of chicken broth and the mushrooms her mother picked. Perhaps Mr Pennyman should be a little more afraid of Meg, perhaps she knows people and things that he does not. As her mother said, now is not a time for listening only. Meg wipes her tears away in the darkness of the pig shed and takes a deep breath.

She's getting ready to tell, and when she does, they'll all have to listen.

Every last one of them.

The afternoon begins to fade. The snow makes it feel like it's January even though it's March, light peeps through the gaps in the pig shed walls. Meg spends more time than she ordinarily would there because when Nana sees the mark on her face, she will be angry, not that she won't already know. This is North Burton. You only have to belch and someone will find out what you had for breakfast. As the light from the weak sun makes long shadows against the trees, Meg walks down the track towards the livery yard and hopes that there is nobody around. When she gets home there will be another enquiry as to why Mr Pennyman struck her, and it will be her fault, again, in Nana's eyes. Meg can hear the horses breathing behind their stable doors, at rest. The Farthing girl, Julia, must have finished her duties and all is quiet as she moves out of the livery courtyard. At the gate, a figure melts out of the half-darkness, tall and slim. It is Mr Farthing with a white handkerchief round his thin neck.

"Thought you'd gone home," he whispers.

"I've been busy," she answers.

"You know we had to shoot Ruby?" This is news to Meg. "She broke her hind leg on a hole in the snow. She's too old to get better after that. I just thought you'd want to know as it was your fault." It wasn't Meg's fault, at all. She keeps quiet because there is no point arguing with him, Meg would be arguing with his position also and his knowledge. She does not have the fighting spirit that Nana does.

"I need to get home, Mr Farthing, my Nana will be waiting up." He makes a scoffing noise through his nose at this.

"I've heard your Nana can more than take care of herself." Meg puts her hands on the gate to push it open and Mr Farthing places his hand also so she cannot. There's no force there on his behalf, but there could be. He takes a deep breath. Meg readies her hand to go for the hairpin that still holds her curly hair in place. There's a cough in the darkness behind the thin horse master and then a voice.

"It was not her fault." It's Miss Charlotte speaking. "The error was mine." A lamp comes into view and the gate to the livery yard is illuminated. The small frame of Miss Charlotte appears under the hurricane light held by the tall coach driver, Mr Reed. The warmth it gives seems to worry Mr Farthing, and he steps backwards.

"I won't have you repeat that, please, says Miss Charlotte. It was my decision to take Ruby, not Meg's."

"Aye, Miss Charlotte. I didn't mean anything rude… to you or Meg here."

"Quite," says Miss Charlotte in a level manner. "Meg, may

I walk you back home?"

"Yes, my lady," she answers. She has no choice.

"Mr Farthing, goodnight." The man disappears into the early evening behind as Mr Reed opens the gate.

Meg and Miss Charlotte walk down the track in the darkness. Mr Reed holds the light a few paces in front so they can see where they are going. After a minute, when they are away from the manor house, and she feels she is safe to talk, Miss Charlotte begins.

"I'm sorry for what happened today," she says. There's a stiffness to her voice. Mr Reed, of course, is listening too but she trusts him. "May we talk freely, you and I, Meg?" Meg nods but it's now too dark to see. Again, she has no choice but to accept.

"Aye, Miss Charlotte."

"If I speak with you truthfully, will you keep it to your own counsel? Will you keep it to yourself?"

"Yes," she answers. Despite Mr Reed with his lamp, there could be anyone from North Burton listening to them tonight, Adam Gamble could be in one of the bushes. Even Carrick the rector could be outside the wooden door of St Michael's looking up to the cold night sky. Miss Charlotte is so unworldly, she is like a child.

"My father had no right to strike you today, Meg. For this, I apologise. There's a person with him, that Captain Salter, the one with the red coat. I think my father wants to seem… more of a man than he is. You see, this Captain is here to hunt someone down, someone with a price on their neck. It was not fair that my father chose you as an example. I'm sorry. It should have been me." Meg cannot stop herself as the words come, hot and wet from her, too rude to be polite:

"Any other man would have broken my cheek." She wishes she had not said this straight away.

"My father is a good Christian, Meg and he has been kind to all you folk in the cottages over the years, and he will be

74

kind to you in the future, so, allow him this one error and do not judge him too harshly. I ask you only this."

"I'm sorry, Miss Charlotte." Meg controls herself. Though this girl appears to be weak and mild, she could still have Meg, Nana and Richie tossed out into the fields if she so desired.

"He's not himself. This Captain's brought the devil out in him. He thinks he's some sort of general. It's not my father."

"Who is The Captain looking for?" Meg asks. She thinks about Dandy Jim on the hill, inside the copse of dark trees with his blue eyes and his silver buckles.

"There is a beast he hunts," she says. Her voice is suddenly hushed. She stops and tall Mr Reed holds the lantern in front of Miss Charlotte's face. Her cheeks are smooth but her brow is furrowed in the soft light.

"A beast?" asks Meg.

"Not a bear or a wolf, something worse. The story is that there is someone in this area who is wanted for crimes that are almost too bad to be spoken of."

"A robber?"

"A murderer. A spy. Captain Salter is under orders to find him. It seems that a letter was sent by this beast through the postmaster here at Beverley. That would mean that he's here."

"There are plenty more villages that send a letter through Beverley, Miss Charlotte."

"Yes, and The Captain will examine each one. He's a hunter of some renown in York and London." Meg thinks again about Dandy Jim and her own Robber in the little cottage not two hundred yards away. Miss Charlotte smiles and her teeth are smooth, even and beautiful.

"So he's not a highwayman then, this one The Captain is looking for?"

"Goodness no, Meg. Have you ever heard of a highwayman in North Burton?"

"The road to York passes but four miles away, John Nevison himself would have ridden there on the way to York.

I've heard stories of them before." Miss Charlotte shakes her head but in her polite way.

"John Nevison is already dead, Meg. He rode from Rochester to York, and would have passed through Doncaster, he wouldn't have been anywhere near North Burton. So, you don't need to worry about people like that. We'll keep you safe. My father or this Captain Salter wouldn't let harm come to anyone, and even Mr Reed here has a musket underneath the seat of his carriage. I don't want you worrying about highwaymen." Meg tries to smile but there is no smile in her. There's still a pain in her cheek from Mr Pennyman's slap, and without showing it, she bristles with indignation. It was Nana that told her the famous highwayman John Nevison rode close to North Burton on his two-hundred-mile ride to York.

"Thank you," says Meg, like she is a child. Her mother warned against her temper and told her many times that she should not let it get the better of her. They have walked past the frozen pond and are nearly at the little row of cottages.

"Will you be safe from here, Meg?" asks Miss Charlotte.

"Aye, Miss, thank you."

There is no need to tell Nana what has happened. She will already know. Nothing of any consequence goes on in North Burton without the old woman finding out, Granddad Blackwood might have told her, or Mrs Farthing. She will know that Mr Pennyman hit her, but Meg does not know how she will act. You can never quite guess what Nana will do.

It's black when Meg opens the door and Richie rushes to greet her. The fire is low. Nana sits in her chair and watches as Meg goes over to it and begins to add some of the coal from the day before. Dutchy looks from the bench with her wide green eyes. Richie is upset. The old woman is unusually quiet, especially since something has happened. Meg goes to the bottom of the ladder to make her way up.

"Mr Pennyman isn't the sort to hit folks, you know, Meg. You must have rubbed him up the wrong way. Granted he's a bit of a fanny, but he isn't cruel. That's something new. You want to watch your temper." Meg gives the old woman a black look with her hair falling across her face. "Richie has been awful upset, he was worried someone would take you away." Here it is. Nana thinks whatever happened was Meg's fault too.

"Nobody will take me away, Richie," she says as she stares at the lad, "and if anyone tries to, I'll take you and we'll run. We'll go as far as France if we have to get away, or Holland." Her voice is bitter. She knows that this will frighten Nana, for without Meg, who will do her bidding? The two women look at each other in the flickering coal light.

"I want that Robber out of here, Meg. If Mr Pennyman gets wind of it, we'll be in front of the magistrates, both of us. I want him gone."

"I'm fixing him," says Meg, "but it isn't going to be quick."

"Can't you do something to hurry it up, whatever it is?" Meg goes to the mantlepiece above the fire and picks up the candle holder with a stub in it, she bends down and lights it from the fire. "Candles cost money," says Nana.

"If you want him to walk out of here then I have to look at him," she whispers. "And since when do you do anything to make any money?"

"This is my house," she bellows as Meg collects her medicine bag and starts to climb the ladder. "A widow's allowance," calls Nana. "Mr Pennyman himself told me so, he read it from his book on Parish Law." When Meg gets to the top, she can still hear Nana complaining in loud huffs.

The light from the candle illuminates the darkness of the upstairs platform, and Meg kneels next to The Robber. She puts her arms on his shoulders and gently, rolls the body onto its back. Her fingers go to his brow and there is a cold, light sweat with a weak fever.

He is fighting.

She examines his face by holding the candle up to his features. His beard has grown a little and the crow's feet from his eyes seem to have got deeper. She moves the light down to his torso and then takes off the cloth that she covered the wound with the day before so she can examine it. The skin is swollen and puffed up, but not yellow. He's lucky it's so cold. If it was summer, it might be infected already. Meg covers him over and manoeuvres herself so her back is against the wall next to the chimney, she lifts The Robber's shoulders and sets his head in her lap. Then places her hand on his forehead.

Years ago, when Meg was a little girl, she used to wheeze and sometimes so much so that she could not go to sleep. Her mother fed her warm water and honey and set a hot wet cloth on her chest, and perhaps these things helped, but they did not help as much as the tender way she massaged her forehead and hair with steady pressure. This was what calmed Meg's chest. It's what she will do for this Robber. She reaches down to her bag to fish out some of the dried mushrooms from yesterday. She rubs one between her thumb and forefinger until the tips are oily with residue from it. Then, she puts her hand down to The Robber's face and rubs some into the man's lips gently. It will work slowly on him, maybe it will work itself into his dreams.

"Come closer, Richie," she whispers, and from the darkness comes the little boy who crept silently up the ladder behind her. He snuggles next to Meg in the darkness. "I'll tell this story to you and my Robber here, so that you shall both have fine dreams." The little lad smiles at her in the darkness. So, Meg begins with one hand gently rubbing the forehead of The Robber and the other on the nape of Richie's neck. She looks into the darkness in front of her and realises that there is no story she has to tell. She is not Nana in front of the fire or Granddad Blackwood with his elbows resting on the wooden bar of The Bay Horse across the road. She has no anecdotes to amuse or confound. Meg's mother told her to tell and that's what she'll do. Dutchy the cat creeps low and nearer to her from the rafters with big wide eyes, she finds a spot on Richie's knee. The lad will be asleep in less than a minute, and The Robber is not in a fit state to hear or remember anything and so, it does not matter what she says, nobody is listening. In the darkness, Meg tells, everything, in a light and low whisper, from her childhood in the fields at Etton, to her wedding day four years since, and she tells everything in between, what she is afraid of and what she dreams, how it feels going to the pigsty every day, the smell of summer flowers, the sorrow of marriage to a man you do not love, and the weight of duty to a family.

She tells of how it would be to get away from North Burton and how it would be if she were free.

CHAPTER SIX

It's pitch black. Morning again. The sun is half an hour from rising and Meg has left Richie sleeping upstairs next to The Robber under the heavy black cloak. Nana would go mad if she knew he was that close, but the old woman can't get up the ladder with her legs, so she says. Nana snores with her head back and a blanket over her lap. The air is still and quiet. Meg considers the old woman's bulbous face, the sagging cheeks and the thin wispy short hair. She claims she can't walk, but last midsummer, when Mr Pennyman ordered all the old barrels of ale to be poured away so they could make more, Nana managed to make it all the way up the hill to the house with Granddad Blackwood. There, she supped as much as she could with all of them, danced a jig to Adam Gamble's singing as well, and made it home. Meg has seen her struggle to the pot to relieve herself but that's all and never more than a few steps without a lot of assistance. She's worked her life, says Nana, and deserves the respect that a widow is allowed. Meg has been taught not to look down on folk, but she can't help it. She throws her cloak around her shoulders, opens the door without a sound and she is outside.

There has been no snow in the night and the road is a solid block of ice. As the sun struggles up, Meg passes the Thorne Farm. At the gate in a black hat with the sides pulled down over his ears is Farmer Thorne. He leans against the brick of the farmhouse, his arms are folded and the bulb of his long clay pipe is in his right hand, with the tip in the side of his mouth. His face is pained as he sucks in smoke with one cheek. Meg tries to hurry by.

"You off somewhere?" he calls. Farmer Thorne is normally a busy man and doesn't have time to smoke his pipe unless he's drunk or it's Sunday morning. It means there must be something wrong. Meg tries not to catch his eye because he's looking at her.

"My mam died, Farmer Thorne, day before yesterday." Meg does not pause and makes her answer seem like it is as matter a fact as collecting eggs, or fence making, or going to the pump to collect water.

"Aye, I heard," calls Farmer Thorne, "but you'll not get over the hill to Etton, our Meg, the snow is deep and it's iced over. Your mam's not to be buried until Sunday week." Farmer Thorne calls those that have worked for him 'our', not out of arrogance but because he cares for them.

"I have to see her, Mr Thorne." The big man steps off the wall with a puff of smoke rising into the cold morning.

"Hang on, Meg, slow down," and at this, she must ease her pace and turn her head to the older man. Farmer Thorne looks pale today and his beard seems more grey, the fingers are huge from a lifetime of work as he removes the pipe from his mouth. "You'll make it there and back, lass but it won't be easy." Meg wrinkles her nose. What's he doing having a smoke when there are things to be done?

"What's happened?" she asks.

"Two of the big girls went in the night. Frozen up." He refers to his cows and has a faraway look to him. Farmer Thorne may be considerably richer than Meg, but it does not mean he feels any less when he loses animals, they are his livelihood and his family as well.

"Which ones?" Meg would have milked them last summer.

"The two brown ones I got from Driffield."

"The cold got to them?"

"Aye."

"Mother and the girls are cutting them up now. I don't know how long we can stand this, our Meg. If the ice doesn't melt soon then how will we get the seeds in, what will the harvest be like? What will happen next winter? We'll all starve." Like most rich men, Farmer Thorne is not so concerned with what is happening today, rather, what may happen tomorrow. He does not really want Meg's advice, he just wants to tell someone outside his immediate family. Meg is harmless anyway.

"We'll pull together, Mr Thorne," she answers. "I think I might try to make it through to Etton anyway." Farmer Thorne looks down at his boots and then back up at her.

"I heard about what Mr Pennyman did," he says. "You'd not be hurt here on this farm, lass and you'd be free to stay in one of the back rooms." He is a good man to work for, honest and fair, but Meg is not a young woman anymore.

"I'm married now, Mr Thorne, I have me mother to think of and Richie and my husband, when he comes home." Farmer Thorne nods. He has forgotten the thin, non-descript John she married all those years ago, and forgotten too that he has not yet come home. Most people have.

"Aye, you do. I was sorry to hear about your mother, Meg. She was a good woman like her daughter is." Farmer Thorne taps his pipe on the brick of the farmhouse to empty it and looks her up and down. "If you ever need anything, if you're hungry or you need a friendly face, then our door is always open. Nana's not the easiest woman to get along with. I've known her a good many more years than you have." Meg smiles to cover up any emotion she might show.

"It's all fine, Mr Thorne, we get on well. She dotes on that lad Richie. Sir, I have to be on my way if I'm to get back before the sun goes down." He nods.

"Be careful up on the hill. There was a robbery on the York Road two days ago, so I've heard. Robbers made off with a tidy penny."

"The York Road's half a day's walk from here," says Meg.

"Aye, but that's only an hour's ride, I'm sure they're long-gone lass, I mean what is there here? Just keep your eyes open."

"Yes, Mr Thorne, thank you," and she is off again with wide strides and the odd slip. Mr Thorne watches her make her way down the track to the fork that leads off to Etton. He sighs and goes back to the wife and the girls back in the barn.

Meg is not going to Etton.

There's no need anyway, now Farmer Thorne has explained that her mother's funeral will be Sunday week.

Meg is going to do what she should not do, she is going to see Dandy Jim. *We'll see you before you see us* - that's what he said. She'll go past Etton altogether and then north along the fields to get to the forest of Dalton Park where Dandy Jim said he was hiding.

It takes Meg an hour to get up the track, through the trees and to the bottom of the hill that separates North Burton from Etton. On a sunny day, it's a fine walk, but the wind has whipped up, and walking through the iced-over snow is difficult. She wraps her cloak around her and puts her head down as the wind drives on. There's not a soul in the white, sterile landscape, and nothing moves. Half a mile in front is a dry-stone wall and behind that, the trees that make up the forest edge of Dalton Park. She struggles on. How is anyone meant to see her in this?

At the drystone wall, she stops and checks behind and around her. There's no movement on the horizon in any direction. She clambers over the stone and her legs sink up to the knees in the snow of the field on the other side, she glances behind her and makes an audible gasp when she sees him. It's a man dressed in ragged clothes and a woollen hat. Not Dandy Jim, but someone equally odd. He squats out of the wind with his back to the wall so he can't be seen and, as soon as he notices Meg, he puts one of his thick fingers to his lips to indicate she should be silent, then points for her to sit down a few yards away, as he is, with his back against the stone. He doesn't seem surprised to see her. Meg notices, at once, the long musket across his waist with his large hand on one end. He wears a grey frock coat and a scarf tied around his neck in the fashion of a gentleman, but there is nothing gentlemanly about how dirty he is, the scarf that may once have been white is thick with grime and his straight hair is slick with grease under the black woollen hat. Along the right side of his face is a wicked mess of burn scars as if he was caught in a fire in the past, but in his eyes, Meg can see a steady soldier's attention to detail. She follows his orders and puts her back against the drystone wall. Out of the wind, her ears begin to go red with the warmth.

"Were you followed?" he asks. His voice is low, smooth and almost hoarse.

"No," she answers.

"I followed you," he replies.

"From where?"

"A while back." There's a gap in the top row of his teeth. "We'll follow the wall here along to the edge of the forest over there, see?" Meg nods. "You go first, and I'll try to keep your pace, but don't go too quick, will you?" He smiles and his teeth have black edges. The man is easily as dirty as Miles Blackwood but has a steadiness of action and his eyes dart over the landscape around them. "I am Carlos. Dandy Jim told me about you, he said you'd come back." She nods but does not smile. There's no need to give men such as these the wrong impression.

As they walk along the wall where the snow has not fallen as deep, Meg considers that she may have made a mistake coming here. Part of her did not expect to find the man she encountered a few days previous, Meg is not certain why she is here, or what she is going to say and is afraid suddenly, for she does not know this man behind her with a heavy musket in his hands as he follows. Nor does she know how many men there may be in the trees in front, suddenly there is an urge to run. Perhaps she has misjudged. She looks back, and the man who said his name was Carlos, is right behind her with a serious look on his face and the scars showing bright in the glare from the snow. Meg swallows. He is not the same at all

84

as The Robber she has in her house back in North Burton, not nearly as well kept nor as well dressed. His hands wrapped around the handle of the musket are thick and the fingernails are dirty.

"There's no need to be afraid," he says. This is what Carrick up at the church once said to her before he tried to push her into the back room of the vestry after Sunday service. It's what Christopher Saunders had told her when she was fourteen in the haybarn back at Etton before he tried to kiss her. She glances back at Carlos again. He has huge shoulders and a thick tree trunk neck. He nods his head for her to keep moving. There's no getting out of this. The trees are just up ahead.

A few metres into the forest and Meg feels a rush of movement and footsteps behind that are much too agile for her to avoid. She is pushed forwards and a deft, strong hand grips the back of her neck as a sack slips over her head, the movement is sleek and there's a voice, this time, Dandy Jim:

"I'm sorry for this, lass, it will only take a minute. You'll have to trust me." Meg fights with her legs as she is pushed forwards further, a rifle butt knocks her knees out of place, more skilled than rough so she stumbles but doesn't fall, very much like Farmer Thorne might encourage his milking cows into the barn. Meg is led through the darkness with the sack over her head, tripping on roots that she cannot see, but not allowed to fall by strong hands on her shoulders. It takes a few minutes and at every turn she hears the voice of Jim, formal but in no way a gentleman, telling her that it will be fine. She wishes she had put her hair up with that hairpin, if Nana had been awake, she would have reminded her. As quick as it was on, the sack is whipped from her head and gentle pressure on her shoulders makes her sit down on a log. It takes a minute for Meg's eyes to adjust.

It seems as if it's dark but she senses bushes around her and the grey sky between thick but bare trees above. There are three big logs arranged in a triangle around a tiny fire. Meg sits on one, Carlos another, and the third bears Dandy Jim with his legs crossed, hat off in his right hand and a big smile across his face. His hair is smooth and combed. It could do with a trim around the ears and the back, but he has made a good job of it. He smells also, of the same scent that Meg's Robber has on, it's exotic and fresh.

"I am sorry we had to do that," he explains. "It wouldn't do you any good to know where we are." Meg takes a breath. It's strangely warm in the thicket of bushes. Even with the fire, nobody would guess anyone was camped in these woods. She looks at Dandy Jim and then to Carlos. If they were going to do anything to her, maybe they would have already done it. The three of them are close, enough so she could reach and touch the smooth fabric of Dandy Jim's coat. Meg should be scared, these are robbers no doubt, there's the shiny silver tooth at the back of Dandy Jim's smile, the soft leather cloth that Carlos wipes his musket down with, the smell of tobacco and the faint aroma of something stronger. Meg should be in tears and yet, she feels a sense of calm with these men. They are more like she is than Mr Pennyman or Miss Charlotte, they occupy the same space somehow in the great ladder of the world. Meg is at the bottom because she has no choice, these men are at the bottom by design. They are kin.

"I told Carlos you'd be back," says Dandy Jim. He points at his colleague. "Didn't I?" he asks. The marksman just nods.

"Did you find our man?" he says. "Did you find our Pearlman?"

"Is that his name?" asks Meg.

"No, but that's how it's referred to in the business," says Dandy Jim. "What's known as a pearlman is the member of the gang who sniffs out where the prize is going to be. Me being the organizer and captain of this little band, it's my job to work out how to get it, and Carlos has the role of shooting those that attempt to stop us, but only if he has to." Dandy

Jim does not have the turn of phrase of an educated gentleman, but he does well enough.

"I thought there would be more of you," says Meg.

"Lads like us go in three," answers Jim. That's what Nana says too. "Now, what have you come to tell me? Did you find a man, a good six-footer he is, thin as a rake and with a wry grin and a big open stab wound on his stomach?" Meg has not come here to tell them about her Robber.

"I haven't seen him and I've heard nothing neither," says Meg. Carlos looks at Jim and shakes his head.

"He'll be dead," he says. Now they are nearer each other, Meg can hear his voice has a gentle lisp because the front tooth is gone. He blinks at Dandy Jim. "I say we cut our losses and get moving, let him be, whatever's happened to him."

"There's no way he could have left North Burton, not in his state, and not with the lanes like they are. He's still here somewhere."

"Probably face down in a ditch."

"If that is the case, he'll still have the silver on him," says Jim. "We could still find him."

"What happened to your Pearlman?" asks Meg. Dandy Jim turns to her and gives her a smile. Not an evil one. More playful.

"Now, if I am to take you into our confidence, Meg, then you will know things that you maybe shouldn't know. That could have consequences for you, in the long run, understand?" She looks at Carlos and then back to Dandy Jim, smells his perfume in her nose. She doesn't quite know what she is doing.

"You can tell me," she says.

"You sure?" asks Jim. "Once you know too much about Carlos and I here, you'll be a danger to the people of your village behind you and also to us. Are you ready for that?" Meg narrows her eyes.

"If you want me to help you find him then you'll have to

tell." Jim smiles again.

"We call him Dale. Carlos knew him before I did."

The big musketeer begins:

"I met him when I walked under the Duke of Marlborough's banner across the continent. I was with him when I got this," Carlos points to the burns that do not make him look ugly, more interesting. "He's a handy boy, our Dale and he knows his cards and he knows how to swindle alright. He can scrap as well as any of us but it's his tongue of pure silver that's his gift."

"I found these two down in Nottingham holding up old ladies on the road out of the city," says Jim. "A couple of lads who weren't soldiers anymore and had no idea what to do with themselves. Carlos here still keeps his redcoat uniform from his days with the Duke, he keeps it rolled up in his kit bag." Carlos grins at the truth of this. "It was me that took them under my wing, showed them what was what. Taught them how to look after themselves and dress well, how to speak like gents, to smile and bow." Meg looks at Carlos with his dirty grey frockcoat and blackened teeth. Dandy Jim nods as he reads her thoughts.

"You should have seen Carlos here before he met me, and also, you can lead a horse to water, but you can't make it piss. We're a good band, the three of us. We know how to get things done and, more importantly, what's worth doing. The plan was to rob the coach and then lay low till the snows died down and then, up to York for a drink down Micklegate. Our Pearlman, Mr Dale, knows the place well, he says he was born somewhere round here too." Meg frowns as she thinks.

"Did something go wrong with the robbery?" she asks. There's a thrill talking to thieves.

"Not so much with the robbery," continues Dandy Jim. "Like all pearlmen, our Mr Dale has a greedy disposition, he always wants more and he always wants what he can't have. That's why he so good at what he does, he sees the value in a thing. Whereas you and I may see a simple pair of boots, Mr Dale will know that they are crafted by Fly's of Oxford Street, London and worth a pretty penny. Over conversations with myself and Carlos here, Dale seemed to think that he would like to settle down, take a wife and perhaps get a property with land. He wanted out of our little arrangement." Carlos's face darkens as Dandy Jim explains. "Dale wanted his share of that silver for himself, to start afresh. As I said, he always wants what he can't have. That's when we had our disagreement. Our Pearlman believed he had the right to walk away from his commitments and take his share with him. Carlos didn't like that, did you, Carlos?" The man opposite Meg taps the long handle of the dagger tucked into his belt with a dirty finger.

"I wasn't gonna kill him, it was just a warning." Where Carlos sounded serious before, his voice now has the quality of darkness as he looks down his nose at the fire. Meg understands the wound on her Robber. "With a little help, he'll make it through," says Carlos. "You learn a lot about what will kill a man as a soldier, little nicks can finish you off in a week or two but you can go on forever on an open wound." Meg should be more scared than she is of these two but, there is an ease to them that men of authority and power do not have, they have nothing to prove and nothing to laud over her. Meg blinks back at Dandy Jim.

"And he took your money?"

"He did, all of it, he managed to get away even after Carlos stabbed him, but, it's not really our money, Meg, it's none of it our money." Dandy Jim speaks with the weight of knowledge. "We're men of the road but we're not thieves. We use the money we take for our expenses, Carlos here needs bullets, I sometimes need a new hat, but most of it, what we take, goes back to those who it was stolen from in the first place. People like you."

"Nothing's been stolen from me, Sir. I've never had anything that could be taken."

"Do you work hard?"

"Aye."

"Does the Mr who you work for have more than you?"

"Aye, Mr Pennyman, he's well to do."

"Does he work as hard as you?"

"He does things that I cannot do, he runs the farm."

"I'd wager," says Dandy Jim, "that there are good, hardworking folk down in North Burton that run that farm for him. They know the animals better, know the land better, work harder and longer and yet, it's this Mr Pennyman that sleeps in a warm bed and has roast chicken, and the upper crust cooked for him. He's stealing from you alright, probably all of you. He steals your time and your work." This talk has made Meg's head spin. "It's men like your Mr Pennyman who steal the money – we just take it back." Meg glances across at Carlos and the sharpshooter nods in agreement. "Our Pearlman, Mr Dale, he was starting to think like one of those who are above their station, he was starting to think the money belonged to him and that he could settle down." Meg looks into the tiny fire with the black pot over it. There's a chill in the air from the forest around her.

"What is it you've come to tell us, Meg, if you don't know where our Pearlman is?" asks Dandy Jim. Meg remembers what she thought she might say.

"It's Mr Pennyman," she remembers the slap across her face and the condescending look in Miss Charlotte's eyes afterwards, Nana shaking her head in the darkness of the cottage. If these men are going to leave North Burton and leave her Robber alone, and by default her, then they will need something to make them leave. Why not let Dandy Jim help himself to whatever Mr Pennyman cannot be smart enough to protect?

"What about Mr Pennyman?" asks Carlos. "I've never heard of him until today."

"He's a rich man. Not showy rich like the ladies in Beverley of a Sunday morning, but he has deep pockets. He could afford a lot more than he has."

"Are you offering to be our Pearlman, lass?" asks Carlos.

"I don't know what you mean," she answers.

"I mean you get us into his estate and we'll nick his stuff." Meg's mother warned her against her anger. It never does any good and only gets you in more trouble in the end, but the fire is still burning in her belly. Mr Pennyman deserves to have the grin wiped off his face.

"I'll get you into his yard," she whispers. Dandy Jim lets out a snort with a smile and stands, his voice takes on an oratory tone in the darkness of the forest.

"Didn't I tell you, Carlos, that there was something different about this Meg, that she was more than just a village girl? Didn't I tell you?" Carlos nods as he looks at her.

"He did say that."

"Can you remember what I said, Carlos?"

"You said she'd be our way out of here, and the key to a good bit of coin." Meg is suddenly sure of herself, but she should not be so surprised. Men like Dandy Jim have a way of knowing who is who in the world. He can spot a lad who knows how to handle himself in a fight in a busy pub, he can tell you which of the rich gentleman along the street have their mind on other business and their wallets in the open pocket of their jackets, he can see honesty at fifty paces and a liar at a hundred, so to see that Meg has something special about her is as simple as picking out pennies from a wishing well.

"A one job Pearlman," says Dandy Jim as he looks down on her. "The best and hardest thing there is to find."

CHAPTER SEVEN

If it were winter proper, it would be dark. The freezing afternoon is grey as Meg makes her way past Farmer Thorne's gate once more. Though it's only four o'clock or so, the families of North Burton will be settling in for the night, there's no point being outside when it's this cold. Meg's fingers have started to take on a blueish colour, so she fancies, again, but it's not done for her yet, she has a job to do up at Mr Pennyman's house with the chickens.

That's not all.

She reaches her cottage and lifts the latch to open the door. It's dark inside and the fire is ablaze with coal. Richie is in front of it and his face is black with a line of soot. Nana sits in her chair, at the sight of Meg, she fills her lungs with air through her nose ready to bellow at the girl for leaving her and the boy on their own all day, again. Meg holds her finger up in front of her to calm the old woman.

"You just hold your tongue, Nana," she whispers, and from the big pocket in her petticoat, she pulls out something wrapped in brown cloth that she hands over. The old woman's breath comes out in a shocked sigh when she unwraps the package, it's deer, a back leg all the way to the buttock where there is still a little bit of meat. Nana looks up in fear. Where would Meg get this? Deer are not to be hunted, by Mr Pennyman's orders. "Now, listen," whispers Meg. "There'll be no sharing of that, I'll get rid of the bones when you're done with them." Nana does not have anything to say and this is unlike her, but, if they have food, they should share it, this is how North Burton works.

"It's only fair the Blackwoods get a bit of it, Meg. Them lads won't ask any questions and they won't say nowt to no Pennyman. They got all that leftover chicken from yesterday." All the anger and fluster has gone out of the old woman because, short of a bottle of brandy, a leg of venison is perhaps the best present Nana could ever get. From the other side of her petticoat, Meg pulls out an empty glass bottle. Inside there's a thin line of brown liquid. She hands it to Nana who pulls the cork out with a low pop and downs the few drops.

"I found it on the road back from Etton," says Meg, preempting any questions.

"The bottle or the meat?"

"What do you think?"

"It's not my business to care how you came by it, lass, but I'm grateful." This is unusual talk for Nana, the shock of good food has put her out of her normal mood. "It'll take all night to cook it properly. Slip next door and tell Granddad Blackwood to bring his big chopping knife, will you?"

"We can't share it," repeats Meg.

"We have to," says Nana flatly.

"They'll talk."

The old woman scoffs.

"A Blackwood has never spragged, not as long as I've been alive. Now if it were a Farthing then I'd agree, we don't share with them, but the Blackwoods, Meg… well, we'd none of us be alive if it weren't for them. Where do you think the rabbits come from? The duck they brought in last week, they get it from Pennyman. Just enough so he doesn't notice. We never say a word, and they won't either." Meg knows Nana is right. The Blackwoods may be as thick as they are strong but they really would never blab. It's not them saying anything that Meg worries about, it's any evidence they might leave.

"Don't let them have any bones, Nana. I don't want that daft bastard Miles Blackwood picking his teeth with bits of deer in front of anyone." Meg backs away to the door. It's not like her to swear.

"You'll not use language like that in my house," adds Nana.

"I have to go," says Meg.

"Where?" says Nana. There's sudden worry in her voice.

"I have to see to the fowl up at the house. I didn't do it this

93

morning. The pigs as well."

"It'll be dark, you'll break your neck. Leave it till the morning, Meg, you've been out all day as it is."

"I have to," she answers. Meg closes her eyes in worry, but in the grey, she knows that Nana won't be able to see.

"Just make sure you're back for when this leg is done." It's an order from Nana and her voice is flat and cold.

"I will," says Meg.

Outside, the air feels welcome on her face and the weak sun is just beginning to go down to the west behind her. It's not unusual for Meg to visit the fowl at this time, there may have been other things she would have been busy with, just as long as she gets there. Meg passes the front door of Granddad Blackwood and then The Farthings, she sees that one of the hinges on the Gamble door has fallen off. Up the hill she walks again, towards the Church and opposite, the great house with the farm behind. There's no wind and it's still light enough to see well, even though it's grey and cold. Carlos told her the moon would be out.

She goes through the big gate to the Pennyman House and to the livery yard where the horses are closed away in their stables with the doors and top shutters fastened, Meg can hear them moving about inside. There are footsteps in front of her and a figure looms out of the grey.

"Shouldn't you be at home, Meg?" It's the coachman, Mr Reed, with his hands in his pockets and his straight blonde hair spilling out from under his cap.

"I could say the same of you, Sir," answers Meg. "There's one of the pigs is lame. I wanted to check on her, make sure she settles." The man in front nods. Danny Reed is okay, as far as Meg knows. She has seen him, on more than one occasion, make an obscene hand gesture behind Mr Pennyman's back when he was not looking, she knows also that Mr Reed likes cards and that he pilfers bottles from the

Pennyman cellar and sells these to the Blackwoods, but not too often to be considered a thief. Despite this, Danny Reed looks like he is someone you could trust, has a reasonable church education from the Grammar School in Beverley and, even though he has not been in North Burton so long, Mr Pennyman has made him a constable of the peace. It's he who could make an arrest, and along with Mr Pennyman, could sentence criminals if needed. Not that there are any criminals.

"Right you are, lass. I'll be locking the gates soon, so don't take long will you." She nods. Meg does not let it show, but she is worried for this tall blonde-haired man. He has done nothing wrong to her, far from it. She does not like to think of what Dandy Jim might do to him if he were to stand in their way tonight. She brushes past onto the pig shed and hears him whistling down the steps to the front gate of the house.

Meg goes into the shed and the smell is rich and hot. She checks that the big sow is not sitting on any of the littler ones with educated taps of her boot. The pigs do not give her any trouble. Perhaps they can sense her unease as she uses the wooden spade to scoop up their doings from the day and piles it just behind the door to remove it properly tomorrow. Dandy Jim had assured her she was doing the right thing, especially after Meg told them both about the incident with Miss Charlotte and the horse. Rather than laugh it off, or blame Meg, the two highwaymen listened with serious faces and scowls. Carlos had mentioned that he would like to teach Mr Pennyman a lesson in manners with the blunt end of his musket; but despite how warm this makes Meg feel, there is still the pressing problem of the prone robber upstairs in her cottage. In no way can these men find him, nor anyone else, perhaps the very survival of Nana and little Richie rests upon this. She hopes that Dandy Jim and Carlos can take something and go, maybe then Meg will never see them again, and she can heal The Robber, collect his silver, and everything can return to being as dreary and dreadful as it has always been.

She hears a light whistle from outside the shed, faint enough to be a bird in the undergrowth calling out before it goes to sleep.

This is the signal.

Meg drew them a map on the forest floor. If you track the side of the field behind, from a few miles away, you don't need to go through the front gate. At the back of the pig shed, there is a section of the hedge that you can climb over. Meg crunches through the snow behind the sow house and the bushes covered by a great, barren oak. She takes a deep breath before she does the noise, the same whistle that Carlos showed her. She waits in the fading light, blinking at the undergrowth wound tight with roots, and wonders if they have heard or if she should whistle again. There is a flash of something in the grey, the glint of Carlos's musket plate and a toothless grin on his face. They have made no noise at all as they came over and there has not been a snapped branch or even the crunch of snow. Dandy Jim appears next to him, dressed in his big hat like he is going to a fine dinner somewhere and not about to rob a country house. He taps Meg on the shoulder in thanks and she moves away from them down to the pig shed. From here, her job is done.

She rubs her face with both hands.

She can't help thinking she has just let the devil in.

The darkness is nearly on her as Meg reaches the front gate. Mr Reed stands with his hand on one of the metal bars ready to close it for the night as she makes her way to him. He smiles.

"You have a good night, now, Meg," he says as she walks through the opening. She swallows and turns back to him, suddenly, she does not want anything horrible to happen to anyone at the Pennyman House, not Mr Reed here or Miss Charlotte, not even Mr Pennyman himself. She does not know anything about Dandy Jim or Carlos, those will not even be their real names. What will they steal? Who will they hurt?

"What's wrong?" asks Danny Reed in the darkness.

"Nothing," she answers too quickly.

"If it's about the other day with Mr Pennyman, Meg. Miss Charlotte was most upset about it. I haven't seen her that angry with her father before and behind closed doors, Miss Charlotte can give as good as she gets, more so. The cook told me that when that Captain Salter was out of the way, she tore a strip off her father for the way he treated you. I'm sure, she will make it up to you." Meg blinks in the darkness at this man. Mr Reed is more one of the servants than one of the house, although he straddles both worlds. She wants to warn him. How would he fare if he came up against Carlos? Would he stand up to Dandy Jim?

Meg knows that if she says anything, there will be more trouble than she can handle, she will set into motion a chain of events that may well destroy her, Nana and little Richie as well.

"He didn't hurt me, Mr Reed. Us from the East Riding are made from stern stuff." He smiles and nods as he closes the gate with him on the inside.

"Goodnight," he adds. Meg can hear him fitting the padlock through the holes in the gate clasp as she walks down the hill. She rubs her face. She has to hope that Dandy Jim will make good on his word to rob what little he can find and get going before anyone can catch him. Isn't that what he said in the forest on the hill? They don't seem like killers. Then again, there's a deep stab wound on Meg's Robber that Carlos said he did, not deep enough to kill. If he can do that to someone who is meant to be part of his gang, what will he do to someone who stands in his way?

Nana has no acid words for Meg tonight.

The deer leg has been cooked and eaten, already shared with the Blackwoods no doubt. Richie has saved Meg a wooden bowl full of the meat but mostly it's just the water it was cooked in. She squats next to the fire and looks up at Richie sitting on the bench and Nana in the high-backed chair like always. They both seem solemn. It's not normal to eat venison, even if it does taste good. Meg takes a sip on the broth and it's divine, like warmth running down her throat and into her chest.

"Where's the bone?" she asks Nana.

"The Blackwoods will grind it up and drink it," says Nana. "What have you got mixed up in?" She is not accusatory or berating Meg, it's just a question from a wise old woman. You don't always know how Nana is going to be, she could fly off the handle about the smallest detail but when it's something big, she's rock calm.

"I'm not mixed up in anything, Nana," she replies, "and anyway, we're up to our neck in trouble already with that Robber upstairs." Nana adjusts herself in her chair and the wood creaks against her weight.

"He's been making noises," says the old woman. She shoots Richie a glance and the lad nods and grins. "Unnatural noises. Grunts and such. How long will he be here before he gets better? He smells too." Meg goes to the bottom of the ladder carrying her bowl,

"You're one to talk," she says, "with the stink of your feet." Here Nana is about to respond with her classic aggression, but she catches herself before she does.

"You better go to him," she whispers. In the flickering light from the fire, Nana seems uncertain, even a little afraid.

The upstairs space of the cottage smells of man and hot breath. He is still laid on his back next to the chimney breast with his black cloak over him and his eyes closed. Richie has brought a candle and put it on the floor. Meg sits The Robber up and leans his back on the warm brick of the chimney breast, just like she did the night before. She fishes for the leather pouch in her herb bag, the one with the dried mushrooms so favoured by the Innkeeper's daughter. Richie watches her as she adds some to the remaining half of the venison water and stirs it in with her finger.

"What will that do?" asks the lad.

"It will keep him asleep and dreaming so he can get better." As previous, she uses her fingers to open his mouth, push aside the tongue and then, with a wooden spoon she adds some of the broth straight down his throat. "You best get some sleep there Richie, I'll be here for a while." The boy nods and scurries away and down the ladder, leaving the two of them alone. As before, Meg knows her voice can soothe and heal as much as the broth and the mushrooms.

"I know who you are now, Mr Dale," she whispers. The man's face does not move. "And I know you're a pearlman and I know that you tried to run out on your associates. Now, you wouldn't do that to Nana and I. We made an agreement that you would walk out of here and walk out of here you will. Nana's fussed about the silver but not me, I just want to see the back of you." She stops spooning the broth for a minute to look at this man's face, the stubble is a little bigger and his cheekbones are proud and high. Meg is not sure she would like to see the back of this man, really. There is something about him that she is drawn to, the light smell of his perfume wearing thin now, the way he breathes in and out, even and slow. Meg leans forward. She wonders what his silver tongue would sound like and if this is a good or a bad thing.

"You could be my Robber," she whispers into his face in the flickering candlelight. "You could take me with you when you go. In the middle of the night, we could leave, out the front door while Nana is asleep, we would go down to Farmer Thorne's yard, right to the back to where he keeps Jamie, the biggest gelding he has, and we'd steal him, the two of us. We'd rob him and head away over the fields to wherever is not North Burton." Meg sits back, a little embarrassed she has said this, but it feels good nevertheless. She glances over her shoulder to make sure Richie is not still there, listening in the darkness. As she adds another spoonful to his mouth, she thinks of the boy, then leans in and whispers at The Robber once more.

"We would take Richie with us," she adds. "We would go somewhere new with the silver you've hidden and we would make a new life." Meg thinks of Nana. None of this is going to happen anyway, so to hell with the old woman. She goes back to her story with her face up close to his. "I would take the wedding band that my husband, John, left here, the one he did not want to lose when he went to war. You'd wear it, and we'd say we were married and that Richie was our son. I know you wanted to leave those others, Dandy Jim told me as much and you would be free as well as I. No more would I be struck by Mr Pennyman or looked down on by men like Mr Farthing. We would not have to live in fear of that monster Carrick up at the church. We could leave it all behind and start afresh, just us three." Meg pauses. Her heart is beating in her chest and she is breathing through her nose. "We would be in love," she whispers. At this, she moves away from him, her face at once ashamed at what she has said.

It is fantasy.

She will not leave Nana, ever, and these words she dreams up are only as real as the dragon's footprint pressed into the stone at Rudston.

She resumes feeding The Robber with the wooden spoon.

"One thing is true, Robber," she says in a clear voice. "You will walk out of here on those two legs. You will get well again and you will leave, silver or no silver. Then, you will leave North Burton never to return again. You will leave us in peace."

CHAPTER EIGHT

There's banging on the door in the grey morning. Meg is already awake and making the fire. The thumping sounds again, too rough to be anything but trouble. Richie blinks from his sleep, he's still dressed and in his boots, it's too cold to take them off - he doesn't have anything else to wear anyway. Meg lifts the catch on the door and opens up. Standing smaller than her is the red-faced Captain Salter she saw the day previous. His ginger moustache ends in two points at each side of his nose and the gold buttons that fix his red jacket together glimmer.

"Out," he yells. "All of you, out, now!" As soon as he has given the order, he moves to the next house along and begins to bang, furious, on the Blackwood door. "Out, all of you," commands The little Captain. "Out all of you and stand before your properties on the road."

Meg steps out into the lane and the snow is crisp underfoot. She looks down the line of little houses as The Captain bangs on the doors; the simple folk of North Burton empty from their ratty cottages despite the bitter cold. The two Blackwood men turn out rapidly, Miles with his battered top hat and teeth clenched, then old Granddad Blackwood with his blanket around his shoulders under a red face. The Farthings are next, the mother, Hannah Farthing, looks like she is done up for Sunday church already. Mr Farthing has managed to comb his hair but his daughter is a mess with her mean eyes in a scowl. Little Archer Farthing stands and looks like he is still asleep. At the end, Adam Gamble has helped his old father to stand at the front door. Nana struggles to the street also, using her stick, she peers round the corner of the door. She wouldn't want to miss the drama.

It's not just The Captain outside. To the right stands Farmer Thorne with his arms folded, a stern look on his face and his wide-brimmed hat pulled down over his eyes.

Opposite is Mr Pennyman dressed in a black frock coat that does not look suited for the cold. Mis Charlotte is present also and behind her, stands tall Danny Reed with his eyes wide in fear. Alone in the street, is the figure of the rector, Carrick, dressed in white robes and with the dog he calls Bear at his side. When they are all out of the houses, The Captain stands on the front steps of the ruined ale house opposite. It makes him slightly taller than he really is. Something bad has happened, reasons Meg. She'll have to confess - confess everything, at least that way it might be only her that goes to the hangman and not little Richie as well. The Captain calls out to all gathered. She wants to glance behind her at The Robber that she knows is up the ladder in their little house but to do so may give her away. Her stomach grumbles.

"You all know why I am here?" begins the little man in a voice that seems too loud for his body. They are not really sure why he is here. "There was an event last night that confirmed suspicions I had when I first came to North Burton." Meg's hands clench with tension and the floor seems to be suddenly uneven under her feet as she listens to this little Captain.

"Last night a man was killed," he yells. "A man was murdered right here in the village of North Burton. His body lies, even now, in front of the gates of Mr Pennyman's house." There are gasps from the villagers and Hannah Farthing puts her hand to her mouth in shock. "We have not yet managed to discover who this man is, and this is why we need you, all of you, to follow Mr Pennyman up the hill to see the body, perhaps you can identify the poor wretch." He gives the information time to settle in. Suddenly this silly little man is more vivid, and the foolish idea that there might be someone dangerous in a place like North Burton, real. Farmer Thorne calls out:

"Is it the work of the man you seek?"

"Yes. The body you will see has been throttled in a most horrible way. You will see that the neck has been broken and there is a bruise in the man's Adam's apple. You will see for yourself." Captain Salter has a way of overly explaining things that makes him less genuine. Farmer Thorne does not look convinced under his frown. Mr Pennyman beckons the working people to follow him up the hill towards the church and his estate. Meg turns to Nana sitting in her chair in the doorway.

"Can you make it up the hill?" she whispers. Nana nods. "I'll get the blanket," says Meg.

It does not take long for the workers from the four cottages to begin up the hill towards the church. They follow Mr Pennyman in a solemn procession past the frozen pond towards the house like it is Sunday. Outside the gate, Captain Salter has hurried in front and he stands beside a prone body in the snow. The Farthings go first, owing to their station perhaps, the mother and father and then the children. They look down on the corpse and then up to the red-faced Captain, shaking their heads. They do not know him, this dead man. The Blackwoods have never seen him before and Adam Gamble does not know him. With her arm around Nana, Meg struggles up the hill. The old woman's legs and ankles are swollen and with each ten or so steps, she lets out a pant of feigned agony and stops to rest on her stick. Meg does not say anything, but she is certain that if The Captain were to draw his pistol and point it in Nana's direction, the old woman would make it to the top with a spring in her step. When they get to Captain Salter he steps to the side.

"Should the boy see the body?" asks Meg. "He's not even five years old."

"He may know who he is," comes the curt answer. "I saw my first dead body when I was about his age, woman, and it did me no harm." Nana gives Meg a glance and they share a moment of understanding. This Captain is a liar. You can spot his sense of self-importance without effort.

Meg steps forward first. She does not want to see who it is so she keeps her head down and only looks at the body for a fraction of a second. It's enough.

The big swollen hands, the dirty black socks.

It's Carlos.

His face is utterly pale and his wide eyes stare up at the sky, blood has frozen all around his mouth and his shirt is ripped open to his chest. The neck and head are at an impossible, broken angle. Meg looks up, into the eyes of The Captain next to her. Only yesterday she had seen Carlos smile, listened to him joke with Dandy Jim, watched him rub his musket down with an oily rag. Now he is a grotesque manakin of how he looked alive.

"Do you know him?" asks The Captain.

"No," says Meg.

"Look again," he commands, so she does. She sees the muddy boots and the dull silver buckle on his belt, sees that the burns Carlos had on his face stretch down his chest also. She looks back up at The Captain.

"I do not know him." It's easy to lie, because, if she does not, she will be swinging from the gallows on Hangman Lane in Beverley on the edge of the Westwood pasture.

Nana steps up next with Richie beside her. The old woman does not know him for sure and so she can take her time about it. She looks up and down the pale body and to his face with blood frozen around his lips. She examines him.

"Someone has knocked out one of his front teeth," she says. The Captain steps up to confirm. The old woman is right. He had not spotted this but he cannot let on that he didn't.

"Do you know him?" he asks.

"He's the look of the Simpson family out of Etton, but those scars," she shakes her head. "Why anyone who had seen him before would recognise him."

"Do you know him, old woman?" Nana shakes her head.

"What about you, boy?" The Captain points to Richie who

104

grips Nana's hand tight. He looks like he is about to cry. "You have to look, boy," says Captain Salter. Richie does not want to.

"It'll be okay, Richie, nobody will hurt you, just have a quick look," says Meg. He steps forward, glances at the body of the heavy-set highwayman musketeer and then bursts into tears. The Captain's voice is high over the sobbing.

"Do you know him, child?" Richie takes a deep breath and shakes his head with his eyes closed tight. The Captain does not seem satisfied with this. "You need to look again, boy, look again. We need to know who this man is, where he came from and how he is dead on the street for everyone to see. Look again!" Meg puts her hand on Richie's shoulder and he is shaking. She guides him back to the body, best give The Captain what he wants.

"Just have another look, Richie, it's only a body, it can't hurt you, I promise." The little lad opens his eyes, he is closer now and he can see the wide, pale face of the highwayman. He sees the scars on the bare chest, the purple and black bruise on his neck where he was strangled.

"Do you know him?" shouts The Captain.

"No," cries Richie and Meg scoops him up into her arms and he buries his head into her shoulder as he sobs. Captain Salter takes a deep breath in through his nose.

"Enjoy frightening children, do you, Captain?" It's a deep voice from behind the red-faced man, the huge hulking figure of Rector Carrick. He is twice as wide as this little man and at least a foot taller. Around his neck, there is a white scarf tied in a knot at the front near his Adam's apple. His face is without emotion. Meg has never seen him wear such a scarf.

"I see you're dressed for the weather," comments The Captain.

"I'm not afraid of a little cold, Sir, like I'm not afraid of an opportunist footpad."

"Do you know who this man is?" commands The Captain.

Carrick steps to the body and looks down upon it with mild disgust. His eyes read the shape of poor Carlos. Meg can see a scratch just under his hairline.

"I do not know this wretch, Captain but I will add that, if he had stepped into my church, I would have done this to him myself."

"Do you think he is a robber?"

"Of course he's a robber. What else would a man like this be doing so close to The Pennyman Estate? You know yourself there was a stagecoach robbed on the way to York a week or so past."

"It's a distance from here, so I am told by Mr Pennyman." Carrick huffs at The Captain's words.

"Men like this can move faster and further than you can imagine, Captain. See his burns? Where would they have come from?" Carrick points at the robber.

"A musket blown up in his face, I imagine."

"Aye, whoever this is, he is a soldier gone rogue. Someone must have found him doing something he should not have been doing and finished him off." Carrick steps closer to The Captain. "I'm glad they did."

"It is not anyone's place to take God's laws into their own hands, Sir. We are a country of order and under the laws of God, any criminal - any robber, must be tried and found guilty or not guilty. This is the way we live, Rector. This is why I am here. I am to find who has been responsible for this." Carrick scoffs again. The Captain may be arrogant, rude and self-obsessed, but, he is a military officer in the first instance, and there are ways of doing things that he cannot ignore.

"Good luck with that," says Carrick. "I would wager, Captain, that this man's accomplice or accomplices did for him. No doubt so that they could keep more of whatever they stole."

"We are checking if anything has been removed from the house as we speak," replies The Captain. "What about the church, has anything been taken?" Carrick grins.

"Nothing has been taken from my church, Captain. That I can assure you. I guard my own. If anyone had tried to get into God's house, we would be looking down on a body that had been killed by the teeth of a hound."

The two men stare at each other in the icy morning. Their breath making steam in front of them. The Captain turns back to Meg with Richie in her arms.

"Back home with you, woman," he commands.

Meg carries Richie down the hill. He has stopped crying. Nana doesn't huff with each step and keeps an acceptable pace for her swollen ankles. There is silence except for their feet crunching in the snow.

It has not at all played out as Meg expected.

Where is Dandy Jim?

Why kill Carlos? Where is that musket that never leaves his side? What did they take from the Pennyman House, if they took anything?

Inside the little room in their cottage. Meg helps Nana into her chair and the old woman lets out a genuine sigh of pain. It's not always drama. Meg pokes the embers of the fire.

"You did well, Richie," says Nana. "You didn't blab about that Robber upstairs. You were strong. Meg and me are proud of you. Isn't that right, Meg?" She turns and nods. She is proud of him.

"You did a good job too, Meg," says Nana.

"How so?" she answers.

"You knew that dead man, didn't you?"

Meg looks down on the old woman. What's the point in lying to her? They are all in this together now.

"Yes," she says. "I knew him."

CHAPTER NINE

Their robber is getting better. His face has more colour and his skin is pink and as cold as it should be. Meg would rather he didn't wake up just yet but then again, she does want him to wake up. They all do.

It's been half an hour since they saw the body of Carlos. Meg comes down the ladder and Nana is boiling some water in the iron pot over the fire. The old woman has not asked anymore as to how Meg knew the dead man or what else went on.

"I best be off," says Meg. "Them chickens won't look after themselves."

"We need him out of here, Meg. We need him out, now. There'll be no bluffing our way out of this one." The old woman looks pale.

There are two sharp bangs on the door. Meg looks at Nana and Richie with her nostrils flared. She opens up and there is Granddad Blackwood with his bald head and white hairs behind his ears. He steps inside.

"They're doing a search," he says. "Every house. They've done up at the Pennyman's and across at the church and nothing is missing. The Captain is seeing to it himself."

"Have you sorted your own place?" asks Nana. Granddad Blackwood will have several things in his house that should not be there. Perhaps a knife or a bottle of something, a stolen plate or some trinket.

"Aye, Miles has put it all down the back of the fireplace."

"That's the first place they'll look," says Nana.

"We'll build the fire big in front, it'll be too hot to touch. I thought I better give you forewarning."

"Where are they now?" asks Meg.

"They're just arriving at the Gamble's, there's Mr Pennyman, The Captain and that Danny Reed. He's not our sort that Captain, Nana, make no mistake. He's a rat born with a silver spoon. He'll find whoever killed that poor bastard and anyone in his way will be for it as well."

Nana nods in thanks. She can see that Blackwood is nervous. Mr Pennyman has never searched the cottages, nor his father neither and so this is a surprise for both of them, but then again, a man has been killed, and that has never happened in North Burton either. Granddad Blackwood backs off and out the door and Meg puts her head into the frozen street, along the four buildings she can see Danny Reed outside with the Gambles. Young Adam stands in front of his two ageing parents. Meg pulls her head back in and closes the door. Her mouth is suddenly dry as she swallows back fear.

"Get yourself up that ladder, throw a blanket over him or something. I'll say my legs are too bad for me to stand up." This is what Nana always does anyway. "Richie will stay with me. Get to it, Meg. We'll pay for this with our necks if we can't get it right." Meg nods and then climbs the rungs of the wooden ladder. At the chimney breast, she removes the cloak that covers The Robber and immediately sees the pistol tucked into the leather holster at his side. There will be no way she can hide him, but she must do the best she can. She drags the man across the rough floorboards to the far corner. Grey sunlight bleeds through the thatched roof and mounting ice, catching the silver handle of his pistol to make her notice it once more.

What was it her mother had told her? That it was not Meg's time to just listen anymore. She feels for the bottle of black gunpowder that will be on The Robber's belt and finds it just under the gun. She opens another pouch next to that and removes an uneven round bullet. Without ceremony, she tugs the gun free from the holster. It's heavier than it looks, the handle is smooth dense wood and there are deep scratches in it. The pistol doubles as a bludgeoning weapon, it takes too long to load when someone is up close. She has seen Danny Reed arm his musket and watched Farmer Thorne fire his

Murdock pistol at the summer fair. She looks down at the body of her Robber on the floorboards. She can spend this time hiding the body effectively, or she can load his gun. She will not have time for both, even now she can hear The little Captain's voice through the walls of the cottage. He must already be next door with the Blackwoods and it will not take him long. Meg blinks in the grey morning. If The Captain makes it up the ladder, he will find the body, he will probably smell him from the front door anyway. Meg pours some of the black powder from The Robber's bottle into the nozzle of the gun. Her hands are shaking. She drops the bullet into the end and pulls out the ramrod that slides along the underside of the barrel, then uses it to pack the ball and the powder tight. She flips the pan in front of the flintlock and fills that too.

There's a knock on the door downstairs. She holds the pistol out level and uses her left hand to cock the flintlock, it's stiff but Meg grits her teeth. Farmer Thorne told her that a bullet from such a gun can blow a hole clear through a man. The muscles in her legs tighten. She looks down the ladder as Richie opens the door. Captain Salter steps inside, Meg hears his voice, loud and rude as he snaps at Nana.

"I ask you to wait outside woman."

"Where are your manners, Sir? This is my house, a widow's house. I'm a cripple and these legs have seen a lifetime of work and service." Richie goes to stand behind Nana's chair and looks over her shoulder at this little man with his eyes wide in fear. Dutchy is under her chair as well, terrified.

"That's as well, woman, but I'm on official business and if you can't get out that chair and into the street, I'll drag you out. Pennyman told me you'd be the one to give us trouble."

"I just don't understand, Sir, why I'm to go outside while you go through my things. I shall stay."

You should not take Nana on at her own hearth. This is where she has sparred verbally for most of her life, with her dead husband, the son who has gone off to the army perhaps

110

never to return, a string of neighbours, and now with Meg. The Captain steps forward towards her and his boots click on the hard ground. His nostrils flare.

"Listen to me, woman," he says in a calm voice. "You can stay here while I look around, but the first thing I want to look at is that chair your sitting on." Nana snarls at him.

"I hope you get treated like this when you're an old man. I've worked my fingers to the bone, I have, to bring up a family and work for Mr Pennyman's Estate and I didn't do it so that some Captain can come here and rifle through my things. We have laws in this country and I shall not get out of this seat."

There is more to the chair than Nana would like to admit. First, there is the dagger she has hidden in the side, next there is the money, and there may be other items there that Nana should not really have. The silver cross she found some years back when she was working in the fields, letters that have been delivered to her that she cannot read. Her son's wedding ring that he left for safekeeping. She does not want The Captain to get his hands on these things because, as far as Nana's experience goes, men like The Captain here will take them for himself.

At the top of the ladder, but out of sight, Meg stands in the grey morning with the pistol held in her shaky hands. She's afraid. If Captain Salter lays one hand on her Nana, then she'll be forced to do something that she doesn't want to do. The floorboards creak below her feet.

There is silence as The Captain deliberates his next move. Meg knows that he will not show any mercy, wasn't it he who encouraged Pennyman to strike her? This path that Meg is on now, the one that started as soon as that Robber came in through the door, this path has already taken her out of the humdrum world of pig muck and chickens. She looks down at her Robber, wrapped in his cloak. What if she did descend the first few rungs of the ladder, level the gun at Captain Salter's head and fire? What if The Robber woke up at the shot? What if they walked out the door as free as you like and down to Farmer Thorne's livery where, at gunpoint, Meg relieved the old man of his best bay, Jamie, and the two of them made off over the hills to York and a new life. A life where Meg could be more than just Nana's punch bang or the poor, stupid girl who worked the foul and the sows. She is letting her mind run away with her. Below, The Captain has made his decision. He steps outside the door:

"Mr Reed," he calls. "In here." Of course, Captain Salter is not going to drag Nana out by her hair, that would be beneath him. To get his own hands dirty would be, unsettling. Danny Reed appears at the door. The Captain stands back and points at Nana.

"Toss this woman into the street, driver." Danny Reed blinks down at this little man. He knows Nana. He has sold bottles of stolen things to her, taken her advice on the weather in the past, sat next to her in church, shared a joke at Mr Pennyman's expense in secret. Danny is not the kind of man who has experience of tossing women into the street either. He is about to protest when he sees the stern anger on this little man's face.

The situation is spiralling out of Meg's imagination. She cannot shoot Danny Reed.

There's a shout from down the road, a boy's voice coming towards them. It's Adam Gamble yelling for Captain Salter at the top of his voice.

"Captain Salter," he pants as he gets to the door. "Miss Charlotte has found something in the church grounds." The boy struggles to catch his breath. "She wants you to come at once." The Captain glances down at the boy and then back inside at Nana in the chair.

"Can't it wait?"

"Miss Charlotte says you're to come at once." Salter curls his lip up in disgust.

"Very well then, I'll attend. Mr Reed, see this house is

112

searched." The blonde-haired man nods but does not give a grin of relief until the little man has turned away.

When The Captain and Adam are twenty yards up the road, Danny Reed steps into Nana's house and closes the door. He holds his finger to his lips to stop Nana from speaking. He will not search this place because he knows, like Nana does, that he will find something he does not want to find and he will have to act on this, as a constable of the parish.

"Do you have any information on the man they found dead, Nana?"

"No," says the old woman. This is not a lie.

"Where's Meg?"

"Up top," answers Nana.

Meg has set the gun on the floor and now descends the wooden rungs of the ladder. She gives Danny Reed a nervous smile over her shoulders as she comes down, but she's pale with the shock of it all.

"Do you have anything to tell me, Meg?" he asks. She shakes her head. "I'm not going to search this place but I'll take it that you don't have anything to do with the murder. I can trust you, right?" Mr Reed really does trust Nana, he trusts her because if she goes down, she will blab about the thefts from the estate larder and that he plays cards for money, that she has heard him blaspheme. Small things can become big.

"You can trust us," says Meg. The man nods in thanks.

"Then I'll bid you good day." Mr Reed, turns and lifts the catch on the door, he closes it respectfully behind him and the three of them are left alone. Richie steps out from behind Nana's chair, he looks white with fear. Dutchy makes a dash for it now there is space and crawls under the bench.

"I want him out tonight, Meg," whispers Nana. "Tonight and I bloody mean it. If we have to bury him, I want him out. You better get me that pistol as well, lass, we might be needing it."

The pigs don't like the cold but they huddle together and there is earthy warmth in the sty as Meg works. The big black sow is in a mood for some reason and Meg has to keep her away with well-timed kicks and a prod of the fork.

The hens are not laying as well as they should because of the cold. Once she has cleaned their coup and replaced their straw, she collects the eggs in her basket, covers them with a cloth and takes them down the big path towards the gates of the house. Today, the eggs belong to the villagers and Meg will share them between the four cottages.

The body that lay outside the house walls has been moved. Carrick will have it somewhere in the churchyard ready to be buried. The death will be recorded by The Rector and Mr Pennyman alike and, when the path to Beverley is clear, the magistrate there will be informed also. Meg looks at where the body was and the blood spots have been shovelled over with fresh snow. She liked Carlos. She liked him in the same way she likes Miles Blackwood or little Adam Gamble. He was someone she could trust, straight away. You can sense that sort of thing, like one bird of a feather finding another, then again, she remembers the stab wound on her robber. Meg walks down the hill to the cottages and wonders what happened last night. Carlos is not a small man and not an inexperienced soldier either, Dandy Jim said so. Whoever did for the musket man, must have been twice as powerful as he. Coming up the hill is Carrick with his Bear at his side on a rope leash. He gives Meg a wide grin that is not at all genuine, and she can see that his teeth are black at the gums. The dog eyes her as they walk past.

"A fine morning for it," says Carrick. He looks cheerier than normal, considering there's been a murder.

"If you like the cold," says Meg.

"It cleanses sin, girl, the cold does." She nods and hurries past him with one hand clasping her cloak together in front of her. Meg does not yet know what Miss Charlotte found that was so important for Captain Salter to be called away. Ordinarily, she would be hungry to hear any of the village gossip but now, she just wants the whole thing to disappear. She wants to disappear.

At the bottom of the hill, she can hear children's voices. On the big duck pond, Adam Gamble and the Farthing girl have cleared snow from a long section at the back where huge oaks grow over the water, and they are sliding on a skid patch. Little Archer Farthing takes a run-up and launches himself across the ice on his front to land in a pile of snow at the far side. Meg has done this before on Etton pond. She would do it now if she were allowed. Archer struggles out of the snow and his face is red under his black hair and he has a big grin. He is wet through. Meg stops to watch Adam Gamble take a turn across the ice. She smiles. What else do you do when you find out there's a killer in the village? Carry on as normal.

"Take care at the back there," bellows Meg. They are her mother's words. "It's deep water and you'd not want to fall through. The roots will pull you under." Archer Farthing looks out at Meg standing by the side of the pond with the egg basket in her hand.

"It's as hard as stone, Meg," he shouts as he stamps one of his little feet. If it were anyone else, Archer would have said Mrs or Miss or Ma'am but as it's Meg, he is free to call her by her first name. It's not that Archer is rude, he just does as everyone else. His sister Julia Farthing looks up across at Meg also:

"You're not our mother," she calls. Julia has heard her parents talk about this woman like Archer probably has but Meg continues to smile at them, even though it does not seem to fit on her face. Adam Gamble waves and she nods back as she watches them for a minute more, Julia takes a good run up at the slide and sits down on her bum as she crashes into the snow at the end. It's a pity they haven't got ice-skates like Miss Charlotte. Meg makes her way past the pond and, just as she

115

does so, she hears a high-pitched yell from the back and a little scream. Then Archer Farthing's voice high in the cold morning,

"Help," he yells. Meg goes back to get a better look and sees Adam Gamble laughing at the little boy who has somehow managed to fall through the ice at the back, where Meg told them to be careful. She puts down the basket of eggs and steps over the fence onto the ice. It complains under her weight with a creak as she walks, unsteady, out to where the two children stand looking at Archer Farthing. The boy is in shock from the cold water with his legs in the green pond and his arms out in front on the ice. His face is too surprised to cry. It's been frozen for months, how can Archer Farthing have fallen through?

"Help him then," says Meg to Adam and Julia who both think it's hilariously funny and do nothing to assist.

"He can climb out of that," says Julia. Archer's eyes do not now have the same playful glimmer. He looks frightened as he clutches onto the side of the ice he has just gone through.

"Don't struggle," says Meg and Archer looks up at her as she approaches him and drops to her hands and knees with her hand outstretched. There's something faraway about the boy already. Adam Gamble stops laughing.

"Hold out your hand, Archer," she says. Meg does not want to go too near to him because, if the ice is thin enough for him to fall through then it could crack for her as well. "I told you not to go near the back," she whispers. Meg edges closer with her arm out, but Archer in the water has stopped moving. The hand he was going to hold out for Meg has slipped under the water and then, languid and terrible, his shoulders sink also, so the water is first up to his neck, then his chin, his nose and then, as slowly and gracefully as the winter sun setting across the Wolds, his whole pale head is under the water and he is gone. Meg looks back at Adam Gamble and Julia Farthing aghast behind her, they are frozen in horror.

"Get help, Adam," says Meg and the lad bolts off the frozen pond slipping as he goes over the skid patch they made and then leaping over the little white fence. Meg turns to the dark hole that Archer Farthing has disappeared under. She knows this pond, she's swum in it before and fished in it too, it's deepest at the back under the oaks and their roots crisscross the dark floor. She glances back at Julia Farthing, whose hand is at her mouth in concern, and her face already as pale as her brother's before he slipped under the water.

There's nothing else for it. Meg will have to go in after him. It's not the cold now that bothers her, it's more the cold later, for once she gets wet under the water, it will take her many hours to dry out, she does not have any other clothes and there will be nowhere to get warm. This is what Meg thinks as she leans into the ice and reaches down to try to feel for the boy. Her hands grasp at the deathly cold water and she stretches far, takes a deep breath and then sticks her whole head in, under the water to find him. She closes her eyes and feels the cold run down her back and her muscles spasm in shock, she is already angry that she has not caught hold of the boy for this means she will have to go even deeper and get her underclothes wet as well. This will make it an uncomfortable evening also, and an unpleasant night, but Meg can't give up. Even though she does not care for Mr Farthing or his mean faced wife and bitter daughter, Meg will do everything she can to help the little boy. If he were to die, not that he will, it would be her fault as the only adult person there, just like it was her fault when Miss Charlotte wanted to ride her horse through the snow, just like it's her fault if a sow dies or one of the hens is egg bound. It will probably be her fault anyway.

Meg must get this little boy back.

There is nothing else for it, but to let her whole body slide into the water. Gravity allows her to fall forward, headfirst with her arms out and finally, sinking into the freezing pond, she grabs hold of the collar of Archer's shirt deep under the water and yanks him up. Julia Farthing watches as Meg's body slides into the water after her brother.

Meg curses Archer Farthing for falling in. She has him by the scruff of his neck, but no way to pull him out, she'll have to swim under him, somehow. The water is thick with mud and chips of wood and branches, Meg's legs move below her and her feet brush the floor of the pond. At the same time she pushes the boy upward with her arms and his head breaks the surface, above, Julia Farthing is there, on all fours like Meg was. She grasps hold of Archer under his arm and yanks him out of the water and onto the ice as he coughs and splutters into the cold air. Alive and frozen, but alive. Julia smiles at him as they lay back on the ice. Meg is still deep under the water. Just like she had told the children a few minutes before, there are roots on the bottom of the pond, roots that can pull you under if you get to the deep bit. Meg's right boot has got caught in one. Impossibly. For roots do not drag you under and Meg had only said this so that the children would be more afraid to fall in. Even so, her foot is stuck. As she twists to get it free, she feels the root move and lock into place. She struggles upwards to the light. Her eyes blink underwater and sting in the cold and dirt.

Shock and panic flood her veins, she wants to take a deep breath but stops herself.

This is drowning.

Meg has seen Farmer Thorne drown rats before in the metal cage he has for them. She has watched them claw at the bars as they wriggle and fight against the water. Seen their black eyes bulge as they stare upwards.

This is how it must feel.

Meg sees her mother again, sitting in the little chair in her cottage with her back bent in age and her frail hands on her lap. She remembers what the old woman told her – that if she is ever in trouble, all she need do is ask, and the long line of mothers that stretches far into the past, into time itself, will send help. Meg struggles with her foot and her lungs complain as they run out of oxygen, yanking at her leg trapped below her in the mud and weeds with renewed vigour. She pulls her foot like her life depends on it, because, as her hands go down to her knees to assist, her life really does depend on it. She looks up and opens her eyes to the world above the water. Her mind races. She should call on the help that her mother offered her before she died, but somehow, Meg knows that there is nothing in it, just an old wives' tale that was a comfort to a woman as she died. How can they help her?

Like those rats trapped in Farmer Thorne's metal cage, Meg becomes frantic. Nobody is going to pull her out. No big hands will reach down and yank her to freedom, like everything else, like The Robber upstairs in her cottage, like Nana's supper, unless Meg sorts this, it will not get sorted. She twists her ankle, franticly, and wriggles her toes out of the boot somehow, leaving the heel trapped in the root as her foot slips free. She struggles upwards through the black, muddy and frozen water to the world above and bangs her head on the ice.

Just like a rat trapped in the cage.

The ice breaks from a heavy blow up top and the thud reverberates in the water around her. Meg is nearly out of time. The ice cracks from another strike against it and splits, Meg's face finds the air between the broken pieces and she takes a huge, gasping breath then sinks back into the water once more. A hand reaches into the darkness and grabs her. The grip is not strong, but strong enough to pull her up. Meg's face breaks the surface again and she sees the slender hand that has hold of her and the pale face of the woman who is laid on the ice. It's Miss Charlotte.

"Grab the end of the gun, Meg," says Danny Reed. It is he who used the handle of his musket to smash the ice. Miss Charlotte has her teeth set in effort as she stops Meg from going back under and Danny offers the handle of the long musket down to her. Meg clutches it with both red arms and he pulls backward, dragging her up and onto the ice. She lays on her side and coughs, then spews out pond water that has gone in through her nose. People have gathered at the edge of the North Burton duck pond, Mr Farthing now has Archer in his arms wrapped in a heavy cloak. Miss Charlotte puts her hands on Meg's shoulder.

"Just take a minute," she whispers. Meg coughs out more and vomits again, wipes her face and then gets to her knees. She has lost one of her boots and bloodied her legs, her eyes weep from the dirty, stagnant water. She looks across at Miss Charlotte's face opposite and feels nothing but shame. She is shivering and red-faced but conscious that she is not to make a fuss – that would be the worst thing.

"Is the boy okay?" she asks.

"He's cold but he'll be fine," says Danny Reed standing a few yards away resting on his musket the wrong way up. "Pond nearly had you there, Meg," he says. She blinks at him and manages a weak smile.

"We need to get you off the ice," says Miss Charlotte.

The sky has turned a dark grey and it must be near noon. It takes her a few seconds to get to her feet and limp to the side of the pond with Reed and Miss Charlotte following. There's a look of disgust on Mrs Farthing's sharp face as Meg climbs over the fence.

"I'm sure he could have got himself out," she says loud enough to be heard. Meg catches Mr Farthing's eye and he nods in thanks but is silent.

"Thank you very much for your help Miss Charlotte, and Mr Reed," says Meg in her best Sunday voice. "I'll be on my way now, I have things to see too." Meg looks down at herself. Her skirt is torn and the toes on her bare foot are bloodied. Her hair must be a mess also, and there is sick down the front of her chest. The water is already beginning to freeze on her.

To lose a shoe is perhaps the worst thing that could happen. Where is she to find another? She'll have to make something herself.

"And what about our eggs, today is Wednesday," it's Mrs. Farthing again.

"The basket is here," says Meg pointing to where she left it ten minutes ago. Miss Charlotte surges forward to the whicker work basket and picks it up before she hands it to Mrs Farthing, who is not now allowed to pull any sort of face.

"You'll come to the house, Meg," says Miss Charlotte with authority. "You'll come to the house, get cleaned up and get dry. I'll see if I can dig you out some shoes as well." Miss Charlotte flares her nostrils and looks directly up at Mrs Farthing while she speaks Meg. "You've done a good deed and we're grateful for it. Imagine if this little lad had drowned in there?" If it were anyone else, Mrs Farthing would give her a straight and barbed reply, but they have not been in North Burton long enough and if Miss Charlotte so wanted, she could release Mr Farthing of his position.

It's much better for Hannah Farthing's sour lips to remain still. Meg looks at Miss Charlotte and the two exchange a glance.

CHAPTER TEN

For the first time in her life, Meg is upstairs and inside the Pennyman House. She walked up the big staircase and to one of the large back bedrooms and into Miss Charlotte's chamber. There's an open fire opposite the four-poster bed and Meg has been asked to stand behind a screen with oriental designs on the painted white slats. There's the smell of lavender in her nostrils.

"Take your clothes off, Meg," says Miss Charlotte on the other side of the screen. She is a little older than Meg in her mid-twenties but she looks younger, her hands are not manly from work and she's slight, clean and well-mannered. Meg struggles out of the rags that are her clothes, the one battered lady's boot, the ripped petticoat. The lavender overpowers her smell and in so doing reminds her how bad she must stink. Meg pulls off the loose corset and is down to her undergarments. Over the top of the screen comes a fresh, brilliant white pair of frilled knickers. Then a long petticoat. Meg looks worried.

"I can't take these, Miss Charlotte," she says.

"Yes, you can," answers the woman from the other side.

"I can't afford them."

"They are gifts, Meg, from me to you. There's no payment needed."

Meg's face creases with worry behind the screen as she takes the long knickers. Miss Charlotte continues:

"If that boy had died today, how much do you think my father would have had to pay?" It's rhetorical. "There would have been a funeral and fingers pointed, and we might have lost the Farthings altogether. Father and I waited for a long time to get a pair like those two who know so much about horses. You saved this Estate money as well as that little boy's life." Here is the Pennyman gift that Meg does not have, Miss Charlotte here sees the full picture. Unlike her father or

Captain Salter, she does not look down on the workers in the cottages or the chickens in their coups. She feels Christian guilt that they are down there with their hands in the mud and cold, while she is up here. As she looks through her old boots, Miss Charlotte, who has never done a day's work in her life, believes that Meg will like her the more for what she is doing, but the working poor do not need charity. If by some magic, Miss Charlotte could spend a week at hard work, with the knowledge that this really was her life, forever and ever, and the solid drudgery of the cold would be her lot, then she would not look to the rich for help. She would want to better herself, she would want to shake free of The Pennyman Estate and the nasty glances of women like Mrs Farthing or her haughty daughter, like Meg does. Miss Charlotte finds a pair of smooth and short ankle boots with a tight buckle that look about right. She places them at the side of the screen, then puts three pairs of her best woollen socks by the side.

"I'll only need one pair, Miss," says Meg.

"Stuff the other two in your pockets," comes the reply in a monotone voice. Meg steps out from behind the screen and looks cleaner than she has ever done before, perhaps since she got married. Though her body is still stagnant with pond water, her clothes are fresh with a dull grey skirt and a brown petticoat. Miss Charlotte smiles at her. Even the boots look like they are a good fit.

"I thank you, my lady," says Meg. "I'll be on my way now." Miss Charlotte walks to her dresser and picks up her brush.

"Would you stay awhile, Meg? I can do your hair. It's in a terrible state." In Beverley or bigger houses than this, there may be girls who would attend a woman like Miss Charlotte, who would do all manner of things that a body should be able to do for itself. Mr Pennyman however, does not like too many helpers in the house, they cost money. Of course, there are servant girls who dress Miss Charlotte of a morning but they double as kitchen and house maids, there is nobody there to attend to her all the time.

"I couldn't, Miss," answers Meg. Her hand goes to her blonde and curly hair. It is matted with dirt and pond water.

"Please," asks Miss Charlotte. "It is my Christian duty."

Meg sits down and looks at herself in the big dresser mirror, over bottles of perfume and necklaces in boxes. It's the first time she has seen herself in a mirror so large and ornate, the world is vivid through it and she seems uglier within. Meg tries not to notice herself, only looking at Miss Charlotte with the brush in her hand. It will be a nasty job to get through Meg's hair.

"What do you think of the murder?" asks Miss Charlotte. Meg gives an imperceptible smile. Here could be the real reason she is sat at a rich lady's dressing table.

"We are all shocked by it," she answers.

"Do you think anyone knew the man who was killed?"

"I have not heard any talk of it, Miss, and neither has Nana, and she knows everything. We heard that you found something in the churchyard."

"Yes, I did. Something very out of place."

"What?" Miss Charlotte stops and looks Meg in the eyes through the mirror.

"It was a hat. A fine and dandy hat. I believe it one of quite some worth also, for inside the rim is the printed name of Atkinson of York, one of the finest hatmakers in the country."

Meg does not alter her expression.

She knows a man who has such a hat.

"Where would that come from?" asks Miss Charlotte. "Certainly, no footpad would wear such finery, even the lords and ladies at Beverley Races of a summer day might not think to wear something so nice, or well made. And certainly, nobody who had such a thing would want to lose it."

"Unless they had stolen it, my lady," answers Meg without thinking.

"Quite," she answers. "Our Captain Salter will find

whoever the murderer is, I'm quite sure of that. He seems to think he is on the trail of someone. Does it not worry you, Meg, that there might be such a man around?" Miss Charlotte has done a good job of getting the knots out of the back of Meg's hair without hurting her too much.

"I have nothing that anyone would want to steal," answers Meg. "Nana says that a robber would not stop for even a split second at our door, nor the Blackwood's neither." Miss Charlotte pauses from combing Meg's hair again. "Who is he hunting, this Captain?" asks Meg. Miss Charlotte can trust this girl, she thinks, but she also knows that any information she gives now, will be given to the whole village, she should be careful what she shares.

"The Captain says the murder is the breakthrough he has been waiting for. The man he seeks is said to be one who can fit in anywhere, one who arrives and then blends in with the world around, until, as has happened here, their instinct gets the better of them. Salter has known about this someone for many years, he says, the person was a part of The Duke of Marlborough's army on the continent, a spy, someone who gave away details that cost men dearly, someone who must be made to pay for what they did. All the same but by some chance, he knows that his target has come here, to The East Riding of Yorkshire and south of the Wolds and now he knows that the someone is in North Burton and that they have been here not too long, less than two years." Meg blinks back at the mirror and Miss Charlotte working on the other side of her hair. She is doing a good job. They both begin the mathematics of it.

"The Farthings came here last summer, not even a year."

"Mr Farthing, kill a man?" asks Charlotte. Meg can imagine he would, his wife more so.

"The priest, Carrick, why he came to North Burton not so long back." Meg does not quite remember.

"He's a man of the cloth, my father checked his credentials

himself. The papers came from the Archbishop of York where Carrick served previous. He is a man of God, however he looks."

"Danny Reed has not been in your service long, Miss Charlotte." She gives a little laugh.

"Mr Reed is beyond suspicion, Meg. He is a constable of the peace here and a trusted member of this household."

"I was not accusing him," says Meg.

"I know you weren't," she answers. "How long have *you* been in North Burton?"

"I was married four summers ago." Is that all it is? It feels like a lifetime. Miss Charlotte puts down the brush on the dressing table and pulls Meg's hair back. With clever fingers, she makes a plait that runs down past her shoulders and she ties it with a band from around her wrist. They look at each other in the mirror once more.

"I'm not the Captain's murderer, Miss Charlotte."

"I know," she answers. There's feeling in her voice.

"This hat that you found. Does Captain Salter think this is related to the murder, somehow?"

"If I'm to be honest with you Meg, I don't think our Captain knows his arse from his elbow." It's not like Miss Charlotte to say such a thing. She steps back to show that she has finished and Meg stands up from the stool, it is amazing just how quickly she felt at ease, now the familiar sense returns, faced with those of privilege.

"I'll be on my way, Miss Charlotte. Thank you." They stand facing each other, Meg, taller and with broad shoulders and her rich, wavy blonde hair now in a plait. Miss Charlotte with her black hair pinned up and much shorter.

"There is one more thing, Meg."

"Yes?"

"If you need anything, you should know that you can come to me. It's my duty to help those that work for my family. It is my Christian duty. I know that you lost your mother and that… that your husband has been gone for longer than he should have been." Miss Charlotte's eyes are stern with conviction. It makes Meg feel embarrassed. She looks at her new boots and then back up to her supposed benefactor.

"Thank you, Miss Charlotte," she says.

There's a part of her that really means it too. It seems like everyone wants to help Meg, at least that's what they say.

It is late afternoon when Meg gets home. At this time of year, the folk of the East Riding should be shrugging off the cold winter, opening their shutters on their windows to let fresh air into their houses, planting onions and carrots that will feed them in the next winter and enjoying the sun on their faces. Not so now. As Meg walks home, snow begins in the darkening grey sky. Perhaps it is a punishment as Carrick says, for their sins. Meg pulls her new cloak around her shoulders and wishes she had been given the opportunity to sin more. Yes, she has always taken Nana for granted and sometimes little Richie, but at the feast last harvest festival in The Pennyman Estate barn, there was nobody to make eyes at her, her cup was only filled with beer a few times and when she danced the jig to the fiddler that had come all the way from Hull, she only got to dance with Adam Gamble and then Miles Blackwood who stank of cows. Perhaps the cold is punishment for things to come. If that is the case, then Meg has got a lot of sinning to do. A whole lot, and she thinks of The Robber again, wrapped in his thick, expensive cloak and the smell of his perfume in her nostrils. The snow begins. By the time Meg is at her front door, it is a blizzard.

Inside is the familiar shape of Nana, on her chair with the fire blazing next to her. She does not say hello.

"You've built that too big," says Meg. Nana scoffs.

"Like you care – you've spent all afternoon at The Pennyman House. Let's have a look at these new clothes you

127

got then?" Word will have spread of what happened, through a servant girl to Granddad or Miles Blackwood perhaps. Meg stands in front of Nana in the weak light. The old woman scoffs again. "All that for fetching Archer Farthing out of the pond. She's soft is that Charlotte Pennyman, soft, I tell you, and if she inherits the estate from her father, God only knows what will happen to North Burton. We'll all be penniless within a year." Nana believes in those of a higher station. Meg is not so sure.

"If she offered you new boots, you'd take them," says Meg.

"Aye," answers Nana, "but I wouldn't beg for nowt else." Nana's voice is unusually loud and her eyes wide. She sits with her arms across her middle and her hands are fidgeting. Although she is saying unpleasant things, they do not have the normal, relaxed sting. There's something wrong. Meg moves closer and the old woman holds her fingers up to her lips to indicate silence. She beckons Meg forwards.

"We heard him moving around up top," whispers Nana with her creased finger pointing to the wooden ceiling of floorboards above her. Meg looks up out of habit when someone points. She nods. Nana continues talking loudly in the worry that The Robber upstairs might be listening to her:

"A bloody new cloak as well, anyone would think you were getting married." Meg moves to the ladder and looks up into the darkness of the roof. Unlike Nana, she has to do something about the problem, rather than wait for another to solve it for her. She rests her hands on the smooth wood of the ladder and feels a lump in her throat, she takes a deep breath. Looking at her from next to the fire, Nana and Richie are frightened. Dutchy also peers at her from the corner, she is afraid to climb up into the roof where she would normally go when Nana goes off shouting and ranting. What if he is already awake up there? What if he is waiting in the darkness with his pistol cocked or his long dagger drawn? Nana nods with vigour at Meg in an effort to make her get on with it, the woman takes two steps up and then, noiselessly, returns to the ground and approaches Nana with her hand out. Nana frowns.

"The knife," whispers Meg.

"You don't want to kill him," rasps the old woman with her nostrils flared. "He's got to walk out of here, remember."

"What if he kills me?" asks Meg. To this Nana wrinkles her nose and rolls her eyes back with drama. She is not going to give up her knife.

Meg goes back to the ladder and looks up once more. Where will he position himself if he really is awake? She glances at Nana one last time. What if the old woman has got it wrong, it wouldn't be the first time, what if she's just heard him trump or roll over and he isn't awake at all? That's probably what it is. It's Nana who thinks John Nevison rode past North Burton and that there's a dragon's footprint in the stone up at Rudston. Meg starts up the ladder and is at the top step in a few powerful pushes, she calls back down behind her.

"Richie, bring up a candle." Her eyes scan the darkness of the roof space and she sees the shape of The Robber, laid out, just as he was in the flickering of the candle that Richie is lighting down below. She frowns. He has not moved since she left him there this morning, but Nana is not stupid, misguided perhaps; Meg should be careful as she steps onto the boards that make up the floor. She breathes slowly through her nose as she approaches, the shape does not look any different from the morning, but she pauses. It's been a strange day for Meg, sunken and trapped in the freezing ice of North Burton duck pond like it was the deep sea, clothed and pampered by Miss Charlotte in the great house of The Pennyman Estate. The hairs on Meg's arms stand up, her eyes narrow into the darkness and her legs begin to tremble. She takes a few steps towards him.

It's not the same, somehow.

He's moving.

Like a snake from the forest floor, The Robber uncoils and

snaps his open hand out and upwards towards Meg's neck. She's quick, especially with a split-second warning, but not quick enough for The Robber. He reads her movement to the left and adjusts so that his slender fingers clasp her by the throat. She expects that the grip will be rock solid, and it is tight but not painfully so. As he grabs her, he kicks her legs away and pushes her to the floor. He could do this with force, but he takes some of the weight with a hand on her shoulder. When she hits the boards, the wind is not knocked out of her, it's more like being danced with than attacked. Then, in the darkness, the smooth blue eyes of The Robber, also known as the Pearlman from Dandy Jim's gang look down on her. She takes a breath.

"I mean you no harm," he whispers. His accent is familiar somehow, similar to the way Meg speaks but smooth, with the consonants pronounced clearly like he could be talking to Mr Pennyman. "I need you to make no sound. I am to leave when the darkness falls."

Richie has reached the top of the ladder and the candle illuminates the area sending shadows to the underside of the thatched roof and the spiderwebs in the corners. He sees The Robber over Meg with his hand on her throat and the boy freezes. The blue eyes of The Robber look over to him.

"I will kill her, my boy, leave me alone and I will be gone at midnight," he says. His voice is calm and warm. "Go back down, please." There is a serenity to this Robber and a sense of gallantry to his manner, so that even in violence there is still time to be polite. Richie's wide eyes blink across the floorboards at the man, the candle in the holder rattles in his little hand as it shakes in fear.

"Put the candle down, boy. I'll not hurt her if you do as I say."

"Do as he asks, Richie," says Meg. Her voice does not sound fearful either. The boy sets the holder down and slowly, climbs back from where he came from. Meg looks up at the man Dandy Jim called The Pearlman and he stares down at her. He is different from how she imagined now he is awake, his eyes are softer and his manner more gentle. She can feel his breath on her face, and it gives her goosebumps, her heart quickens. He is not as she had imagined. Not at all.

He is better.

There's clattering from downstairs, bellowing too. The scraping of a chair on the stone floor and Nana's voice yelling,

"What in God's name…" she cries. The ladder creaks under her heavy weight and the voice sounds nearer. "Not in my house, I can tell you. Who in God's name does he think he is, Richie, after all we've done for him? Typical bloody man." Nana's head appears at the top of the ladder and her eyes blaze with anger. This is Nana who cannot get up from her chair most days, who needs Meg to help her get to the toilet sometimes.

"I'll repeat what I told the boy, woman," The Robber's voice is light but commanding. "Go back down. Stoke the fire if you wish, for when midnight comes, I will leave. I do not want to hurt you, but I surely will if you do not do as I say. I will start with this one." He nods at Meg.

"You'll get your bloody hands off her," demands Nana. The Robber draws in air through his nostrils and the grip around Meg's throat tightens. It is not the first time he has been in a difficult situation, a steady temperament helps such episodes go smoothly. "Get off her, you sod," Nana whispers. From her side, she produces The Robber's pistol in her shaky hand and levels it at him over the uneven boards that make up the floor. His face is not shocked.

"Are you sure you loaded it?" he asks.

"I fired Farmer Thorne's pistol at the summer fair. Meg pinched your bullets and your black powder from your belt, we know what we're doing, Robber." Nana frowns and points the gun at him, while her other arm grips the top of the ladder. "You get up off her or I'll put one of your bullets in you." The robber considers his position and his mind whirls as he calculates. They would have killed him already or handed him over to the local constable if they had wanted to. Perhaps this old woman does know how to load a gun. He has examined the wound on his side already and it has been neatly stitched and cleaned. They are perhaps more capable than most, these two. One of the reasons The Robber has been so successful has been his ability not to underestimate folk.

He sits back and holds his hands up. Meg scrambles free towards Nana. The old woman is in a right mood.

"What now?" asks The Robber.

"Meg, fetch down some of that twine that holds the thatch on, we'll tie this bugger up." The pistol is shaking in Nana's hands but she is too angry to feel any pain. "You're gonna pay up on your end of the bargain, Robber. You promised us silver, if you remember." The Robber smiles and his teeth are straight and white.

"I do remember, and I had no intention of breaking it." Both he and Nana know that this is not true. As soon as this man leaves the cottage, he will never return. It would be too dangerous, even if he wanted to.

"We kept our end of the deal. Meg here fixed you up, like you asked."

"You will have to let me go first to get your silver."

"We will. You'll see. But Meg here will be going with you when you leave and she'll not cut your bonds till you pay." Nana is just saying the words as they come into her head, as she does. Meg has pulled off some heavy twine chords that keep the big bunches of thatching in place. She approaches The Robber and he holds out his hands together for them to be tied in front, perhaps a little too willingly. She shakes her head and indicates that he should hold his hands above one of the roof beams. He gives her a wry smile. Now he knows these two are not fools, he will not underestimate them. Meg has tied big sows' feet together because they wriggle when they get their throats cut, she's fixed hedges and rooves and made tourniquets on legs, the slender wrists of this Robber are easy enough to secure. She ties a series of deft knots and tests the strength but they are not as tight as they should be, she remembers the way he clasped her neck and made sure she did not crash into the floor. She does not want to hurt him, somehow. Even being close makes the hairs on the back of her neck stand up.

"Do his feet as well Meg," says Nana. "Then tie him to the corner. At midnight… then, we'll think about going for a walk." Meg glances over at Nana still standing at the top of the ladder with the gun pointing at The Robber. The words just tumble out of her mouth without plan or consideration. Meg whispers back at her:

"You mean *I'll* take him for a walk?"

"Aye," says Nana.

"And put that pistol down."

CHAPTER ELEVEN

There's no way to know what time it is. On summer nights Adam Gamble will ring the church bell at eight but the carriage clock they have could be wrong. Truth is, nobody knows what time it is really and why would anyone care. This is North Burton, it's not like there's a coach coming through or anyone but Mr Pennyman has important business. You get up when the sun rises and when it's dark, there's nothing else to do but go to sleep.

It's been perhaps an hour since Meg tied The Robber to the corner roof beam. She didn't bind his feet. Nana and Richie are next to the fire and the man upstairs has not made a sound since, this bothers Meg as she pokes the embers. If she had tied anyone else like that, Granddad Blackwood, Julia Farthing, even Dandy Jim perhaps, they would have cried out, complained and shouted down the ladder that the rope was too tight. Not this Robber, not the one Dandy Jim called his Pearlman, the man who they said was named Dale. He sits as quiet as a church mouse against the beams with his eyes closed, and not a word. Meg remembers how quickly he moved to grab her previous, his hand around her throat and the way he manoeuvred her to the floor. The hairs on the back of her neck stand up again when she thinks of his breath on her face and his blue eyes, the thrill of it, she has to put these thoughts from her mind. Meg has peeked out of the shutters also and the snow has stopped. The stars and a weak moon twinkle, lighting the night. This might be the moon Carlos said would be out the evening previous. The conditions are perfect.

"Where do you expect me to take him?" she asks Nana.

"I don't bloody know," she answers. "He's the one that buried the silver, that's where you're to take him, my Meg. Take him right to where he put it and fetch it back here."

"And then what?"

"You'll have to do something." Meg frowns at Nana in the

134

same way a mother might look down on a foolish child. Nana only calls her 'My Meg' when there is something extra required.

"There is no silver, Nana." Meg's voice is cold and flat. The old woman looks across at this girl who has become a daughter to her, the girl has learned a lot. Nana takes a deep breath and settles back into her chair with her head against the flat backrest.

"I know," she says. "There's no silver." Her voice is slate grey and without emotion. "People will tell you anything you want to hear when you've got a knife to their throat, and men will lie till their throats are raw."

"That's why there's no silver, Nana. He's too calm, anyone else would be fighting like a donkey and I don't like him." Meg does not like him but she is drawn to him, intoxicated by him almost, more so now he is alive. She cannot put her finger on his manners and his relaxed way. "He's like a gentleman," she says without thinking.

"They're the worst bloody kind, Meg, believe me and he's no gentleman. A man who carries a pistol like that is not someone you can trust." Nana nods to the flintlock gun that they have set on the floor in front of the fire. Orange glints from the silver mechanism.

"Did you really load it?"

"Aye, it was still loaded from when you did it," says Nana.

"Would you have shot him?"

"If he'd hurt you, I would, and I will if I have to." Meg looks down at the gun. If there is no silver, then what is there to be done? "I care about you, Meg, as if you were my own," continues Nana, she leans forward and her eyes are bright. Meg has seen this before and heard it many times. It begins by Nana telling you how important you are, how much you mean to her and how worthwhile your life is. She's seen the old woman use it on Granddad Blackwood and even Danny Reed. It's the patter of a saleswoman making an offer or a priest that is about to provide salvation in return for something. Meg narrows her eyes. "You're my own, you know." Meg moves in first.

"I'm your daughter. I married your son, I'm part of your family. As to whether I mean anything to you, well, if there were someone else who would make the fire, fetch your eggs, cook your tea, sweep your house, wash your clothes and listen to your complaining all day then I'm sure she'd mean a lot to you as well." It's deliberately cruel talk. Nana responds:

"I took you in," she calls.

"I married your son."

"I let you marry my lad."

"No one else would," answers Meg.

"You did," her tone is condescending. Meg looks up at the fat woman, sitting like some queen in her high-backed chair. Let her have it. Isn't that what her mother said? That it was time to tell and not to listen?

"You've got a nerve," says Meg. "I'm only here for what you can wring out of me. If there were anyone else you could choose, you'd have them, but you're stuck with me." Her voice sounds different somehow, fatalistic with the solid weight of reason and truth. It's the same tone Meg's mother took when she had to put a cow out of its misery or tell a new mother that her baby is already gone. Nana tries to counter:

"I do a lot for you, Meg. It's me who pays for your new clothes at Christmas, you get to live in this house and I've never asked you for a single penny. I let you bring little Richie up here and I treat him like he's my own as well." Nana is now moving onto the second part of her game, from praise she will move to emotion, perhaps tears. Meg responds.

"Richie here is your boy, Nana, as you've been at pains to explain. We only live here because of the work I do at the farm or else you'd be tossed out into the mud." Meg is about to carry on and press home her advantage but the old woman's chin quivers and her nostrils flare. She's about to cry. A row that would usually last a day or even two has been supercharged because of The Robber upstairs. They have to fight to get to a place where they can talk.

Meg has to stop this. It will do them no good.

"Dry your eyes, old woman," she bellows. Her voice is clear and loud. "We have a thing to do here and blubbing or fighting won't get it done." Meg knows what Nana wants her to do. It's plain. It's as plain as the gun on the floor in front of the fire but she does not know if she dare tell it out loud.

"You can't say things like that to me," says Nana as she wipes her face with her chubby palm.

"We both know there is no silver. So, what is it?" Nana sniffs back her crocodile tears and points down at the pistol on the floor in front of the fire. Her eyes are keen.

"Back of his head Meg, as close as you can," she whispers because The Robber upstairs will be able to hear everything, if he is listening. "Take him out behind the pastures of the Pennyman House, to the north drain and plant a bullet in the back of his head, let him drop into the water, and it'll wash him all the way to Arram Beck and he'll be in The River Hull by high tide, and then God knows where they'll find him." Nana has not thought this through either but the plan comes fully formed.

"Why don't we just let him go? Cut his bonds, give him his gun and let him be on his way."

"He wouldn't get far."

"What do you mean? His wound is healing."

"That's as maybe, but he hasn't got the strength to get very far, nobody would in this weather. If we let him go now, he'll make it a mile before he collapses into some bush somewhere and someone will find him. Then he'll blab like he did to us, he'll tell to save his own life, just like he did when he sat against the wall right here." Meg looks down at the gun. She's killed pigs before, chickens a plenty and drown rats caught in cage traps; she's gutted rabbits and crows, fish, deer and even a badger but that was just a simple matter, not pleasant but a fact of life. This is different. This would be murder.

"You have to do it soon," says Nana. "In a few hours, it'll be morning." Meg blinks at the old woman. "We'll all of us swing Meg, if they find him here. Whether he's the man that Captain is after or not, we'll swing for sure."

Meg stands before the fire, looks at Richie with a blanket around his shoulders and then to Nana with her hands on her lap.

If she does not sort this, nobody else will.

Upstairs, Meg approaches The Robber as she might one of the nastier sows in the Pennyman pigsty, with a sense of no-nonsense and urgency.

"Wake up, please, Robber," she says. The man with the pale face opens his eyes. He has not been asleep. Without fear of what he may do to her, Meg takes her knife to the tight knot she made previous and his arms fall to his side after she cuts the bond. She does not expect him to react, and he rubs his wrists where the twine was tight, he looks at her as she stands back.

"Have you changed your mind?" he asks.

"I'll explain as we leave," she says.

"Leave where?"

"You are to be free, Robber. We have kept our part in the bargain. Now it is time for you to fulfil yours, you'll lead me to the silver you promised, provide me with our share and then be on your way." He gives a tiny grin. Meg does not need to tell him that she knows there is no silver. The idea is there to make him get to his feet and get out the door. He stands.

"I'll need my effects and my pistol."

"We have them," says Meg. "You'll lead the way. Can you make it down the ladder?"

"I think so, Meg. If you step back and give me a little room." She looks at him with renewed mistrust.

138

"How did you know my name?"

"You told it me."

"When?"

"When I lay here, prone. My eyes were closed but not my ears." Meg frowns at him and wonders what else he heard.

"Just to let you know, Nana has your pistol below." He nods in understanding.

The Robber struggles to get down the ladder and Meg watches him. He is still in pain with the wound, clearly, but he makes a good job of it. He has also been laid on his back for two days and he will be stiff and his muscles sore. He makes it to the bottom and stands to his full height in front of Nana while Meg climbs down behind, The Robber considers them from under his thick black hair. Nana holds the pistol loose in both hands, she has managed to stand. She hands the weapon to Meg who has already wrapped herself in her cloak. Richie looks up at the great height of The Robber and hands him his tricorn hat, as the tall man gives him a wink. Dutchy considers them from the roof rafters with her wide green eyes and her ears pricked up in slight agitation.

"I was in a sorry state when I hid the silver ladies, you understand. I may not be able to find it so quickly in the darkness, and, as you can see, I'm not strong enough to move as fast as I normally would." His accent is smooth and yet familiar, persuasive and with relaxed humour to it. Meg can see why he may have been a Pearlman in Dandy Jim's gang but she can see none of the ruthlessness that Carlos told her about, perhaps this is hidden deeper. She wonders if he is using the silver tongue on them that he is famed for.

"I'm sure you'll do your best," says Nana. "You're from York way on," adds Nana.

"Aye, how can you tell?" he answers.

"It's in your voice, lad. You can't wring Yorkshire out of a voice when it's been put there by God." Nana comes out with some right shite when it's not needed.

"Do you want to tie me?" he offers.

"No need to," says Nana as she motions to the pistol.

"You wouldn't want to wake the neighbours, would you?" asks The Robber.

"Why would you care about that, you'd have a hole in your back?" Nana's tongue is quick and sharp. "Meg will lead you out to the fields and you can cut back to the York Road."

Outside, thin grey clouds cover the moon, but here and there are patches of sky with stars twinkling in the cold. There's not much light to see by, but just enough. The snow that fell a few hours earlier is still fresh. It makes the going good. Nana has told Meg to stay close behind The Robber and keep the pistol out of sight. They have taken the track that goes off behind the cottages straight to the fields, Meg does not want to walk down the main street of the village. Even though it's the dead of night, you never know who might be watching, someone like Hannah Farthing probably doesn't even sleep. The track goes up a little hill following a low wall, it's the way to the back of The Pennyman Estate and the north drain that Nana spoke of. He moves slowly just in front of her, his feet slip on mud that has frozen and he uses the wall to keep himself upright. Meg should be cold out in the night, but she does not seem to feel anything at all as she watches the man in front struggle to walk. Maybe Meg deserves to be hanged, maybe Nana too. They should have told someone about The Robber the moment he knocked on their door. Nana's greed brought him in and Meg's stupid fantasy made him well again.

They walk for perhaps five minutes before he slows his pace and looks back at her in the grey light of the stars, she returns his stare with a stony-faced one of her own. Meg has put beasts out of their misery before. Why should this be any different? If she doesn't sort this Robber out one way or another, then he will sort her. They were foolish to have taken him in on that night he appeared at their door, foolish and greedy and this is the price. Under a leafless oak that grows this side of the drystone wall, The Robber stops and turns, slowly. His face is dark with pain and exhaustion. This is not some animal that she has to deal with, this is a man. The Robber wraps his cloak around him tight and then leans against the trunk of the tree. He has not complained once.

"Are you stopping for a rest?"

"Do you want your silver?" he whispers. Meg stands a few feet away. They are far enough from the cottages to talk, and in the distance behind them is the silhouette of the big Pennyman House overlooking the frozen, snow-covered fields.

"There is no silver," she answers. The Robber smiles and she can see his white teeth under his black hat.

"People say that country folk are plain and foolish. I know that's not true. I was a country lad myself, once upon a time. If you want your silver, then I do not believe it is this way. I came to your little village by the York road, this way is going due north. Do you not want your silver?"

"We know there is no silver, Robber." His face darkens.

"Then where are we going?" Meg does not answer. "Are you going to shoot me? Shoot me with my own pistol?"

"Once you catch your breath we walk," she explains.

"Why not give me my pistol now and I'll be on my way?"

"You are wounded. You'll not make it two miles away from here. Like Nana says, there will be questions if they find you."

"Will you find some sort of ditch to put me in, is that it?"

"Aye, something like that. I'd like to have it done before sunrise as well, Robber." It helps Meg not to give him a name even though she knows it is Dale.

"I wouldn't agree that country folk are backward but they do lack experience. What makes you think I'll walk to my death?" She is now cold. Meg does not know how to answer this. Her feet are freezing and her hand shivers with her fingers

141

around the ornate handle of this man's gun under her cloak.

"Your Nana is not a stupid woman, Meg." He uses her name again. It's unnerving. "She cares for you and Little Richie. She cares for you both almost as much as she does her own son, the one who has gone off to war and will probably never return. She worries that the Farthings will take her house when she dies, that when Granddad Blackwood passes on there'll be nobody for her to trust in the whole of North Burton." Meg moves closer. How could he know this? How could he even know her name? She swallows dry to her throat.

"How do you know about us?" she asks. He looks at her and a little smile creeps along his mouth. The air is still.

"You told me. You told me everything. While I lay there with the wound in my belly, all I could hear was your voice. Many times, I wanted to give up for good but then I'd hear you, whispering something or other. I know about that bastard Pennyman and Carrick The Rector with his big dog, Bear. I know that you never loved Nana's boy John and that he never kissed you like you wanted him to. I know that if you could, you would march into Farmer Thorne's livery yard, fetch his big bay, Jamie, and be off with you to a new life, with me and Richie riding alongside." He pauses to let the words sink in as the world around them twinkles from the starlight and the ice. Every blade of pale grass is silver and the branches without leaves of the oak are smooth with ice jewels.

"I know you, Meg. I know you because you told me, and I know you because I have lived this life as well. Not so many years ago I lived north of here on a patch of ground fouler than North Burton, far fouler. At sunrise, I went to the farm and returned at sunset, as you do, like an animal just to keep a roof over my mother's poor head. When she died there was not even enough money for a coffin in the ground, and the rector had her wrapped in her own sodden cloak with a wooden stick for a gravestone. I knew then that I had to change or die, to leave that place and see what I could make

142

of myself." Meg breathes deep, transfixed by this man who she has told every detail of herself to, every detail that she has never admitted to herself.

"So, you became a robber?"

"Aye. A good one at that, one of the best. Whatever Dandy Jim told you about me, know this. It is the same feeling I have now, that I had when they buried my mother, the need to change and grow and find out what I can become. There is silver. A whole two bags of it from the carriage we robbed on the way to York, there is silver whatever your clever Nana thinks. I want to end this life that I have had on the road. Jim and that Carlos have been that way too long, they wouldn't know how to live on the land, they're men of war. Neither of them could understand that I needed to be out, and so that big half Spanish bastard tried to run me through with his knife but, you Meg, you made sure that he didn't kill me. I find it hard to understand that a woman who could care for a body as well as you do, would be able to kill the same thing just as easily." Meg puts her face in her hand. She is out of her depth. He sounds like he is truthful. She did not know if she was going to kill him or let him go, perhaps Nana knew this as well.

"You know your Carlos is dead?"

"I heard. He was my brother in war. I asked him if he would give it all up with me and leave but, he was built for that way of life. I cannot say I will not grieve, but when you live like we did, on the road, death and injury are never far. You know, I can make this easy on you, Meg."

"How?" she answers.

"In my cloak here, sewn into the lining is a pistol that fits into the palm of my hand, listen as I draw back the flintlock." There is the crackle of a mechanism under his cloak. "Even now this gun is trained on you, Meg, and before you could raise up the pistol you have, you would be dead and I would be on my way, albeit just a few miles more."

"This is how you make it easier for me?" asks Meg.

143

"Now you can tell Nana you were tricked. How were you to know I had a gun sewn inside my cloak? You didn't even find the knife stitched into the bottom of my trousers."

"So, what would you have me do?" The Robber steps forward so he is just in front of Meg. She can smell his perfume still and she looks up a few inches to his face with his black half beard and hat tipped back. His eyes are blue in the moonlight as he looks into hers.

"We will return to the cottage and, on the next full moon when this damn weather has lifted, when the light is good enough to see, we will slip into Farmer Thorne's livery yard, to the back where he keeps the bay horse, Jamie. We will lead him away and in the moonlight along the York road, I'll show you where I hid the saddlebags with the silver and then, I'll climb on Jamie's back and you'll jump up behind. In an hour we will be as far away from North Burton as you have ever been." He takes hold of her shoulders and his grip is firm and honest. "I owe you my life," he says. Tears are beginning in her green eyes.

"What then?" asks Meg, already she can imagine her arms around his waist as they ride, with the world and the pigs and Mr Pennyman and North Burton and Nana falling far behind them. His spell is working.

"Then, my Meg. I will use the silver I have to buy a place that I know well far to the north on the Tyne, a house and land that will last a woman like you and a man like me a lifetime. Honest work and a family and everything that comes from it. That is what I wish for. I feel like I have been reborn." A tear rolls down Meg's cheek. No one has ever spoken to her in such a way. It makes her skin tingle and her stomach groan.

She holds the pistol up and offers the handle to The Robber. He collects it and swiftly returns it to the holster under his cloak, then pulls his hat down over his eyes.

"Not a word to anyone, mind," he says. Meg nods.

His spell has worked. Perhaps he has cast it before.

CHAPTER TWELVE

Nana is angry. It's her seething anger that she doesn't let out, the worst kind. Usually, Nana's opinions spill like a waterfall out of her mouth, but with Meg opening the door and ushering the tall Robber back into her house, the old woman narrows her eyes in fury.

They have been gone less than an hour and the dawn is coming fast, people will be awake and about their business. The Robber stops at the foot of the ladder and looks directly at Nana. From somewhere within his cloak he pulls out an uneven silver coin and holds it out for the old woman to take. She collects it quickly and spirits it into her chest.

"There's more where that came from," he says. He is earnest and his blue eyes have steel in them. "It wasn't her choice to bring me back either." The Robber shows Nana the small pistol he had cocked previous, she can also see the larger gun tucked back into its holster under his cloak. "We had an agreement, you were to get me better and I was to provide you with half the silver – I aim to make good on my half, as Meg did on hers. When the moon is out next and the going is fair, I'll get you your money."

"I want you out of here," whispers Nana. "This is my home."

"All in good time." The man makes his way up the ladder and each step complains against his weight. When he reaches the top, they can hear him walk a few steps and slump to the floor with a light thud.

Nana turns to face Meg. Her eyes are black with fatigue.

It's Sunday. The day of rest. At first light, just a few hours after she returned with The Robber, Meg moves little Richie off her chest and swaps places with him, tucking him under the thick blanket. They have slept upstairs at Nana's request. She looks across the floorboards at the black, motionless shape of The Robber wrapped in his cloak. Down the ladder, Nana has her mouth open and she is snoring from the back of her throat.

Sunday.

It may be a day of rest for some, not for others.

The girls who milk Farmer Thorne's cows will already be at work, so will Adam Gamble as he sweeps the floor of St Michael's ready for the morning sermon. While Miss Charlotte gets out of bed and slips her feet into her soft day shoes, Meg is already in the hen house with the birds around her feet as she scatters their seeds. Her face is hollow and she is hungry.

The words of The Robber bother her greatly for many reasons, they bother her because she cannot be sure they are true. It is the same as the first evening they met him, when he sat against the wall holding his wounded side and looking up at Nana with his pale blue eyes while he told her there was silver to be had. Like Meg, Nana knew this was too good to be true and not to be believed but, there is always that nagging doubt – what if it were real? It is the same as The Rector, Carrick who will stand at his pulpit in the church across the road and tell of the riches of heaven and how devotion to God can guarantee eternal happiness. Meg cannot be sure this is true either, in all honesty, what would God want with her and why would he give her anything at all, and yet, what if it were true? She thinks back to the way The Robber held her shoulders in the starlight the night previous, how his eyes looked into hers. She knows he is a robber, she knows he is the kind of man every young woman is warned about, that he is probably a murderer and by his own admission, a thief and that his heart will be as black as coal and yet; what if it were true? What if he did want to start a new life? Meg moves the pigs out the way while she forks down some of the hay from the shelf above. What would he see in Meg? A woman who is already too strong from work with long matted hair and weather-beaten skin, what would he see there? She leans against the wall for a moment as the pigs fuss with the new straw in front of her. Here she is, the girl who looks after the sows and chickens, what can she offer him? Then comes the *what if* again. Meg healed him, Meg fed him the mushrooms her mother used to kill pain and bring dreams, Meg whispered to him everything that she has thought, about her life and her hopes – he knows her. It could be true. She could be happy. All Meg knows is that she has to find out, and if she is wrong, then they'll put her in irons and hang her by the neck from the gallows in Beverley until her eyes pop out of their sockets, and the world will be black. At least there will be no more Nana or pigs or chickens or cold.

When Meg returns to the cottage, it is just before eight o'clock in the morning, the day outside is clear and the sky is blue with the sun bright on the snow. It is the time that the great and the good of North Burton walk up the hill and to St Michael's in their Sunday Best. It's also against the law not to go to church.

Nana struggles out the front door of the cottage with a huff and Meg hooks her arm, the old woman leans on her as she puts one foot in front of the other. Although they've only walked a few yards, Nana Jackson makes a good show of it with grunts at every ten or so steps just so that anyone around her will know what kind of pain she's supposed to be in. Richie follows behind, he's fallen in with Archer Farthing and they are chatting with their heads very close together. Everyone has had a scrub up. Nana has her best red shawl over her shoulders, Meg has brushed her hair and put it in a loose plait, she has wiped all the mud off her skirt and from Richie's stockings, they have washed their hands and faces too. In Beverley or off in York, these farmworkers would be considered beggars, but here in North Burton, it's clear they have made a Christian effort for Sunday morning.

Mr Farthing tips his best hat as he and his wife pass Meg

147

and Nana. She smells of flowers and has a plain white bonnet with frilly edges tied under her chin – the impressive thing about this is how white it is, emphasis of how smooth and pure Mrs Hannah Farthing must be, on a Sunday morning.

"You are a brave thing, Nana," she comments, "with your legs, coming all the way to the church." This is the kind of thing Nana expects folk to say.

"I try my best," says the old woman as she huffs into another step.

"She was a lot quicker when there was beer on at the Pennyman cellar," she adds with just enough volume that Meg can hear but Nana can't. Hannah Farthing gives a clever look over her shoulder. The fact that Meg yanked her son out of the pond yesterday has slipped the woman's mind, already.

The Blackwoods come next. Miles Blackwood has cleaned his battered top hat and his teeth are still tight from his permanent lockjaw. He looks almost older than his father. Granddad Blackwood steps past with a whistle.

"You should have married me, Nana. I've lasted the course, still fit and strong I am, lass, and I've still got thoughts in my head."

"Well you can keep them bloody thoughts to yourself," snaps Nana. She likes Granddad Blackwood.

"Do you want me to take over, Meg?" he asks.

"Goodness no," calls Nana. "I'd be on my arse with you by my side, Blackwood. That's where you'd want me." The old man gives a broad, toothless grin. They have been knocking chips off each other for many years.

As the Blackwoods march ahead, Nana turns.

"What about the Gambles?" she says.

"They're not coming. Adam says it's too much trouble to get them up the hill. Mrs Gamble can't get out of bed and the old man won't leave her." Nana thinks on this as she turns back to the hill.

"Lucky to have a bed, isn't she?"

148

Standing at the big wooden church door is Carrick The Rector with a long white gown over his massive frame. His face is red and looks freshly shaved. Mr Pennyman is opposite at the other side of the door in a green frockcoat covered by a black cape with a white fur-trimmed collar, his boots look new and have been polished. Next to him is Miss Charlotte with her long black hair silky over her shoulders and a blue dress that bulges at her hips with a shawl. She strides out as she sees Meg and Nana coming up the path and her face breaks into a wide and open smile.

"Let me help Nana," she says. They can refuse Granddad Blackwood's help but not Miss Charlotte's. Meg unlinks her arm from Nana and steps backwards while the lady takes her place. "It's the very least I can do after what happened with young Archer yesterday," she says. Mis Charlotte is radiant and she smells of flowers and turmeric. Nana does a kind of grin that is meant to be polite, they could not be more different, these two, and neither has the faintest clue of the world the other inhabits. Meg and Richie follow behind into St Michael's and the darkness within. Mr Pennyman goes inside too and Carrick waits by the big wooden doors until the folk of North Burton have taken their seats.

St Michael's is not by any means a great church. It does not have the majesty of The Minster at Beverley or the sweeping grandeur of Lincoln or York, but neither is it drab or stale. The two stained glass windows behind the raised altar depict the story of St Michael's battle against the devil on one side and David and Goliath on the other. There is craftsmanship in the pews behind the carved stone pulpit, up in the roof there are faces and gargoyles formed along the seams. There is simple art here, a fitting tribute to God from those who work the earth and live within the seasons. They take their seats. Nana and Meg take the third pew with Richie in between and Miss Charlotte joins her father at the front. It might be one thing to assist Nana into the church, but she would never sit down next to her. Meg counts the heads in front. Four for the Farthing family. Two for the Blackwoods. Three for her, Nana and Richie. On the other side of the church, there are five servant girls from the estate behind Farmer Thorne, his wife and three of his workers. Right at the front sits Danny Reed, and beside him, Miss Charlotte. Mr Pennyman and the little red-faced Captain Salter sit together. Behind the pulpit, with a white smock over his shoulders is Adam Gamble, the only choir boy, his right eye is swollen and he looks sullen. She wonders if Carrick has hit him again. It is a sorry congregation, Meg remembers when the pews were full and people had to stand at the back and the door was open to the summer outside. Rector Barret was a big man with a round stomach and a curly ginger beard under red cheeks, he was a kindly soul with an ear for anyone. Carrick couldn't be more different. His church is stale and cold.

The door slams shut and Carrick's boots clack as he walks down the aisle to the pulpit at the front. His strides are wide and strong, he takes the steps three in one movement until he is above the little congregation, looking down on them with his big bible open already on the lectern. He wears a frown and his face is red and smooth. Meg wonders if anyone wants to be here. They don't even sing.

"What do you know of hell?" he asks. There is an iron silence on the air. It's a stupid question. Everyone knows what hell is, even little Richie, even Archer Farthing.

"Hell is a place of white-hot fire. Heat, so intense that it can melt stone and if you were not already dead, it would sear the flesh from your face and your eyeballs would melt out of your face." Mr Pennyman wrinkles his nose. He has spoken to Carrick about this kind of language. Not that the big man has taken much notice.

"That which is hot is the work of the devil. Hot liquor, hot stomachs, thoughts that are hot and impure, hot tempers, hot bodies where warts and boils can fester and bubble." This is not a sermon from the book. Mr Pennyman takes an uneasy breath and glances at his daughter. He'll have to speak to the rector again.

"Heat is part of the devil," continues Carrick in his booming voice. "From the bowels of the earth itself. We have, all of us, asked ourselves why this winter lasts for so long, why, when we should be out in the fields with the animals, are we still huddled next to our fires with our stomachs growling? I will tell you why. Like everything in the world, it is God's will. It is a punishment. Clear and simple. God has seen the manner in which we live, the sins that we cannot wash away and he has sent this cold across our island to purify and put out the hot fire of evil. Ask yourself, each one of you, if you look inside your heart, truly, have you never sinned? Have you never felt jealousy or resentment for a neighbour or perhaps even desire? Are you as devoted to your family as you could be or your duties? The reason this winter persists, dear friends, is that the purification through ice is not yet complete. This has happened before, and not just within the pages of the book. Did God not send the plagues to Egypt? Was it not God who burned the foul city of London almost to the ground some forty years ago in 1666, and, six years ago, he sent the Great Gale to blow rotten sailors and pirates into the icy North Sea." Carrick's face is flushed red but not yet fully angry.

"Even now, one sits among us who is prepared to commit the terrible act of murder. It is of no consequence that the man killed was a vagabond, it does not matter to God. He is the only one who can judge a man, truly and so, one of us here, sitting in their Sunday best is responsible for this. We all know that the snow and the lanes are too bad now to get in or out of North Burton quickly. Someone has blood on their hands."

Meg's face does not show any emotion.

It's not new that the people of North Burton have been up to no good. There is always something getting lost from Mr

151

Pennyman's cellar or from the church pantry itself, especially when old Rector Basset was around. Chickens go astray, Miss Charlotte's best pants that are hung out to dry on a summer morning disappear, Adam Gamble manages to get into the kitchen and take two fresh loaves that have just come out of the big oven. They are permanently in trouble somehow, whether it be with each other or God and so, now that something truly terrible has happened, Meg does what she always does, what Nana has told her to do – say nothing.

The little Captain stands up next and makes his way to the pulpit. He wears a different, more pristine dark blue coat with highly polished buttons and gold stitching across the front. The Captain's moustache is curled at each end with wax and his hair is smooth and combed. In his hands he has a leather pouch and he holds this up in front of him so everyone can see. The man has no real power for speaking, unlike Carrick.

"Here are ten guineas," he says as he holds the pouch aloft. "Ten guineas for whoever gives me information that leads me to the killer. No questions. I am a man of God like all of us here, but through me, he will encourage the devil to make himself shown. This whole afternoon, I shall be in the Pennyman House kitchen, waiting." The Captain eyes the little congregation before him, from the cool green of Farmer Thorne to the frightened face of little Archer Farthing squashed up next to his mother's big skirt. "I will tell you about the man I seek, so that you may see why I'm anxious to find him." The Captain takes a deep breath as if he does not want to say what he is about to – it's just for drama but he is not a very gifted actor.

"I have led many men into wars, on the continent in France and in Spain also. I always found it was best to be honest with them. If they knew a little of the plans that I had, then they may be better able to carry out their duties, with a full picture of the field." He wipes his face for dramatic effect. This is not true. The Captain has been to war in Europe but he did not lead soldiers into battle. Like other men of position and some wealth, he was far behind the fighting. Of course, it was dangerous, canon fire can go astray, but he did not ever speak to his men as he does now in front of this congregation. What would commoners know of war and what is true? Indeed, in such a place as North Burton, The Captain can allude to himself in the same sentence as say, The Duke of Marlborough or even Prince Eugene of Saxony.

"The man I am looking for is a deserter, a murderer and a liar. A man who caused The Duke of Marlborough's army on the continent a great deal of damage, and loss of life. A spy, in short, a shapeshifter, a doppelganger who worked in the service of our crown, and who betrayed it. It is little more than five years since the Battle of Blenheim along the banks of the Danube, and that victorious event may well have gone quite a different way if our spy had been successful." The Captain sets the leather pouch on the lectern in front of him and, reaches inside his jacket pocket to withdraw a slip of paper. He holds this up, it is an envelope, yellow and a little dirty.

"This, people of North Burton, is a simple letter. It is addressed to a Field Marshall in the king's garrison based at the fort of Westminster, London. The seal is from Beverley. It is my belief that our spy is here. They will be a newcomer, they have most certainly been here less than three years and they will be an expert in what they do. They will blend like a rat in the darkness, and man or woman, I do not know. The Duke himself does not know, this is the nature of a spy. Among you, I believe, is the one I seek and I will find you and I will take you back to London, alive and you will stand trial or, be carried back dead in a box."

This is a new development.

The people of North Burton have ritually been told they will go to hell and their souls will be burned for eternity. They have been told that Mr Pennyman will cancel the summer fair and that there will be no ale for a month, but never have they been threatened like this – with something real. Nobody looks at each other. Yet.

The Captain climbs down from the pulpit and Carrick steps back to tower over the big open bible which he has not looked at. He leads them in the lord's prayer. Meg does not open her eyes as they murmur the words together. When The Captain finds her Robber, which is only a matter of time, he'll be pinned as this spy, somehow, and anyone who has helped him will swing, Meg, Nana and if he's unlucky - little Richie too.

After the service, it does not take Nana as long to get back down the hill, firstly because it is easier and secondly, there is nobody to watch her struggle. Meg has linked her arm with the old woman, as her hips move, the little grunts of pain are real but suppressed. They pause for a break on the railings of the duck pond where Archer Farthing fell in the day before. There are no children on it today and the sky is a brooding grey, their breath makes steam in the fresh cold. Nana's nose is red from the temperature.

"It's going to snow," she says. Meg nods and rubs the old woman's back.

"The quicker we get home, the quicker we can get you warmed up, Nana."

"Aye, and the quicker you can get on up to the Pennyman House."

"I'll have to make sure the animals have water."

"Not for that. Didn't you hear The Captain?" she whispers. "Didn't you hear him say he would be in the kitchen all afternoon? Waiting?" Meg did hear this, but she does not yet understand what Nana wants from her. "You'll go to him, Meg. You'll go to him and we'll have that 10-guinea bag."

"How so?" she asks.

"Our Robber."

"What do you mean?"

154

"Our Robber, he does not intend to leave us in peace. I know men, Meg and believe you me, when the darkness comes he'll be on you… on you like a beggar on a scrap of bread. Well, yesterday, we gave him his chance to get away but he was too clever to take it. When we get back, you'll say you have to go to the animals and you will, but after, you'll go to Captain Salter sat at Mr Pennyman's kitchen table, and you'll tell him that a robber has holed himself in our upstairs, that he's threatened to knife us and our Richie if we tell anyone." There's a wry grin to Nana as she struggles with her weight on unsteady legs. "Then those ten guineas will be ours and what's more, when the snow lifts, you and Richie can go up to the York Road and look for his silver, once he's been hung." Nana seems pleased with herself.

Adam Gamble hurries by with his head down. He will have been up at the church setting things straight after the service.

"You there," says Nana. "Young Adam, let me see you." The boy stops but does not look back round at the two women. "What's wrong with you?" says Nana.

"Nothing, I'm on my way home." Nana has a way about her. She knows when something is not right and she knows too that anyone who says there is nothing wrong, means there is something wrong.

"Turn and look at me," she orders. He does so. Across his face is a red mark and his cheek is swelling in a bruise. "Did that bloody Carrick do that? Again?" asks Nana.

"I fell, Nana."

"You fell," she repeats. "He'll keep on hitting you, Adam Gamble, like he hits that horrible dog of his. Tell Mr Pennyman or Miss Charlotte for that matter. If I were in my youth, you could tell me and I'd go up there and put one on the big bastard myself. I was a strong lass you know. I won Walkington wrestling at the village fair in 1685, against men twice as big as him." Nana repeats this fact as often as she can and it brings a grin out on Adam's honest face. "If you don't

155

tell anyone, I will. Meg is going up to the Pennyman house this afternoon, she'll mention it, won't you Meg?"

"Don't Meg," says Adam Gamble. "Rector Carrick wouldn't like it."

"Bugger him," says Nana.

"And anyway, I fell," adds Adam. The old woman huffs. Nana does not like to see her own get hurt, and neither does she like to see bullies win.

"We'll get that Carrick one day, young Adam Gamble, you'll see."

"Not if I get him first," says Meg. It's not usual for her to say something like this. Adam Gamble considers her green eyes. There's something about Meg that you might be afraid of, he shakes his head and hurries away.

"You want to watch that temper of yours, Meg," says Nana. "It might get you into trouble one day."

Inside the end cottage, Meg can hear whispering coming from up the ladder. It is Richie's voice. He ran home ahead of them after the service as he does. For little lads like Archer Farthing and Richie, North Burton is a fine place. There is always something to do or steal, or someone to upset or talk to. It seems Richie has taken a liking to their Robber. Meg helps Nana into her chair and pokes the fire back into action, above, she can hear low words spoken by The Robber. The old woman looks at Meg through narrow eyes and nods,

"As we agreed," she says. "You'll get on up to the Pennyman house once you've got changed."

"I didn't agree," says Meg.

"I think you did," answers Nana. They hear Richie laughing from up the ladder. The two women look at each other. Perhaps it's for the best. They can get rid of their Robber for good and keep their lives, and most importantly, Richie's.

Meg climbs the ladder and steps up onto the smooth

floorboards of the upper level. In front of her, cross-legged opposite each other are Richie and The Robber, between them on the floor is the silver pistol that he usually carries in the leather holster at his side. Duchy the cat is curled up next to The Robber like she never does with anyone else but Richie.

"What in God's name are you doing?" asks Meg. Her words are sharp. The Robber turns his head and holds his finger up to stop her from talking.

"Observe," he orders. "Go on, Richie." The boy picks up the gun and uses his thumb to flip the pan open that is behind the flintlock, his little hands are quick and clever. He puts a packet of black powder to his mouth and rips it open with his teeth, pours some in the pan and the rest down the nozzle. He takes out the ramrod and packs the whole lot down before he cocks the flintlock with both thumbs and sets it down on the floor where he had picked it up. He beams up at Meg with a wide grin.

"Five seconds that," nods The Robber. "He learns quickly does this lad."

"You're letting him play with your pistol?" says Meg with incredulity. She does not want to shout because of the neighbours but her words are harsh.

"It doesn't have a bullet in it."

"The flash could blind him. What were you thinking? He's a child." Richie looks up at Meg and his eyes have lost their sparkle.

"I'm sorry, Meg," he says.

"It's not your fault, Richie," she answers. "This gentleman should know better than to put a little lad in danger." Meg is conscious as she says the words, that they could easily be spoken by Nana or Mrs Farthing or someone equally as angry about little things. She does not want to be that woman. "Richie, could you go down, please?" The boy moves away quickly and The Robber picks up his pistol, uncocks it and sets it back in the holster on his belt, under his cloak. Meg walks past him to the corner and the chest that is open with their clothes inside. She takes off her best brown cloak and folds it. This is Meg getting changed, the cooks in the Pennyman kitchen probably wouldn't use her clothes for rags.

"Are you feeling well?" she asks.

"Aye," he answers. "You did a good job on that cut. I can feel my strength coming back to me. What have you got for the pot?"

"There is nothing for the pot. This is North Burton and the coldest winter we have ever known. This is how it is. It's a pity you didn't knock on Farmer Thorne's door that night you came here, he might have something to eat." The Robber grins. His teeth are white and straight and his eyes are blue under his black, smooth hair.

"When is the next full moon?" Meg looks down. She will have to tell The Captain about him.

"I'll find out."

"See that you do, that's when we move." She looks into his eyes and takes a deep breath.

"I'm a simple woman, but I'm not a fool. I have thought on about what you said, and, it seems to me something that you would say to any woman whose help you needed. You are a certain type of man, I imagine you have said such things to a girl before." The Robber's face is suddenly earnest.

"I have lied previous, aye, many times. I have been a robber and a pearlman for many a year, and that role requires such behaviour, but, Meg, I have not had the pleasure of knowing any others the way that I know you."

"You do not know me."

"I do. You told me everything, or do you not remember?" Meg in truth does not recall what she told him when he was in fever in her arms. She swallows.

"What is there to know?"

"That you never loved your husband. That you guard Richie and Nana with your life. That your mother passed you

158

knowledge of medicine, that you are shy with what you say. That you love her and miss her and have not yet had time to grieve. I know this about you. I know that you put others before yourself. This, to me, is something I had not believed to be true." The Robber is sincere and his eyes are watering. "I would like to learn this from you, Meg, how to care for others so that I can leave the life I had behind. Will you help me?"

"This is a fantasy. Whatever I said in the night, I will not be leaving with you. My place is here, with Nana and Richie and my duties to The Pennyman Estate and in time, the people of North Burton and my medicine. This is all I am. If you know me, then you know I will never leave, and, there must be a thousand women in the alehouses in Manchester or London who are the same as I, who will put you before even themselves, and women who have rich fathers and clothes that are not ruined, that have curled hair and white makeup and hands that are not broken from work." It makes Meg sad to speak so plainly, but it is true.

"I have met these women, Meg. I have met them a thousand times and you must understand, they are not the same as you, not nearly. You have no reason to believe me at all, I know that. So, when the full moon comes, I will leave, but I will make good on my promise and if you do not wish to come with me, I will return in the summer, once my affairs are in order."

"I am yet a married woman."

"Do you think he is coming back?"

"Until I know, I am a married woman."

"If he was part of the war in France, he will be dead. Otherwise, he would be home."

"How can you be sure?"

"I have associates who were there." The Robber struggles with his next words. "I was there also. Those that were not strong and did not have friends to look after them would have

159

died. It has been four years. He is not coming back." She considers The Robber again, sat on the floor crossed legged like a child. This has to stop. This game between them. He does not want her, he cannot. She will have to tell The Captain about him because there is too much for them all to lose if she does not. If he has to die, then that is the way it is, some people are born to riches like Miss Charlotte, some are born in the gutter like Meg, and others, they are born to rob and then to die for what they have done wrong.

"I have to go to the farm," she says.

"Aye," he answers. Perhaps she looks at him too long. "I should have died many times before, Meg. Bullets have whistled past my head, I have fallen from horses, I have fought with men who by strength ought to have killed me. I should have died with the blade that Carlos did me with, were it not for you, I would have. I feel as though my life has brought me here, somehow, I feel like it has brought me here, to you. What can I say to make you believe me?" Meg has walked over to the ladder while he is speaking and she looks down at the room below.

"You can't say anything."

"You don't believe me though."

"No."

"Why?"

"I don't believe anyone could love me, Robber, not in the way a man loves a woman and I don't believe in love either. It's a thing people talk about, but you can't see it or feel it, it doesn't fill your belly or keep the house warm. Duty, I understand, but the kind of romance you seem to speak of is not real. Perhaps in silly stories or songs or poems but not here in the real world and not for a woman like me, and not in North Burton."

"We will see," he says. The Robber does not take his eyes off her as she climbs down the ladder and out of sight.

Nana watches Meg wrap her working cloak around her, she

will have heard every word. The old woman fixes Meg with a steel stare as she stands at the door.

"I'm proud of you, Meg," she says. "I'm proud of the woman you have become and the woman you will be."

As Meg walks the main street of North Burton, past the row of cottages and the well, she feels tears running down her face, hot and wet and though she wipes them away they will not stop coming.

CHAPTER THIRTEEN

Hannah Farthing is in the livery yard as Meg walks through. She has switched her pure white bonnet for a floppy felt hat and is in her working boots.

"It could be you The Captain is looking for," calls Hannah. Meg does not stop walking. "You could at least look at a person when they're talking to you," snaps Hannah again. Meg pauses and turns around. In the hierarchy of North Burton, Hannah Farthing is far above Meg and likes to demonstrate this, as does her daughter. "You know some of your chickens have got loose, they were all over the yard this morning."

"How many?"

"Two."

"Hardly all over your yard."

"If it happens again, you'll be scrubbing up any mess they make." Hannah does not like to be answered back. Meg seems to have got a bit full of herself. "You might fool Miss Charlotte into thinking you're a quiet little country girl, but you don't fool me, you and Nana, scheming away. I know you're up to something, and I know you're mixed up in this somehow. I'm supposed to be thankful to you for pulling Archer out of the pond. He told me he was fine, and there was no need for you to help. Makes for a good story though, doesn't it? Miss Charlotte fell for it."

"Could be you The Captain is looking for," says Meg.

"What?"

"It could be you or your husband The Captain is looking for, you've only been here three summers. You're not from the East Riding." Hannah Farthing steps forward with the brush in her hand. She is a foot shorter than Meg, but like those who have worked with horses all their lives, she is strong and thinks that you get things done by shouting.

"You say that again and you'll feel the back of my hand, girl. My husband and I are as honest as Mr Pennyman himself." Hannah Farthing is angry because the information could be true. Her family are relative newcomers to North Burton, and something did happen down south in Essex that they would rather forget. The Captain worries her, hence why she takes it out on Meg. "Do you understand me?"

"Yes, Ma'am," she offers.

"You better watch yourself. I'm watching you as well." Meg wonders if Archer Farthing could have got out of the pond on his own. She lowers her eyes so as not to make Hannah Farthing angrier and wishes she could stop herself from answering back.

"I'll make sure none of my birds get into the yard."

"See that they don't." From inside one of the stables comes Mr Farthing, he too has changed his clothes and has a black handkerchief around his neck. Day of rest or not, he still has to attend to the horses. He strides out and stands next to his wife.

"We had some of your chickens in the yard this morning Meg, I got them back in but there's a hole in their cage somewhere, I think."

"I already told her," says Hannah.

"Who do you think our spy is then, Meg?" Mr Farthing's voice is jovial.

"I don't know Mr Farthing, Sir."

"Meg thinks it might be us," says Hannah.

"I don't think that," says Meg. "I best get to my chickens and find that hole." Mr Farthing steps forward and his face wears a frown.

"It's not us, we're farming folk, working people just the same as you."

"Yes, Mr Farthing," says Meg. He looks nervously at his wife and Meg knows too, that there is something this pair are hiding. She nods her head and is relieved. If the Farthings have something to hide then they are more like the rest of North Burton than she thought previous.

"We have as much interest in catching whoever The Captain is looking for."

"You don't need to explain to me," says Meg. "I've lived here only a few months longer than you. John and I were wed just before you came. Danny Reed, the driver, he's come from Beverley of recent, can't be more than a year. Carrick at the church, he's new as well, two years after Rector Bassett passed on. Farmer Thorne has a couple of different hands who work for him." Meg finds herself speaking candidly. "I don't believe Captain Salter knows what he's looking for, seems to me like he's someone who only knows how to shout and doesn't get his hands dirty, the kind of man who worries more about his coattails and his moustache than what's right and good. I think The Captain will fit someone up for the job alright, whether they've done anything or not, and soon, and then he'll be on his way and the job will be done." It's Hannah Farthing's turn to step forward now and her face is serious and her eyes cool, she has not heard Meg speak like this before, she respects the thinking because it's what she has reasoned too.

"It'll be a show trial," she whispers, "The Captain will pick the first person to do something wrong, the first one to slip up, and he'll pin it on them, you'll see. It's happened before, this kind of thing, hasn't it, husband?" Her voice is quiet but barbed. Perhaps this is what they ran away from down in Essex.

"We just can't put a foot wrong," answers Meg. She looks Hannah Farthing in the eye without malice. The three of them stand facing each other for a moment before Meg steps back, conscious somehow that she has said too much. She knows that the Farthings will not have anything to worry about once she has spoken to The Captain in the Pennyman kitchen. Hannah will not have to fret. Captain Salter will have his man.

"I best get to them chickens," she says as she turns. Hannah Farthing calls after her:

"Meg," her voice is loud.

"Yes, Ma'am."

"About my Archer, yesterday. You have my thanks, and my husband's thanks too." Meg nods.

It does not take Meg long to find the hole at the back of the run where two chickens managed to squeeze out. She fixes it by threading kindling to make a lattice, and as she works, she thinks of Dandy Jim. This is almost the spot where she let him and Carlos into The Pennyman Estate. She has tried to piece together what might have happened to them that night but it does not make any sense. They may or may not have entered the big house or the church grounds, but how would Carlos end up dead on the road outside, and what of Dandy Jim? Neither of these men were shrinking, they were soldiers. Perhaps Jim is out there somewhere, like some wounded dog fox, silent in the bushes.

The work is good for her. It makes her forget what Nana has asked her to do and what she is going to do. She thinks also about The Robber and his blue eyes as he spoke to her in the cottage an hour previous. He is a handsome one, his words are earnest and he has a soft way about him also. She likes the way he deals with Richie and Dutchy the cat trusts him already.

When she is finished, Meg collects the eggs in her basket and looks down at the hole she has fixed. She has not until now considered why or how it was there, the birds could not have made it, and if it were a fox then all her chickens would be dead. As she is closing the door to the run, she grins. The work of a man. Dandy Jim.

The pigs are in a foul mood because of the cold and Meg gives the big sow a wide birth as she cleans them out. They should be outside already, where they were born to be, in the fields rooting for whatever they can find, but Mr Pennyman has ordered them to be kept out of the snow so they do not freeze to death. A wise move. Meg works more slowly than normal because she does not want to have to go up to the

Pennyman House and knock on the back door, to sit down in front of The little Captain and tell him that the man he is looking for is above her own fireplace. What will happen after that? How will the house of playing cards she has built crumble? No doubt Mr Pennyman and The Captain will fetch their guns and Danny Reed also, as the constable of North Burton. They will storm the cottage with their pistols for her Robber and then, God himself only knows what will happen. Will he go quietly, perhaps he will take Nana hostage or Richie, Meg knows he is a man with fight in him just by the way he fought for his life at that wound on his side. Then what? Suppose they shoot The Robber dead, what is Meg to say happened? That he kept them against their will, how could they have gone to church? It will not wash. What of Danny Reed who was supposed to have searched the house and did not? There will be ripples far and wide when Meg tells The Captain of The Robber, ripples that may cost her dearer than if she had just kept her mouth shut.

Meg closes the pigsty door and drops the metal hook over the catch. She has already spent too long at this, she should be at The Pennyman house already. She carries the basket full of eggs across the livery yard and there is Hannah Farthing, putting fresh hay into one of the stalls. She gives Meg a half-smile, the first one ever. Meg nods. Today she will deliver the eggs to The Pennyman House and the red-faced cook will take them into the larder, so there is a reason for Meg to go into that kitchen.

Her stomach churns.

Meg sees her mother again. The thin figure sat in her chair in the tiny cottage at Etton with her fingers skeletal and the skin on her face drawn tight to her cheekbones. She told Meg it was not the time just to listen anymore, she told Meg that it was time to be responsible, that her happiness depended on it and the happiness of others. Didn't her mother tell her that love was close and that now was her time to speak? So, maybe

Meg does not have to do what Nana says. It's not like she has done so far, anyway.

At the back of the Pennyman House, Meg pauses, puts the wicker basket into the crook of her arm and raps on the wood of the kitchen door. It opens and she looks across and down into the cold grey eyes of The Captain with his cheeks red and his brow crinkled in a frown. He steps back and ushers her inside in silence. Then closes the big door behind her.

The kitchen is deserted. The cooks and serving girls will have already cleaned up after Sunday lunch. The fire is still burning and the room is nice and warm, even though it's big.

"Would you like to sit down?" he asks. Meg shakes her head. The Captain returns to a seat at the table with the fire at his back. His long pipe burns in an ashtray and there are papers on the table with his glasses in a little wooden box. There is a teapot with cups next to it on a tray. Alone in the middle of the table is the pouch with the guineas that The Captain displayed in the church.

"Would you like a drink? It's tea."

"No thank you," says Meg. "I've brought the eggs as I always do."

"Ah." The Captain looks let down suddenly and his shoulders drop. "Very well then, set them down where you usually do."

"Yes, Sir," answers Meg. She walks to the Welsh dresser, pulls open a drawer and begins to pick the eggs out of the basket and slot them in the holes inside.

"Have you been in the village long, girl?" asks The Captain. Meg stops what she is doing and turns around. It's rude to answer a gentleman with her back turned to him.

"I've been here four summers, Sir."

"Four years then?"

"Four and a half, Sir" He frowns at this.

"Did you and your husband come together?" Captain

Salter has taken so little interest in North Burton that he does not recognise this girl or remember that he has been in her house. They all look the same, the villagers, with their drab clothes and washed-out faces.

"I came here to wed my husband, Sir and he went away to fight with the Duke of Marlborough's forces on the continent." The Captain nods with approval. The Duke is a fine man. He has seen him up close, though not as up close as he leads everyone to think.

"Has your husband not returned?"

"No, Sir."

"Then he'll be dead." The Captain has no regard for niceties with this woman. She's worth less than a horse.

"Thank you, Sir," says Meg. She feels only fear as he sits in front of her with a scowl across his face.

"Who do you think our killer is, girl? Who do you think would kill a man and leave him in the street?"

"I don't know, Sir," she says.

"What is it you do here?"

"I look after the chickens and the pigs, Sir. I work the fields also when the weather allows."

"Have you noticed any goings-on? Anything that is not usual with anything or anybody." Here is the question. If Meg is to lie, it is here, and if she is found out, she will hang, Nana as well. Her throat is dry, the room is so hot and the grey eyes of the Captain glare up at her.

"Nothing different, Sir," she mumbles.

"Well, if you do hear of anything, then you'll be sure to let me know, girl, won't you?"

"Yes, Sir."

"Just so as you are aware, if I find anything in this village that leads me to think anyone has been lying, then I'll have you all hung. All of you." Meg swallows again. She is scared because it is perfectly possible for a man like The Captain to do whatever he pleases. At any trial, his testimony will have more weight than anyone. Like Hannah and Meg imagine, Captain Salter is becoming bored by the whole game and needs someone to pin the blame for the crime on. This could easily be Meg. The stress is getting to her. A tear runs down her face and over her cheek. The Captain stands up and his chair scrapes on the stone floor of the kitchen.

There's a knock on the door.

It has broken the moment.

The Captain steps round the table to the kitchen door quickly. So far, Meg has been the only visitor. Because he has a high opinion of himself, Captain Salter believes his plan will work, as all his plans work. This new visitor may have information for him. He beckons to Meg that she should leave and she goes to the door and opens it. There, with her eyes wide and her nostrils flared is Hannah Farthing, she sees Meg and looks down to see the egg basket hanging on her forearms. Then looks back at Meg's eyes and spots the tear that has dried on her dirty face as she moves past her into the kitchen.

Meg does not look back as she walks up the drive.

It's late afternoon as Meg comes round to the front of the Pennyman House and towards the gate. The sky is grey and a little flurry of snow begins. Danny Reed, dressed in a long black coat with shiny buttons crunches in the fresh snow towards Meg, he has a stiff brimmed hat and a wide grin. In this weather, there's not much coach driving for him to do.

"Afternoon," he says as he tips his hat. He sees that Meg is pale and her lips are red. "What's happened?" he asks. She looks back at the house and thinks of Hannah Farthing at the kitchen table and then stares back to the smooth face of Danny Reed in front of her. He wears a frown of concern.

"I dropped the eggs off in the kitchen. The Captain, he means to find someone here, whether they're guilty or not."

"I'll walk with you a minute, Meg, just up to the church." Mr Reed's voice is suddenly serious. She nods. When they are a few steps away from the house and out of earshot, Danny Reed offers his counsel.

"I would be careful who you speak to about anything at the moment, Meg. The Captain is desperate to get out of North Burton and complete the job he's been set, and there's nobody he wouldn't hang if he thinks he can prove it's them. Mr Pennyman himself has had to vouch that he saw my letters of reference."

"Do you not have them?" asks Meg. Danny looks concerned.

"They're back in Beverley with my mother for safekeeping. The roads are still too bad to travel but as soon as the snow lifts, I'll retrieve them to show to The Captain." Danny Reed has not been in North Burton long, perhaps a year at most but he has already made himself liked by all, even by Nana. He would not dream of lifting anything from Mr Pennyman's cellar at the moment, perhaps he wishes he hadn't previously.

"Is The Captain really that desperate?" Danny Reed's eyes are narrowed in concern.

"Captain Salter is a good deal richer than Mr Pennyman, Meg. He's richer and more powerful too. Some fool down in London has sent him on an errand that, to my ears sounds damn near impossible, to find a spy neither he nor anyone else knows anything about. I think someone is making a fool out of him. He has some sort of letter and nobody knows what's written inside."

"You don't think there's a spy?"

"I know a man has been killed, that's all, but Captain Salter will find someone, soon enough."

"He can't just decide that someone is guilty." Danny Reed takes a breath in through his nose. He has spoken to men who work the courts in Beverley, heard the gossip outside The Minster from the lawyers and the businessmen.

"There's a different sort of truth for the rich, Meg, I mean the rich like Captain Salter and to an extent, Mr Pennyman.

170

Whatever they want to be true, is true, whatever they decide is right, is right."

"What about all the laws we have?" asks Meg. "What about you as the constable?"

"Their rules are the only justice there is."

"It's 1709. Nana would say it's not right, not in our time."

"It may be 1709, Meg but it could be a hundred years ago or two hundred or a thousand. Those with the money and the guns do as they wish, the rest of us hang onto their coattails."

The snow has begun again and the afternoon darkens as the two of them reach the big metal gate. Meg pulls her hood over her head. From the church there's the barking sound of Carrick's big dog, it's like gravel being shovelled. They look at each other. The dog doesn't usually bark at all. Danny Reed goes first, crossing the little road and going up the path towards the gate to St Michael's, Meg follows. It has begun to snow more heavily and the sound of the animal is closer and louder. Danny Reed stops when he sees Carrick holding his dog by the collar, the beast is struggling to get away, barking and frothing at the mouth at a figure huddled against the smooth stone wall of the big church. Meg sees Carrick also and hurries forward, for some reason she thinks of Dandy Jim, but the person the dog is barking so ferociously at, is Adam Gamble, the boy has his head buried in his arms. Carrick on the other hand has a jovial look on his big face.

"Go ahead and run, boy," he calls. "Run, and Bear will follow and I don't think I'll be able to hold him."

"Is there something wrong, Rector Carrick?" It's the nervous voice of Danny Reed through the snowfall. The perfect English question. Of course, there is nothing wrong with Carrick, nothing at all, he seems to enjoy putting the fear of God into the lad, so Danny Reed's question could easily be 'What the hell are you doing?'

"Nothing wrong here, Mr Reed, just some friendly games. Adam needs to get used to Bear if he's going to feed him."

"The boy is terrified," says Meg.

"Aye, and you would be too," comes the reply.

"I think perhaps the game has been enjoyed by all a little too much already," says Danny Reed. This is a polite inversion of the truth. Carrick snarls at him and grunts. The Rector pulls Bear back by his collar with a sharp tug and the dog looks round and up. In his left hand, Carrick is carrying a stout baton, he smacks it on the dog's head with a savage blow and there is a yelp. He does this several more times while he is holding the collar and the dog tries to wriggle free, in a few moments, the beast is cowering and Carrick leads it back to the cage under his wagon where it is happy to go inside and be closed in. Carrick is out of breath when he returns, his face flush and he wears an unusual smile.

"Never shout at a dog," he says. "All you need is a heavy hand and they'll be your best friend." Adam Gamble collects himself from where he was huddled against the wall, his face is pale and weak, not at all like the proud and clever lad that Meg knows, the one who used to help old Rector Bassett.

"Is there something I can do for you, Mr Reed?" asks Carrick.

"I heard the dog barking and thought there may be some sort of commotion."

"You were not wrong, if you hear Bear barking then you can be certain that there is some sort of problem, but, as you can see, it was only a bit of lighthearted fun." Like Danny Reed or anyone with an education, Carrick speaks in opposites for the sake of appearing polite.

"Come along then, Adam," says Meg. "Your mum and dad will need their fire building." The lad looks at Meg and his eyes are fearful, the bruise on his cheek looks darker.

"I'm not done with him, yet," says Carrick. "He has to sweep the church out, girl."

"He has an elderly father, Sir, they will need him on a day like this. The storm looks like it's coming down again. We could be under six feet of snow by tomorrow." At this, Carrick cocks his head. She has spoken too much and out of turn for a woman of her station. The Rector is hot-tempered and angered by her.

"If you believe that there is anything more important than God's work, girl, then perhaps you need a speaking too."

Danny Reed steps between them. The snow has begun to fall heavy.

"I do not believe she meant that, Rector Carrick."

"Well then, what did she mean? Do you speak for her?"

Meg shrinks back. She has said too much.

"I do not, Carrick. I will see that she gets home and I will educate her on the importance of making sure that God's house is clean and well swept."

"See that you do. If you speak to me like that again, girl, you will feel my fist." He glares down from his six foot four at Meg as she backs away. "You boy, back into the church and about your duties before I lose my usually cool head." The big man towers over Danny Reed and his eyes blaze. "Is there anything I can help you with, Mr Reed?" he asks. Again, the opposite talk they are so fond of.

"I'll be on my way, Sir," says Danny. He keeps his eyes on the big Rector as he moves backwards then turns when he is nearer the gate.

At the end of the row of cottages, Meg looks in on Adam Gamble's aged parents and builds their fire for them. They have a bed in the little front room where they both sleep, the old woman is so frail and thin that she does not even wake up as Meg busies herself. The old man is not much better. She makes sure they have enough water in their pot and that there is a bowl of rolled oats and water for the father. Adam Gamble's lot is worse than Meg's. Perhaps he sleeps curled up on the floor on straw here, and every morning he has to go up to the church to be shouted out by that bully Carrick, or worse.

Outside the snow falls thick and heavy, it sucks the air from the afternoon as it turns to evening, and young Adam does not return. Meg cannot wait for him and so, she tucks the sleepy father into bed and lets the fire die down.

Meg opens the door against the snow that is already an inch thick on the ground below and steps outside, her new boots crunch, she looks up the road towards the church and thinks about Adam Gamble, perhaps he will be back soon enough. It must be six o'clock but the air is heavy and dark around her and though it is only a minute walk to her house, she does not want to go back to Nana and their Robber. She does not want to have to face them or see Nana's watery old eyes as she whispers that she could not tell Captain Salter about their visitor. Meg wonders why she could not. She is not in love with the man despite the fluttering she feels in her stomach when she thinks about him. She makes her way past the cottages, past the Farthing's front door and then past the Blackwood's and in a few seconds, she is already there, outside her own house and the snow falling at a rate all around her.

She looks up the road again.

Perhaps she should go and see if Adam Gamble is okay.

She looks back at the door and swallows.

She was too afraid to tell The Captain. This is the truth. She was afraid but not for her, for the people inside the door of this house. She does not want the Robber hurt, nor Nana and especially not little Richie. Captain Salter is an angry beast, injured somehow and, like any farm girl, Meg knows that you don't go near an animal when it is hurt, even if you want to help it. The best thing to do with a dog or a bull or a stallion that's been injured badly is to get someone with a gun to come along and put a bullet through its skull.

Meg knows someone who has a pistol.

CHAPTER FOURTEEN

Carrick's palm buzzes from where he clipped Adam Gamble around the head. He told the lad to leave as soon as he had swept the floor one more time. The cruelty will make the boy strong. It made Carrick strong when he was young.

The bulky Rector turns to look at the pulpit and the deserted rows of pews in front of him. The snow is falling thick outside and it makes the church gloomy. When it freezes over in the next few days, people will suffer more, like they have been, like they should do.

There's the noise of a flintlock cocking from behind him in the darkness. He's heard such a sound in the past, many times in days gone by, before he was a respectable man with a church and letter of commendation.

"Nobody will hear the shot," says the figure standing in the darkness behind him. "With the door shut and the snow, and at this time of night, nobody will hear, not even that dog." Carrick does not move or turn, but his heart quickens as he takes a deep breath. He smells perfume and the heavy scent of wine, why did he not notice this before? Perhaps he allowed himself to have too much fun bullying the boy.

Dandy Jim steps out of the shadows with his pistol held up against the back of Carrick's head. He's lost his hat.

"Time for us to play a game," he whispers. "It's in the bible. You'll know it. An eye for an eye."

At the western end of the church, there is a heavy black curtain. Behind this is a table with simple wooden chairs. It is where the previous Rector Bassett used to talk to people who were in trouble. Carrick never uses it, that is, not until today.

Opposite him, lit by a lamp, Dandy Jim sits back on his chair. He is smiling and his legs are stretched out ending in those shiny leather boots crossed over each other. Held loose in one hand, is his pistol with the handle resting against the wood of the table and the barrel pointing at Carrick; in the other a bottle of altar wine from which he takes a good glug, keeping one eye on Carrick.

"Why do they make it so sweet? It's too sweet, don't you think?"

"I don't drink," says Carrick.

"Of course you don't," scoffs Dandy Jim. "You don't enjoy life at all, your sort. Flagellation and God and punishment."

"If you were going to kill me, you would have already done it." Carrick's words are level and without emotion. He is afraid but he has been afraid before, in some ways, he likes it.

"I'll get to it, Rector, I really will. I just want to have a bit of a chat and a drink, you know, enjoy what I'm about to do rather than feel guilty about it."

"There is nothing to steal here, as your colleague discovered the other night."

"Why did you kill him?"

"He tried to rob my church, why wouldn't I defend it?"

"It was only a robbery by distinction, Rector. He was making his escape and had taken nothing. I'd argue that you and your sort robbed us and the rest of the poor people of this land already."

Now it's Carrick's turn to scoff.

"Nonconformist shit," he says. Dandy Jim leans forward.

"My God is not the same as yours, Rector. Nobody needs a corrupt priest and a corrupt enterprise to worship. You killed my friend and I would have killed you that night, if not for the risk of getting caught myself."

"You didn't fight me then because you are a coward, like your associate. You expected to find a kindly Rector with soft hands, and a delicate frame who would be scared by your guns and your angry words. Not so I, Robber."

"You have a history, no doubt, before you settled in this place. Any man who can fight one such as Carlos has been in a fair few scraps before. Where was it?"

"I marched with Marlborough's army."

"Schellenberg? Blenheim?" These were battles on the continent, battles where the English and their allies beat the French and gained the upper hand for the first time in a generation.

"Something like that," answers Carrick. He does not take his eyes off Dandy Jim. "Are you going to be about your business or do you just want to blow wind out your mouth?" Jim takes a double glug on the altar wine and places it down on the table. There's not a lot left of the bottle.

"Have you got more of this?"

"Plenty," says Carrick.

"Fetch me some, then."

"I'm not your boy. It's in the cupboard behind me."

Dandy Jim grins and stands up. He staggers because of the drink and a smile escapes from Carrick's mouth. Jim drags the handle of the pistol along the wood of the table, languid, like he can't quite be bothered to pick it up properly, and, as he has taken his second step, Carrick makes his move. The big man is faster than you might think for his size and more ready to strike than a rector should be. His right hand is tight in a fist, travelling as an uppercut to Dandy Jim's jaw.

If only Carrick could see himself.

Dandy Jim expects this. He has been in brawls from York to Brighton, fights in Edinburgh and murders in suburbs of Manchester that do not even have names. He slides to the left and brings the heavy butt of the gun up to Carrick's jaw. There is a crunch as the wood finds the bone and Carrick slumps forward, his eyes streaming and his brain rattling in his thick skull. Dandy Jim takes his time looking in the cupboard before he finds something a little better than altar wine.

He returns to the table and sets the bottle down. It's brandy and Dandy Jim has a smile on his face. Now it is Carrick's turn to have misjudged. Jim was born dirt poor on the canal docks in Birmingham and he was a scrapper - known for it, a fighter with a tidy right hand and a vicious manner so that, at fifteen, he was bare-knuckle boxing in the livestock market after dark. They were scared of him and his uncle could not get a good bet with the bookies and so, when they moved to London a year later, they affected the image, the fancy cravat, what harm could some nancy-boy in a floppy hat do? After he left the services of the crown as a soldier, Dandy Jim went back to it. Men like Carrick fall for it every time. They think he's either drunk or some foppish rake, wet behind the ears and soft.

Dandy Jim pulls the cork and there is a light pop. He takes a swig and his throat bobs. Carrick's eyes come back round and blood spills from his mouth where Dandy Jim has dislodged a tooth.

"Tell me about your time as a soldier then, Rector, perhaps we can swap some stories."

"Get on with it," mutters Carrick.

"With what?"

"If you're to kill me, then get it over with."

Dandy Jim tuts.

"This is not a service, Rector. You are not in charge. You'll have to listen, and answer and then, maybe before morning, you'll be dead." Carrick effects a grin and his lower teeth are red with his own blood.

"I rode with the Duke's army when they travelled south to face the French, and I was for a time, one of his messengers."

"A big fat bear like you?" mocks Dandy Jim. "You'd break a horse's back after 10 leagues."

"I was not chosen for my swiftness, Robber, rather for my ability to get things delivered, come what may."

"So you were a scrapper then? You're out of practice, you practically threw yourself onto the handle of my pistol."

"You have not witnessed my skills, perhaps it was a move designed to wrong-foot you," Carrick gives a sickly humorous grin. After Dandy Jim and Carlos scanned the Pennyman

House with its locked doors, they made their way over the wall that was no trouble at all. The plan was to enter the church through a smashed window, pilfer what was on the altar and then go back to the Pennyman Livery yard to steal a couple of the geldings which would be worth a tidy price in themselves. Carlos had wanted to leave the church alone but Jim forced him to take a look, just because… because Dandy Jim hates churches and likes to smash their windows and piss all over the pews. When the dog started barking, Carlos and Dandy Jim had not thought to run with great effort from a big rector dressed in his nightclothes in the cold. He overpowered Carlos as they ran from the church, Jim had made off down the lane, laughing, thinking Carlos was behind him and, when he circled back half an hour later, he saw the man's lifeless body outside the church where Carrick had left him. It was already breaking dawn by then. Carlos was in no way a weakling, he had really been with the Duke's men at Schellenberg and later at Blenheim, battles whose thunderous guns Dandy Jim still hears in his dreams. Perhaps he has misjudged Carrick.

"I was with the Duke on that journey south, Carlos too." Carrick curls his lip up in disgust as Dandy Jim says this.

"Marlborough is a bastard and turncoat," says The Rector. Dandy Jim raises his eyebrows as if puzzled, for The Duke of Marlborough is a legend, a hero, he and Prince Eugene of Savoy are the military minds that have so plagued the French armies of Louis the fourteenth. The Duke is also a respected man, even by his soldiers, Dandy Jim and Carlos marched for him, they believed in him, even if they did not believe in the monarch he represented. Carrick continues:

"Marlborough does not serve God, Robber. Like you, he serves only that which he thinks will win. He is a slippery eel fish and he'll face his judgement, as will you."

"I have a feeling, Rector, that my pistol has a more likely chance of allowing you to face judgement much sooner than I. Would you not agree?" Dandy Jim has learned to speak in opposites as those who have money and education do.

"You know your friend, who I murdered out on the lane here? As I strangled him, he begged for his life and you heard him whimpering in the darkness, yet, you ran on. I wonder if he would have done the same for you? You betrayed him." This is a lie designed to cause anger. Dandy Jim has lived in the shadows all his life, on the streets, as a red coat soldier, as an outlaw and a highwayman, he does not care what others think of him, he knows only what he thinks of himself. While there are things he has done wrong in his life, things that he would change, he knows that he would never have left Carlos if he thought his friend was in danger.

Carrick is right, he should get on with this. He'll steal whatever the big man has in the church and wait it out behind the chicken coup where he has been hiding. He'll wait there until the snow lifts if he has to, especially if The Rector has more of the brandy. Dandy Jim lifts the bottle and takes two long gulps, his throat reacts.

The big man sees his second chance.

Carrick was not always a Rector. He is not even a Rector now. He really was once in the service of the Duke on the continent as he explained, as a messenger, but not quite in his full service. At the first opportunity, he sold his messages to the French for a handful of silver and made his way back to England. He is not the man the Captain seeks, but he could be, very easily. The Robber here can take his place. The blow Dandy Jim hit Carrick tells him what he needs to know – that he is a little arrogant, and with each swig of brandy, drunker.

Carrick shoves the table forward with all his weight and the top of it slams into Dandy Jim's chest. The brandy spills down him and the pistol in his right hand fires, too high and over Carrick's shoulder. The big Rector leaps, his knee rests on the tabletop and his big hand goes for Dandy Jim's throat, grasping it between his strong fingers as he pushes him off his chair and up, against the stone wall of the church. Unlike

Dandy Jim, Carrick does not waste time when he kills someone.

Jim stamps at Carrick's knee and it staggers him, and then, the dandy highwayman knocks the big arm out the way and clobbers Carrick in the cheek, feeling it crack under the weight of his fist. Jim cannot afford to stop hitting this one, if he does, he'll face the same fate as Carlos. Carrick has been hit harder before, much harder, he rises and grabs at Dandy Jim and the two of them crash through the curtain into the church proper, Carrick slams into the floor and his head clunks on the stone, but it does not stop him. Dandy Jim tries to strike, but the big man has caught his throat once more in a powerful hand. He squeezes and sees Jim wince above him, feels some of the strength go out of him as well.

They struggle, the two of them, while the snow falls languid outside the stained-glass windows and the night is black and silent. Carrick pushes Jim back and off him with relative ease now, so that the rolls are reversed and he is on the stone floor. Once he is on his knees, he presses Dandy Jim's head back against the stone and puts both his big hands around the wide neck. He grins down on Dandy Jim in the darkness as he chokes him, smells the sweet brandy from his breath and watches his eyes bulge and his chest fight for air. Carrick could squeeze tighter but he likes the sensation of this man being on the edge, between life and death. He holds Jim there, not enough pressure to kill him and yet not enough for him to breathe air into his lungs. Dandy Jim's hands flail out at either side of him, grasping at the smooth cold stone of the church floor where, only that morning, the folk of North Burton, dressed in their finest, attended Sunday service.

"Please," rasps Jim.

It is another two minutes of pressure before the man's face takes on a purple hue, his legs shiver and he wets himself, still, Carrick holds him tight as he feels all the breath and life slip away. He sits back when he is done and looks up at the altar in the darkness.

"This is your work," he whispers to the silver cross. "He was a robber and I killed him as your will dictates." The big man gets to his feet and he is a little shaky, he spits on the body below him and the light from the fallen lamp on the table sends his long shadow across the floor. Carrick looks around him at the quiet of the church and returns to the lamp to pick it up. He will have to consider his next move carefully. Last time it was easy enough to leave the body out in the lane in front of the church. Now he must think about what to do. Perhaps even, it is time for him to move on from North Burton altogether.

There's a noise from the vestibule, the chamber that houses the front door, and Carrick grabs the lamp and quickly steps out into the main church again.

"Who's there?" he calls as he strides forward towards the entrance. The door is closed, but there is movement from the handle. Carrick shines the lamp into the corner and there, cowering against the cold stone, is Adam Gamble with his chest heaving as he breathes in and out.

"The snow was too heavy to go home," he whimpers, "I heard that man attack you." Adam is already working to be of as little resistance as he can to Carrick. He had wanted to leave as soon as he heard the voice of Dandy Jim earlier but, he did not want to draw attention to himself, then, he heard the highwayman murdered some ten yards away, and there is no reason why it could not be him next. Young Adam Gamble is well aware that bad things happen to good people, despite what it says in the bible. He knows The Rector will do something similar to him if he gets a chance, that's why as Carrick draws his right hand back to his face, Adam Gamble dives under his arm into the cold, black silence of the church.

Carrick turns on his heels as he hears the boy scamper away into the darkness. He follows, but not with any sort of speed. There is no other way out of this church, not unless Adam

Gamble has the key to the tower door and is prepared to climb the steps and throw himself off the top.

"You have one chance to save yourself, boy," whispers Carrick in the darkness. "Come to me now and we will resolve this together." The man's voice is unconvincing and more tired than anything else. Carrick does not really have the desire to kill a young boy, and so he hopes that Adam keeps quiet. He's a smart lad who only works for the money that is given him. Carrick steps back into the vestibule and to the door, he takes out the big key from the lock and opens it. The wind is not bad, nor the cold, but the snow is as heavy as he has ever seen, laying quickly. There is already more than four inches on the floor. He does not close the door behind him and his feet crunch as he makes his way to the cage underneath his wagon where Bear will be curled up on his sack of straw. Carrick hopes the boy makes a sprint for it, he'll never outrun the dog and there'll be less to explain anyway, if it was an accident and that Bear got out somehow. Carrick opens the latch and reaches inside to grab the big furry dog by the collar and yank it outside.

"Rats," he hisses into the animal's ear and instantly the beast responds with a low growl and a yelp. Carrick drags it out into the falling snow and to the door of the church where he rags the collar to make the dog angry. It strains against Carrick's grip, ready to hunt for whatever may be within the darkness of the church. "Wait for it," whispers the big man as he holds the dog back with his eyes on the door. Adam will know there is no other way to get out, his only chance will be to make a run for it. Bear pulls against Carrick's arm and a minute ticks by. The dog can hunt him inside the church, it will make a more grotesque story.

"Go on then," whispers Carrick as he lets go of the dog's collar.

CHAPTER FIFTEEN

The world is white again, pure, clean and new, the sky is blue with a weak sun. Meg steps out of her front door into the frosty morning. She looks across to the run-down pub opposite and the heavy snow has completely collapsed the roof. That will happen to their cottage next, she reasons. Nana seemed to understand when Meg explained why she had not told The Captain. Perhaps because of the cold or the creaking from the floorboards above them where their Robber paced slowly from one end of the room to the other.

Meg wonders when the snow will lift. Perhaps it will go on forever until there is nothing left to eat and they freeze up into stone. She looks through the shutters of the Gamble house and there is no movement, she hopes Adam made it home safely last night.

Meg passes the pond and the village green opposite, flat with snow and then, up the hill, all the while crunching through the snow. She has a light sweat when she makes it to the church with the sun on her back, she looks over the wall and all is peaceful with the big door closed and snow along the roof like icing.

Meg has an uneasy feeling as she walks up, through the big gate that Danny Reed will have opened at first light, there are wheel marks in the snow and she can hear voices from ahead. Carrick's wagon is parked up on the drive next to the Pennyman House, but there is no horse. He must have pulled it himself from the church somehow. The big Rector stands next to one of the wheels and Captain Salter is small beside him, Mr Pennyman is opposite, they look out of place this early and together as they discuss something that appears important by the earnest looks on their faces. Miss Charlotte is not yet fully dressed but wears a woollen gown, boots and a fur hat. She approaches Meg.

"We've got him," she beams. "Meg, we've really got him!

184

Carrick caught him in the church last night and strangled him. Look, he's got the brute here on his wagon." Meg walks forward and her world sinks as she sees the body laid on its back on the cart, she sees the black boots that Dandy Jim wears and then moves up to his face, his eyes are closed and his neck covered in purple bruises. She feels like crying. It is her fault, all of this. If she had not been so stupid as to talk to him and tell him about The Pennyman House and the church, then he and Carlos might still be alive. She'd wanted to give Pennyman a bloody nose after he struck her, but vengeance comes at a price. When will she learn her place?

"He was a big one," says Carrick to The Captain. "Not as big as me, but a fighter to be sure." Mr Pennyman has a look of wonderment on his face:

"He gave you a proper thump, I see, Rector," the man nods to the red bruise on Carrick's chin where Dandy Jim clobbered him with his pistol. "That's it then, Captain, you've found the man you were looking for." The little soldier with red hair, already dressed in his coat with a stout belt looks up at Carrick with concern in his eyes.

"Perhaps so," he says. "I'll have to check things through before I can conclude my investigation." The Captain peers over the side of the wooden wagon to the dead body therein, he does not seem convinced somehow. He notices Meg and Miss Charlotte standing and gawping at the scene. "On with your business," he snaps. Miss Charlotte puts her arms around Meg and they hurry past to the livery yard and the rest of the farm, their shoes making footprints in the snow.

"My father will be pleased," says Miss Charlotte as they walk. "He's been so worried, having Captain Salter sniffing round everywhere, you good people and the animals being bothered by him. It's just a relief that it will all be over and we can go back to normal. Aren't you relieved, Meg?" Miss Charlotte's face beams with smooth, pale skin.

"Are you sure it's him? I thought the man The Captain was

185

looking for had lived here a while." Meg wishes she hadn't said this when Miss Charlotte's smile drops. She should remember that she is not required to give her opinion – just agree. Meg already saw the look of mistrust on The Captain's face, like him, she has worked out that the man in the back of the wagon cannot be the person he is looking for unless he can devise some explanation to fit with his current story. This does not mean that the body of Dandy Jim will not become the guilty man, it's just uncertain now. Miss Charlotte, however, cannot be shaken by the weight of fact.

"But it's him, Meg. He tried to break into the church in the night. It's him, it has to be. Who else is there in North Burton who would do such a thing?"

Meg nods. She should not muddy the clean waters of Miss Charlotte's mind further. They are in the livery yard and the two stop walking and face each other. Miss Charlotte looks up at Meg with her big blue eyes.

"And Carrick throttled him?" asks Meg.

"Yes," she smiles back, then her smile drops. Throttling someone is not a good thing.

"You'll be right, Miss Charlotte, it will be the man The Captain is looking for. Thank the lord we have Carrick."

"Aye," she says as the smile returns. It is much better if Meg just agrees with her. "Who would have thought that a village rector could take on a rogue and do him in? We really are lucky to have him. I know father wasn't too sure about Carrick when he first came, and some of his sermons are a bit heavy, but by Jove, he's earned his keep!"

"Yes, Miss Charlotte."

"I want you to do something for me, Meg. I want you to go down into the village, knock on every door and tell them what's happened and that we don't have anything to worry about. Could you do that for me?"

Meg nods. She would rather not but she cannot refuse Miss Charlotte.

"I'll have to check the chickens and the sows first, Miss."
She smiles up at Meg, in a form of admiration for her
commitment to duty. Miss Charlotte does not realise that if
one of the sows should be injured or God forgive, die, then it
will come out of Meg's meagre wage and she will be held
responsible for the death also. Meg will not need to knock on
anyone's door because, by the time she gets back from her
duties, everyone will already know.

"Thank you, Meg. If only everyone was as helpful as you
are." Meg nods and effects a little, half bow. She backs off,
turns, and walks through the livery yard towards the sty, she
does not run although she wants to.

Inside the warmth of the pigsty, Meg puts her back to the
wall and slides down with her knees bent, her face is in her
hands. She liked Dandy Jim, he was one of her own, someone
from the gutter who had managed to crawl his way up and
now, he has been torn back down again. Not only that, his
body and his name, will be dragged through the mud, abused
and used and spat on, like he was a liar and a cheat. He may
have been, but then so is Pennyman and The Captain, so is
poor, deluded Miss Charlotte and arse licker Hannah Farthing
and her sycophant husband. Money wins and you are either
born lucky or you are not. Hadn't her mother told her so? Isn't
that what Danny Reed says too? Money wins over everything,
it can buy loyalty, comfort and it is more important even than
truth. The Captain will have to use Dandy Jim as his scapegoat,
it is too much of a good opportunity to miss.

There is something else.

Meg stops crying and looks up into the half-darkness of
the pigsty. If Captain Salter does decide Dandy Jim is the man
he was searching for, then it leaves Carrick a free man. Carrick
who throttled Dandy Jim, and, she realises, probably strangled
Carlos too. Carrick, who is not much of a rector, who does
not know his scriptures, who has been in North Burton less

than two summers. Carrick, who thinks it's fun to threaten Adam Gamble with his big dog, Carrick who sells bags of coal that were given freely.

He's the man The Captain is looking for. He must be the spy. She stands and the pigs in front seem afraid of her. What did her mother say? That it was time to speak and not listen. Meg feels her fists clench in anger and her teeth clench in rage. She can see what will happen. Carrick will be a hero rather than a rogue. She's tried to be angry before now, she has tried to be angry will everyone, with Mr Pennyman, with Nana, with herself, with the pigs in the sty next to her, but so far, that seething anger that makes her nod in agreement with Miss Charlotte or do Nana's bidding, that anger has got her nowhere at all. She needs to approach this with her mother's understanding and her own sense.

But first, there is someone she has to find and speak to.

Adam Gamble.

Meg knocks on the door of the Gamble House and waits a few seconds. The cottages are so small that it doesn't take anyone long to get from one end to the other. There's no answer so she goes in. There are the old couple from the night before, Mr and Mrs Gamble in almost the same position as she left them. The fire is out and the air is stone cold.

"Where's Adam?" asks Meg. Old Nick Gamble looks up from his bed with red and frightened eyes.

"He didn't come back, Meg. Not at all. I waited up all night." It's not like Mr Gamble could get anywhere on his own anyway. Mrs Gamble is asleep still with her eyelids down on the other bed, the same as last night. Someone will have to come to look after these two while Meg goes up to the church. She swallows when she thinks about Carrick.

"Will you two be okay, while I go look for Adam?" she asks. Mr Gamble blinks up at her from his blanket and nods. "Then I'll come back and we'll get the house warmed up."

"He will be okay, won't he, Meg?" The man's voice is crackly and she can see the thin veins along his hairy nostrils.

"He's a clever lad, Mr Gamble. He'll look after himself as best he can."

"Aye, see you fetch him, Meg, his mum won't be pleased if anything has happened." The old man looks across to his wife, who has not moved or opened her eyes. Meg backs out the door.

Julia Farthing is carrying some horse tack down the Main Street for Farmer Thorne. When Meg asks her, she has not seen Adam, not anywhere.

Archer Farthing and his father are clearing snow from the drive of The Pennyman House with wooden shovels – a little one for Archer. Nobody is too young to work in North Burton. Neither has seen Adam.

"But if you do see him, tell him he ought to be out here with a shovel in his hand," says Mr Farthing.

"His mum and dad say he didn't come home last night."

"He's a big lad," adds Mr Farthing. Adam Gamble is twelve, a year older than his daughter, Julia. "He can look after himself."

The serving girls at the back of The Pennyman House have not seen him, neither has Granddad Blackwood coming back through the thick snow over the fields.

Danny Reed and Miles Blackwood are smoking long pipes and laughing about something by the coach shed. They have not seen little Adam Gamble either.

"He'll be at the church," says Miles Blackwood through his teeth that are permanently together. She nods. She would rather look anywhere else than there.

Meg stands outside the dark church and does not want to open the gate to go up the path. She looks over her shoulder and down the lane at North Burton, all peaceful with a blanket of snow atop the run-down cottages and Farmer Thorne's house in the mid-distance.

She pushes herself on, through the gate and up the path to the big front door. Meg stands there for a few moments, gathering herself and feeling her chest rise and fall. She looks to Carrick's cart and the cage under the back wheel, inside is the huge heavy set hunting dog. It is silent but watches Meg with big orange and black eyes. She feels her legs tingle in fear. Bear doesn't bark unless Carrick wants it to. She looks at the closed door of St Michael's again, and there comes a voice, deep and cruel from behind her. Carrick:

"What do you want?" He stands a few feet away from her back and Meg turns, wondering how a man this big can move so quietly.

"I'm looking for Adam Gamble,"

"Why?" asks The Rector. The big man's face is bruised and it makes him look more fearsome.

"He didn't return home last night," says Meg.

"Really?" asks the big man. He steps forward and looks down his nose at Meg. "It's none of your business where Adam Gamble is, he has important work in the church. Who are you to even ask?"

"His parents are worried, and they depend on him, Sir. They're scared." That tongue in her mouth. Why can't she keep it from waggling? The rector cocks his head.

"You see Bear? My dog, under the cart? I know you do because I saw you looking. I only have to let him out of that cage and he'll tear you to pieces. I did God's work last night, defending this village from some dandy fool robber and you come here, without so much as a thank you, asking where Adam Gamble is, as if I would know." Meg steps back and realises that her shoulder blades are against the door to the church, Carrick has moved forward as she has retreated. She can smell him as she looks up at his battered face, she can stink his sweat and the blood on his clothes.

The catch on the door behind her clicks and the handle turns as it opens from inside. There, his face black with exhaustion and grey with worry, is Adam Gamble. He steps out into the snow.

"Hello Meg," he says. His voice sounds far away and hollow and his cheeks are sunken. Adam no longer looks like the child she knew a day before and his eyes seem to have lost their fire. One of his cheeks is scuffed and his shirt is ripped.

"Where have you been?" she asks.

"He's been working for me, for the church," cuts in Carrick. He moves behind Adam Gamble and puts his big hand on the boy's shoulder. Adam shrinks at this, Meg sees his legs bend and his eyes widen in fear. "Isn't that right, young Adam?"

The Gamble lad nods in panic.

"You're to go home, Adam Gamble, your mother and father are worried sick." Meg can hear Nana's voice on her own as she commands. He moves off down the path, when he gets out the gate, he breaks into a limping run.

It leaves Meg facing the big Rector once more with the Church door next to them. Meg is angry, she cannot help herself.

"If you've hurt him, there'll be hell to pay," she says. Her nostrils are flared and her chest swollen.

Carrick darkens.

"You watch the way you speak to me, woman."

"I'm not frightened of you or your wolf dog." Meg should not be saying this. Carrick will now be a hero. He will be a hero for killing Dandy Jim but he has done something to Adam Gamble. He is dangerous, certainly. If Carrick were to strike her it would be nothing like Mr Pennyman with his half-arsed slap.

"You should be," he growls. "You should be frightened for yourself and your Nana and that lad, Richie. You should be very frightened of a man like me and what I can do, and what I've done." Meg is not afraid, although she ought to be, anger seems to dull her senses, it gives her courage.

"My biggest sow is two stone heavier than your wolf, Rector, a stiff broom handle to the neck would break it. This is North Burton, you might find the folk here tougher than you're used to." It is Meg's mother speaking through her now, despite her anger, she is measured with her insults. Rector Carrick is not a good man of God or the people. He is vain and rude, selfish and bad-tempered like the God he believes he serves. He leans forward and his lips curl in disgust.

"I'll make it my business to hurt you," he whispers.

"If you've done anything to that Gamble lad, you'll pay for it. You better mark my words carefully, Rector, because I shan't say them again. This church stood here long before you came, and it will stand long after you're gone. You should be protecting the folk of North Burton, not threatening them because, however big you are and however nasty your dog is, you can't take all of us on together. You don't strike me as a rector anyway."

If Meg thought she had made Carrick mad previously, she was wrong. The suggestion that he is not a rector has hit a nerve. His arm whips out and catches hold of Meg's neck, he is quick.

"Watch your tongue, lass," he spits, "or someone might rip it out." He brings his face closer to hers so she can see the broken red veins in his eyeballs and smell his fetid breath. "I'm watching you." He releases his grip. Meg's hands go to her throat as she gasps for air, staggering, she backs off into the snow.

"That's it," says Carrick, "off you go."

Carrick steps inside the church and closes the heavy door behind him. He wipes sweat from his brow with his handkerchief and walks down the aisle between the pews. The sun streams through the two stained glass windows behind the altar and he sees the figures there, St Michael on one side, feminine almost with his sword resting on the floor so the hilt makes a cross where he holds it. On the other, the slim figure of David as he approaches Goliath. When he gets to the altar, Carrick kneels.

Events have gone in The Rector's favour in some ways. With the murder of The Dandy Robber, Carrick has finally won the favour of Pennyman and his proud daughter. He looks up to the multicoloured figure of St Michael once more, the sunshine making the red and green colours vivid and unreal. Carrick wonders at the magic of a world that can be so beautiful. He knows he should not have done what he did to Adam Gamble, after he pulled the dog off the boy, but it was better than killing him, a mercy perhaps.

The Rector has never believed that God was anything other than cruel and cold. The snow outside is most certainly punishment for their sins, Carrick's included. He should have killed the boy. The dead don't talk but the living do and, if that Meg knows that there's something wrong as well, Adam will tell her. Carrick has it good in North Burton, better than he's ever had it before, better than as a soldier with the red coats, better than carrying messages, better than selling out his colleagues to the French, better than the brothels in Paris, London and then York. He bought the letters of engagement for the church here at North Burton from a priest in Micklegate, and they cost him everything he had, all the gold he got from the army of Louis the Fourteenth and his silver bracelet and his father's watch. He was to retire here, to this tiny hamlet and live in peace where the people are as docile as sheep and just as stupid, where there are no soldiers or spies and he could melt away, unseen for the rest of his days watching over his flock. Is he the man The Captain is searching for, Carrick could be, but how would such a fool have tracked him all the way to North Burton? It may be chance or something else, perhaps it's divine intervention.

Carrick gives a wry smile when he thinks of this, his God is cruel, that would be just like him. He stands up and bows his head to the two figures.

He'll have to get rid of the boy. He'll have to throttle him, or something, but not here. Not in the church, he'll have to make the boy disappear somehow and get rid of his body.

He'll take young Adam for a ride on his cart, over the hill towards Etton and to the woods at South Dalton, and he'll bury him there. It will be easy. Young Adam Gamble has had enough of looking after those ageing parents, working every day up at the church, he's tired of it all, tired and young and hungry. Carrick will tell them he ran off to York or Leeds, or London and they'll believe him. The big Rector rubs his hands together and grins. He'll have to move quickly. It will have to be today.

CHAPTER SIXTEEN

Adam Gamble is not himself at all.

He hasn't said a word. Meg stands in his little house and watches him build the fire in the hearth around their iron pot. Adam's mother is still asleep and his father has gone back to his normal state of vacancy, sat on the side of his bed now his son has returned.

"What happened to you?" asks Meg.

"I was punished," says Adam, he looks over his shoulder at her and his eyes are blue and wide. Meg has seen the same sort of look before, in the knowing eyes of big sows before the butcher cuts their throats.

"What for?"

"I did something wrong."

"What?"

"Something."

"You can't let him treat you like this."

"I have to."

"Stand up and talk to me," she snaps. The thin lad gets to his feet and faces Meg. "Why do you have to? Go to Mr Pennyman, go to Miss Charlotte, I'll come with you, tell them what he's done to you."

"Please, Meg," says Adam Gamble. "I can deal with this. I have to. There are people who need me." She steps closer to him and looks down into his eyes. He's older than he should be already, trapped into a life of service to his family, The Pennyman Estate, the seasons and now the church. Aren't they all the same in North Burton somehow? All of them forced to look after each other, what other life is there?

"You but have to knock on my door, Adam Gamble, and I shall be there without a word to help you. Do you understand?" Adam Gamble nods. Whatever Carrick has put him through, he has spent his whole life preparing to survive. There are no tears from the lad but Meg can see a little of the shrewd intelligence return to his eyes.

"I'll be grand once I get something down me."

"We'll do something about that Carrick, Adam Gamble, you'll see. He'll get what's coming to him." He turns back to his fire and the iron pot within the flames. This is the real Meg talking now, the one who dreams of running away with her Robber, who lets Richie sleep on her knee, who befriends highwaymen.

"God will judge him," says Adam over his shoulder.

"I haven't got time to wait for that," answers Meg.

In the street, Hannah Farthing steps out of her front door with her usual look of disdain. She sees Meg and gives an unexpected smile.

"They've got him then, Meg," she says.

"Aye."

"It's a relief to us all to know. In more ways than one. Mr Pennyman is having a feast tonight, have you heard?" Meg shakes her head. "He says that it's what we need, all of us. After the winter and this murder business, he's going to open up the big cow barn and there'll be two barrels of beer." Meg has not noticed before, but Hannah Farthing's teeth are uneven, perhaps she has never seen the woman smile. Meg likes her the more for it.

"Tonight?" asks Meg.

"Yes, tonight. In the morning, Danny Reed will take both the bodies to the magistrate in Beverley and it will be done. Winter and all, we can get back to our lives." Meg looks at the blue sky above them and then down to the snow on the ground.

"It's still winter, Mrs Farthing," she says. "It's still cold."

"The snow is firm. You can get a cart over this easier than mud. So it's all set. Julia has gone to bring down the bunting from the loft at the Pennyman House. It will be lovely to get back to normal." Meg nods and smiles. "So you can bring

Nana and Richie up after the church bell sounds at five."

"Does everyone know?"

"Aye, my Archer went house to house and even up to Farmer Thorne as soon as we knew. It's going to be lovely." Hannah Farthing reaches out and grips Meg's hand in friendship, her face is suddenly serious. "I thought you might tell on us, Meg. I thought you might say to that Captain that we had problems where we came from last. I know that you didn't."

"You're welcome here," says Meg. "We all live under the same sun in the end." These are the words of her mother.

"It will be a good night," says Hannah Farthing. "One to remember."

"Aye," says Meg.

Nana has made the fire inside. She has a grin. She must have heard about the party.

"Meg, did you hear? Two barrels of beer and there'll be a feast. Granddad Blackwood thinks there'll be pork from Pennyman's larder as well." The old woman's eyes twinkle with mischief and excitement. "I told Granddad Blackwood that there'd be none of his funny business, if he thinks I'm the kind of woman who changes after a few mugs of ale." Richie sits with a blanket around him and just his head showing. He has a wooden cup with hot water in his hand and a big toothless grin. Dutchy will be under there with him, somewhere. Meg remains stony-faced as she stands opposite Nana.

"What about our problem?"

"It's all done," whispers Nana.

"How?"

"I spoke to him, your tall Robber. We made a deal. As soon as we all leave for the Pennyman House tonight, he'll be gone. He'll go past the Thorne Farm and out to the York Road from where he came."

197

"The silver?"

"We know there isn't any silver, Meg. You were right. Best let him get on his way and we forget this whole episode." Her forehead begins with a light sweat. It has happened so quickly. This is the reason Nana is happy, she will have her ale and pork and when she returns after a fumble with Grandad Blackwood, her house will be free of The Robber Meg healed. Things can go back to normal.

"With any luck," continues Nana, "the weather will turn as well. It can't be winter forever."

"How is it any different from before, he won't get very far."

"There'll be nobody up at the Thorne Farm, he can borrow one of the horses. He says he knows a place half a day's ride where he can rest up."

"So you've sorted it?" Meg asks. Her tone is sarcastic.

"Aye, your Nana has."

She climbs the ladder and there he is, dressed in his cloak but without his hat. He sits with his back against the chimney breast and his legs out straight. His face has more colour than Meg has seen previously. It was not so long ago that he was a pale and white ghost near death laid on the floor.

"Have you come to wish me farewell, Meg?" he asks with a smile.

"Nana spoke to you?"

"Yes. She's a robust and hardy woman. I promised her a bottle of brandy if ever I passed this way again."

"A lie then?"

"A polite lie. She promised me a warm welcome."

"Nana says what she wishes were true, they aren't real lies."

"So, do you think I lie?"

"Of course. When the church bell rings at five, Pennyman's feast will begin but they will all be there way before then, even Nana."

"Will there be drink?"

"Aye. Plenty."

"Maybe I should come too. Will you be going, Meg?"

"When they are all at merriment, I'll return here to make sure you are gone."

"To make sure I am gone?"

"Aye."

"And if I'm not?"

"I'll tell the constable. This has to end, Robber. This has to finish. The snow has to lift, you have to be gone and North Burton has to go back to how it should be." Sunlight is streaming through the gaps in the roof and the dust dances in the air. The man grins.

"Are you coming with me?"

"No." Meg has to be realistic. "You don't need to lie to me anymore. I will help you get away and like Nana says, we don't need your silver."

"We'll need a horse," says The Robber. "A big one at that, for both of us to ride. Getting two would be no good."

"Why do you keep talking about we? I told you I will not come."

"So why are you coming back here when the rest of the village are drinking up at the Pennyman House? Do you want to make sure I lock your door?"

"I want to make sure you are gone, otherwise, neither Nana nor I will be able to settle."

"Bring me a horse, Meg and we'll ride away, you and me." He is doing it again, teasing her with his low, calm voice and educated tones. Meg remembers the look on Adam Gamble's face, that sense of resignation to a life of drudgery and servitude. She almost wishes she did not have the imagination to think it could be any other way.

"Please do not lie to me," she says. "We've helped you. Nana, Richie and I, we've nursed you and sheltered you and fed you, the least you can do is leave in peace." He taps his finger in thought on the wooden floorboards.

"I still need a horse." Now he looks up. "Do you remember your wedding day?"

"Aye," Meg frowns. "What has that to do with our situation here?"

"You told me about it, you told me how the girls gifted you daffodils, about the dress your mother made with the lace she bought from Market Weighton, about the spring sunshine and how you felt like you were the most important girl in the world. You told me how the coachmen stuffed their muskets with feathers and fired above your heads as you left the church, so that nothing harder would fall upon you in the years to come. Do you remember that day, Meg?"

"I do remember. Why must you say that to me?" she has forgotten what she told him while he was asleep.

"I have never had a day such as that because my life has been only war. War to get away from the drudgery of the farm, war as a soldier, war as a robber, war against my comrades, always war and always a fight because somewhere, one day, I hoped there would be peace."

"Please stop," says Meg. "I will get you a horse. I will get you your horse and you will leave without me, today."

"We will see," he answers. She looks into his blue eyes for too long and hears Nana bellowing from downstairs. "We will see," he repeats.

There is a hum to the village.

It's like Christmas.

Granddad Blackwood has dug out his best frock coat and polished the buttons. Danny Reed and Miles Blackwood have been charged with moving the two barrels of beer up to the cow barn and during the move, Miles has managed to pilfer a bottle of ale, Danny has stolen what he hopes is rum. Mr Farthing has cleaned the felt on his best hat and his wife is in one of her wild moods, she cannot choose which of her two pairs of stockings to wear. Meg has boiled up enough water for everyone in the house to wash their faces and hands, she has scrubbed Richie's nails and cut his hair. Farmer Thorne has given all his milking girls the afternoon off, and his cowherd lads will be bringing a barrel of his cider that is three years old by horse and cart. Miss Charlotte and her serving girls have decorated the barn as best they can with bunting from the loft. The house cook and the kitchen girls have made batches of sweet muffins with raisins and apples from the larder. This is how North Burton should be. Everyone at work.

Mr Pennyman sits, already washed and dressed in the dining room of the great house, in front of a roaring fire, a glass of wine in his hand as he listens to the red-faced ginger Captain tell him of the battle of Blenheim for the fifth time.

Julia Farthing picks her teeth clean with a bit of wood she has whittled with the axe, then does a red bow in her blonde hair. There is excitement. Life feels like it might be returning to normal, somehow, even though the snow and ice are still outside. There is a buzz to the place. Nobody has a thought for the first dead body they found nor the second that Carrick killed, it is as if they do not want to be reminded of it.

Adam Gamble does the best he can with his parents, his mother will not wake and his father drools the oat broth that the lad has made. He will go up to the church as instructed by Carrick and he will ring the bell at five. His parents are much too old to make it up to the cowshed, and they would not enjoy the noise or the dancing anyway.

It's half past four by the tower clock of St Michael's and most are already somewhere near the cowshed. Archer Farthing and Richie chase each other around the livery yard. The Blackwood men and Danny Reed are leaning on the coach smoking long pipes and swapping stories. Meg makes her way through the great gate to the Pennyman House with

Nana on her arm. The old woman has forgotten that she is in so much pain and there was almost no drama as she walked up the hill.

"It reminds me of The Walkington Show," says Nana. "Walkington Show 1685, I was younger then, mind. Did I tell you, Meg, they entered me into the wrestling as I was the biggest lass in the village?" She has told this one before. Many times, but the old woman is excited by the thought of food and ale and the chance to see smiles and feel the warmth of comradery. "I got to the final, you know, I was against this big farm lad with hands like shovels, and he stank when you got near him, and he wrestled me to the floor good and quick like he was going to have me, right there in the straw in front of all them people watching." The story changes, this version is shorter because Nana wants to get to the end quickly. "He had me pinned, and I wriggled and wrestled him round till I managed to get me legs around his neck and then, by heck, he went a purple colour, he did, when I started squeezing. At first, he thought it was a joke but he tapped for it to stop soon enough. A lass winning the wrestling at The Walkington Show, Meg! Why, the name of Jackson was on every tongue from here to Thwing, by, that was back when they knew how to do a village feast." Her voice is wistful.

They have moved through the livery yard and see both the Blackwoods and Danny Reed. The men pass a small bottle between them and take sips.

"Are you on it already?" calls Nana.

"I'm just getting myself warmed up for you, lass," answers Granddad Blackwood.

"You'll need a lot more than you've got to handle me, Granddad," she shouts back with a false look of indignation.

The bell in the church gives a low and loud dong. It reverberates around the livery yard and to Meg's pigsty, over the place where Dandy Jim had slept in the bushes and into the dining room of the great house. The sound travels up the staircase to Miss Charlotte, her face powdered as she slips on her soft white gloves. It rings out over the snow and ice and down to the village, to the last house on the end of the row of cottages, to The Robber who gets to his feet and begins down the ladder. The feast is about to begin although it is well before five.

Meg squeezes Nana's arm and the old woman turns to her with her face suddenly serious.

"It's time," she says. Nana nods as Meg unlocks her arm from hers and their eyes meet and hold a gaze for a little too long to be normal. There is something profound there.

"You go then, Meg," says Nana. "Just you go." Her nostrils flare as she takes a deep breath. "And don't you look back neither," she whispers. "You might never get the chance again." Meg nods as she backs away. Nana is as sharp as the knife she keeps hidden under her chair, and Meg, she must be as easy to read as the seasons changing on the wind. The young woman did not consider that Nana might know how she feels, and the old woman has known all along. Nana has lived the same humdrum dull life that Meg lives, but longer. "I saw my chance, Meg, when that big bastard was on top of me," she is talking again about her wrestling match at The Walkington Show all those years ago. "I saw my chance and I took it, if I hadn't, he would have beaten me, make no mistake. You have to take your chances, Meg, when you can. You'll take your chance and nobody will think worse of you if you do." It is so unlike Nana to speak in riddles, it makes what she says much more real. "Now, be off with you," snaps the old woman as she waves her hand, all traces of emotion gone from her face as she struggles towards Granddad Blackwood.

Meg makes her way back down towards the gate and she can hear Nana laughing behind her.

You have to take your chances.

The village is quiet when she walks down the hill. The sun is still up but is beginning to fade; in another hour or so, it will be dark, and all of those up at the cowshed will be drunk. She does not walk quickly, and with each step her guts churn, images of The Robber flash in her brain and Nana's eyes too, and the smile of Dandy Jim also.

She stops outside her own door for a moment and takes a deep breath. She does not know what she will do, truly. There is no way she can go with him but her throat is tight with emotion and her fists are clenched. Was Nana telling her to go? Meg could be free, she could be happy. All she needs to do is open the door and there will be her Robber standing at six foot two with his dark hat and jet-black hair peeping out from under it.

Meg hears the clatter of hooves on the ice coming from the direction of the great house and the church. She turns and there, at speed more than needed is Carrick on his cart with his horse pulling it forward. Next to him on the passenger seat is Adam Gamble, his thin face is pale and hollow in fear. On the back of the trap is the metal cage with the German hunting dog inside. This does not make any sense. They are going away from the feast. Meg steps out into the street with a frown to meet Carrick's grimace as he whips the horse to go faster on the hard snow.

"Where are you off to?" she calls.

"I'm collecting coal from Farmer Thorne," yells Carrick.

"There's a feast on," she shouts.

"We'll be back," Meg watches the cart bump along on the ice towards the farm, and the dog snarls at her through the bars. He should be up at the cowshed like everyone else, just like Meg should be and so, if they are not there, then both Meg and Carrick do not want to be spotted doing whatever it is they are doing. She watches for another minute and sees the cart go past Farmer Thorne's house and drive on.

There's something wrong.

Her front door opens and The Robber stands just as she imagined. The silver buttons on his long, black coat flash and she can see the handle of the pistol peeping out between them.

"Where's the horse?" he asks.

"Follow me," and Meg is off, sprinting over the hard snow towards Farmer Thorne's yard with The Robber behind. Her heart is beating with worry and her stomach knotted in fear.

She'll have to go with him now, just so far, then she'll turn back.

CHAPTER SEVENTEEN

Meg runs down the lane with The Robber following, her boots slip a little on patches of ice but she does not fall. She can hear the man behind her and her back tingles knowing he is there. At The Thorne farmhouse, she puts her hands on the big gate and clambers over in two steps.

"Jamie is at the back of the yard," she yells over her shoulder. She gets a glimpse of him, tall and dark against the white snow.

"You already told me," he calls back as he gets over the gate. This is the dream she explained to him while he recovered on the floor near the chimney breast. This is what she imagined she would do, and now, it's real. Meg disappears inside a door and comes back out with bridle and reins.

"There's no time for a saddle," she says. "We have to get after Carrick." They run on past the stables with horse's heads pointed outwards, and to the last stall where there is the big brown face of the storm horse, Jamie. She opens the half-door and fits the bridle over his head and ears without effort, then does the straps under his mouth.

"I'll ride up front," says The Robber.

"Not on Jamie, he'll throw you," she leads the big gelding out into the yard and the beast nods his head up and down against the reins and the bridle. "We have to get him moving or he'll give us hell," she says. She goes up the mounting steps and swings her leg over the broad, brown back and puts her right hand on the horse's face to soothe him. Her touch is gentle. She holds out her hand for her Robber and his palms are soft as she pulls him up and, when he is behind her, his left arm goes around her waist to hold on. Meg feels her legs shiver with electricity. His grip is firm but not tight. His breath is hot on her neck. Her chest buzzes.

It feels right.

It's like she should be here, it makes her strong.

Meg walks Jamie out of the livery yard and round to the drive where she has not opened the gate. If she does not catch up with Carrick soon then she will not see which road he has taken. She drives her heels into the side of the horse and clicks her tongue and he is off like a rocket, his hooves spraying snow behind him as he builds up speed. Nobody rides Jamie this fast, and then, they are crunching across the icy gravel towards the gate. Like Meg, Jamie is not allowed to do what he wants, she grips his side with her legs and leans forward as they jump, The Robber tightens his hold also in readiness. For a few sweet seconds, they are in the air, the three of them, The Robber's strong arm around her waist and her teeth clenched. Jamie crashes back down into the snow, and without missing a stride they are away, moving quicker than Meg has been before towards the end of North Burton and the junction. One road goes left to Bishop Burton, another straight onwards to the York Road and the right towards Etton. She sees the cart track ahead in the snow and gives chase, off to the right and down, past another frozen pond and then they begin the climb upwards to Etton. Far away in front, they see the cart with the big figure of Carrick and Adam Gamble next to him cresting the hill.

Meg digs her heels into Jamie and he surges forward, she feels the power in his legs and body as he moves, his muscles smooth and even as he ploughs through the hard snow upwards. She does not know what she will do. She never does, but she is sure of one thing, that Carrick killed Dandy Jim and Carlos and that he means to kill Adam Gamble too, and she will not let that happen. It's like her mother said, now is not the time to listen, it's time for her to speak, time for her to act.

Jamie's silky brown body roars on through the snow as the cart disappears over the hill. The snow is powder here and the horse's hooves leave round imprints as they gallop. With the sun out and a cold westerly wind blowing across from the Wolds, if they were not following that cart, they could be going anywhere. They could be free. He is a skilful rider, this Robber, he must be to have remained seated at the jump previous. He too grips at Jamie below him with his legs and knees. Meg allows herself to look over her shoulder and his face is close to hers with his steely blue eyes looking out into the distance in front. She glances down and sees that he has drawn his pistol, and it is resting on his leg. It confuses her for a moment, but she does not have time to think about what it means as they continue at a gallop up the lane towards the big hill above Etton. This is what Jamie wants, to run as free as the open sky as fast as he can, forever and to hell with tomorrow. This is what Meg wants too.

They near the cart up in front. Carrick will not be travelling as fast as they are but Meg can see he is at a fair pace with the two big cartwheels bouncing as they clatter over the hard snow.

"Shoot him, Robber," she bellows over her shoulder against the wind. "Put a bullet in his back."

"You'll tire the horse," he calls into her ear. "Ease up."

She does not.

"Robber," she yells. "Robber, you owe me, shoot him, shoot him in the back of his fat head." The grip of the man behind suddenly tightens, and she feels him sigh in either pain or exasperation.

She has to be realistic.

The Robber has drawn his pistol to threaten Meg, not to shoot Carrick. Why would he care? He has his horse and his freedom. Meg will have to sort this herself, like always.

She gives Jamie a kick with both legs and flicks the reins to power him on. It makes The Robber jerk backwards with the unexpected movement and Meg reaches down to snatch the pistol from his hand. He needs both his arms around her now to stop himself from tumbling off into the snow. She grips the reigns with one hand and with the other, levels the pistol.

Here she is.

Meg.

The girl who looks after the chickens. The one who mucks out the pigs. The one you feel sorry about at Christmas because she is so plain and her husband left her to go to war and never came back. The one who lives with that nasty old woman. Here she is, riding atop a shiny brown bay in the snow with a flintlock pistol held out in front of her. Clinging to her waist in shock, a robber from The Dandy Gang, and the finest Pearlman outside of London. In front, whipping at his horse to get away, Carrick, the foul-mouthed bitter rector to who Mr Pennyman turned a blind eye because he was too weak to stand up to him.

There is no time to think.

Meg points the gun and squeezes the heavy trigger at Carrick now ten yards in front; her hand shakes while the black powder burns and then, the nuzzle roars out with a blast of smoke and fire, the pistol recoils. Meg's aim is poor, and shooting from a horse is difficult anyway, and at a gallop, it's twice as hard. The bullet flies, not at Carrick's head as Meg had hoped, but somewhere to the left and down, the heavy lead ball strikes the axel that connects the wheel to the cart and the wood splinters and snaps. There's too much weight where Carrick sits and the wheel comes loose, the cart pitches forward to the left. Carrick tumbles out, headfirst into the snow as does Adam Gamble and the dog cage clatters off the flatbed over the seat with the animal yelping inside. Meg thunders past and pulls hard on the reins to slow Jamie down. The big bay fights against her but he is tired from the run.

"I doubt even my Carlos could have made that shot, lass," whispers The Robber from behind. He takes the big pistol from her as she brings her leg over and slides off Jamie into the snow. There's no movement from Carrick, but Adam Gamble is groaning and the dog is whining, high pitched and pitiful.

"He'll not be dead, Robber," says Meg. "Ready your gun I

tell you." On the horse, he is doing just that and at a speed that Marlborough himself would be impressed by. Meg makes her way to the mess of broken wood and the noise of the dog. There's a scrabbling sound and then the sharp yell of Adam Gamble as Carrick stands up and drags the boy towards him by the neck, in the big man's left hand is a knife, and he holds this up to the lad's throat.

"Don't you come any closer," he barks. "I'll kill him." Meg stops and looks back at her Robber who slips from Jamie's back with his pistol, now reloaded, pointed in Carrick's direction. The Robber is calm as he examines the two figures he has never seen before, he knows them alright, though, Meg has told him all about them. He knows this is Adam Gamble and the big, angry figure is Carrick The Rector from St Michael's. He levels the pistol as he walks forward, aiming down the barrel with one squinting eye.

"I said get back," yells Carrick. The dog has stopped whining now it can see its master, although the cage rolled upside down, the dog is the right way up inside but trapped still. The Robber takes a few more paces until he is ten yards away from Adam Gamble's wide eyes. A wind picks up on top of the hill. There's a moment of silence as the four of them look at each other.

"If you kill the boy, you have nothing to bargain with," says The Robber. "At this range, there's a good chance that I'll be able to hit you and not him, or if I do shoot the boy by accident, there's the likelihood that it will go through him and into you."

"Shoot him," yells Meg. The Robber with the pistol holds his hand up to calm her. Carrick is nervous.

"What is it you want, Carrick?" he asks. "Perhaps there's a way we can all come out of this situation. First of all, however, I'd like to explain that all I want is for young Adam here to be able to go home to his family?"

"Just who in God's name are you?" asks Carrick as he pulls

Adam backwards towards the dog cage and his foot kicks at the catch that is now the wrong way up. The door does not open and the beast within growls upwards in fear.

The Robber has been in enough situations to know when the time for talking is over. He has only heard about Carrick through Meg, but he can see that the man is not classically trained as a scholar, he holds the knife too well in his right hand, and, even as The Robber moves forwards, Carrick tries again at the cage to set his dog free and give himself the upper hand. There will be no parle with this one. Carrick sees his chance. He pushes young Adam away from him towards The Robber, so he can bend down and unhook the catch to free his dog.

The pistol fires from a few yards and there is the puff of smoke and a flash, but The Robber remains frozen with the weapon pointed at Carrick fiddling with the catch on the cage. It will be three seconds before they know it's a misfire and if the lead ball will fly, red hot from the nozzle of the pistol. Guns can take a few seconds to shoot. Sometimes they don't shoot at all. That's why the handle of The Robber's pistol is solid, smooth and heavy mahogany, perfect for clubbing someone. The first second passes. Carrick can't seem to get the catch for the door open, it has been bent in the accident. Another second passes and The Robber keeps the gun steady as his eyebrows rise. There will only be enough time for this one shot, and if he gets that door open before the black powder lights, The Robber will have to shoot the dog. The third second passes and Carrick rattles the catch, it is about to come free in his hand. The side of his mouth grins.

The gun has misfired. Perhaps the powder was wet. Perhaps The Robber did not load it properly. This is not a rare thing to happen.

Carrick is going to open the cage and his great German hunting dog will be free. Then, there will be no stopping him.

Before he can open the door, out of the winter evening

with her fist tight, Meg bares her full weight down onto Carrick's face. She cracks him just under the left eye and he staggers backwards away from the cage with a grunt. The Robber dances towards him, the butt of the gun ready to finish the job, but Carrick is not for giving up. The man who has already defeated Carlos outside the church and Dandy Jim inside, will not be rubbed out so quickly. As The Robber moves in for the strike, Carrick brings his fist upwards into his thin stomach – the same stomach that less than a week earlier, Carlos cut deep into with his blade. The man Meg brought back from the dead, crumples in the middle and falls to his knees in pain. Carrick now stands to his full height and he wears a dumb, cruel grin as he looks across at Meg and then round to Adam Gamble. The blow she dealt him a few seconds earlier has barely registered.

"Not much of a fighter, is he, this one?" says Carrick as the figure of The Robber groans in pain below him. "I'll get Bear out, shall I?" he continues. Carrick's mood is cocky as he steps over to his hunting dog in the cage. Meg stands next to it with her fists clenched. She is afraid of this big man, but if he frees the dog, she and Adam Gamble will be dead. Carrick stops when he sees her standing over it, and the dog inside has its lips curled back and is growling at her, low and nasty.

"You're going to stop me, are you?" says Carrick. His face has lost all emotion, his eyes are black and narrow and the purple bruise from Dandy Jim's pistol handle on his face makes his skin discoloured and grotesque.

"They'll come after you," she says. "That Captain Salter and Pennyman and Danny Reed, they'll hunt you."

"Those fools? Weak kneed Pennyman? The Captain who thinks he was at Blenheim? Those men will not hunt me, Meg. I'll go back there and they will welcome me with open arms. I'll even take them the body of another robber. They'll thank me."

He steps forward towards the cage and Meg swings for

him. She's not a fighter. Carrick, a good foot taller, slaps her across the cheek with his rough hand and the world shakes in her head. He grabs her by the hair before she falls and slams her down onto the snow, and then, he is on top of her, both his heavy hands go to her throat and his lank, wet hair falls into her face. He uses his legs to get between hers and she struggles. He stinks, his face is rancid and ugly, she can see his rotten teeth as he grins. Carrick pushes down on her, heavy and rude with his big hands so she is powerless to stop him from doing what he is about to do, and yet, there is something familiar about the position Meg finds herself in. There's one story she has heard a hundred times before. It is 1685 and The Walkington Show, Nana has been chosen to fight for North Burton because she is the biggest lass with the biggest mouth. The brute has got her onto the floor, and his hands are around her throat while the Walkington lads laugh and jeer. Carrick huffs and grimaces as he strangles Meg. She reaches up and grabs his own neck with her two hands then begins to apply pressure. Carrick grins and allows this. He smiles. Meg is a child to him, however strong her hands are from all those years of work, they are not as strong as Carrick's neck. He begins to laugh, not wickedly, but genuine, like he is being tickled and this is fun. Meg grits her teeth and tries to dig her thumbs into him, Carrick responds also, putting more weight on her throat. She does not want his ugly face to be the last thing she sees but, like always, if Meg doesn't do the job, then nobody else will.

She feels her strength slipping away, her legs are shivering with exhaustion, her throat is dry, her chest heaves, her neck is slowly being crushed. Carrick belly laughs into the cold early evening air and into her face. Meg should laugh too at how ridiculous it all is, ten minutes ago she was on top of a great bay horse with thoughts of running from North Burton at the front of her mind. Now, she is alone again. Meg, wallflower Meg with her big hands and curly, unruly blonde hair, with her temper and sad eyes who looks after Nana out of duty not out of love. Meg feels Carrick's neck tense as she tries to hurt him. She thinks back to her mother alone in her chair in the cottage in Etton, her tiny body bent forward and her hands skeletal on her lap. She waited to tell Meg, she kept death away to tell her daughter that she was not alone.

It's time.

Meg needs her help.

Aren't these palms that grip Carrick's neck the same ones that held her mother's hand, and they in turn, that held her grandmother's and so on, down the centuries to every woman who came before and worked these fields? If ever you need our help, Meg, her mother had said. Just call. There's a gust of wind coming across the dale up from Etton. It blows powdered snow over the dry-stone walls.

"Mother," she whispers. Meg feels a surge through her, she digs her thumbs into his pale white neck. Carrick stops laughing. She has hurt him if only a little. Time for him to stop messing around and get this job done, but, there is more fight in Meg than Carrick expected.

She feels her world darkening but holds his throat tight. Everything is there in her iron grip, The Robber's eyes, Nana and her nagging about her legs, little Richie sleeping on her knee every night by the fire, the pitying eyes of Miss Charlotte, the ineffective slap of Mr Pennyman, her wet husband John who went off to fight for the Duke of Marlborough and never came home. All of this is here and more, her mother's help is there too, it's what makes her strong. Carrick begins to struggle as Meg presses on his throat, the big hunting dog whines and barks next to them in its cage. Meg's teeth grit in effort, of course, she cannot beat him, but she will not give in.

Adam Gamble appears behind the big Rector, carrying the pistol like a club by its wrong end. He's a good lad is Adam Gamble, a good North Burton lad who won't give up when others might. He swings the handle into the back of Carrick's skull with a hollow clunk, the shock is enough to stop the big man from fighting for a split second and his head lolls to the side, his hands suddenly limp on Meg's throat as she gasps in air. She does not pause, the hands grip his neck yet as his eyes roll from the shock. Adam Gamble swings the pistol handle behind his head and brings it down on the Rector again in a smooth stroke, there is anger behind the heavy mahogany, for everything this big man has done to Adam Gamble and his poor father also. Adam wishes he had done this the night previous when he had heard Dandy Jim suffering. The Rector's brain rattles and he loses his grip altogether as Meg presses home her advantage, his body slumps sidewards and their roles are reversed because Meg will not let go of his neck. She is on top of him now with her thumbs pushing deep into his throat. Meg's temper is in her mouth and her nose is bleeding. His arms flail and grab at her, but she can feel his strength ebbing away as she jerks her body forward to assist her thumbs, so that they dig deeper into his windpipe. His chest heaves and his face begins with a purple hue and still, Meg does not let go. Carrick has taken a fair beating over the last day or so, he feels his eyes going dim and Meg's hands are rock-solid around his neck. The two heavy blows that Adam Gamble landed on the back of his head burn and send pain across his skull and face. Meg's green eyes look down on him, she cannot let go, even if she wants to. It takes a few minutes for Carrick to lose focus and, when his body is still, she keeps her hands tight around his throat, she is shaking.

"Adam," she calls. "Bring me the pistol." The boy appears next to her and holds the gun out. She does not dare to get off Carrick's neck, but she has to, she sits back, grabs the pistol, and, as soon as she has it, smashes the handle into the dead man's face. She hammers it down a good few times till the nose caves in, until Adam Gamble calls to her in a soft, shaky voice.

"He's gone, Meg. He's gone."

Adam Gamble does not look well as he sits on the side of the broken cart. He has a big dog bite on his calf and the wound is nasty. Meg squats down and rolls up his wide britches so she can see. The Robber has recovered himself and finds his pistol from where Meg left it next to the body of Carrick. He wipes blood from the handle with a handkerchief and checks the flintlock action. He looks white and a line of blood runs from his nose.

"Did the wound come apart?" Meg asks him.

"I don't think so." He sounds different. The Robber loads the pistol once again. More delicately this time so he knows it will work. Meg looks up at him and gives a weak smile. He does not return it.

"Why do you need the pistol?" she asks.

"A precaution," he answers. Meg stands and feels dizzy as she does so. Her hands are black with mud and her petticoat ripped, her hair is in knots. The Robber goes back to Jamie and stands facing the horse's body with his head down as he examines his pistol. Meg walks a few paces towards him on unsteady feet.

"Not one more step, Miss," he says without turning around. His voice really is different.

"What is it?" asks Meg.

"I think you can make it back to North Burton, the boy is injured but he can still walk." Meg's legs tingle. She did not believe that she would go with him, but now that Adam Gamble is safe, now that Nana knows she is going, now that they are out in the country with the big bay Jamie in front of them, now she sees that it could be true, she wants it. You can never believe something until it is real. Here it is. It's real. She moves forward. "Not another step," he repeats. She doesn't want to believe it.

"Adam Gamble is a strong lad," she says. Her voice is high and earnest. "He'll make it back to North Burton in time for supper. It's only a few miles. You are overly concerned,

Robber. There is no need to fear for him." The man turns and Meg can see that he has done the buttons up on his long coat and around his neck is a black scarf. He pulls it over his nose like a true highwayman and then, levels the barrel of his pistol at Meg's chest.

"Not one more step," his voice is stone.

"You wouldn't," she whispers. He moves the gun so that it points at Adam Gamble who sits on the broken cart.

"I would," he says. This is not the voice that Meg knows. She steps back.

"All the things you told me," says Meg.

"Partly true, Miss, you have the gift of healing."

"What are you going to do? Get on Jamie and leave?"

"Yes. Is that so hard to believe?" Meg is confused. She knew that they were lies but she allowed herself to believe them.

"What about me? What about us?"

"There is nothing between us, Miss. I apologise. We do what we must to survive. You know well enough, as does your Rector there with his neck snapped. I am a pearlman, a robber, a highwayman. It's my business to lie. You knew this and you told me so." Meg's eyes well.

Her dirty hand comes to her face to cover her nose and eyes, and she sobs, silent and honest. She does not want to cry, not in front of him. The Robber uses the reins to help clamber up onto the horse's back and he steadies himself. Meg steps forwards and he raises his pistol to her once more.

"You could take me with you," she says. Her voice is broken. "I wouldn't be any trouble. I don't take up much space and I can see to your wound." The Robber grabs at Jamie's reins with his free hand and he kicks with both legs. There are no words needed now.

She watches him ride away down the track, his black cloak billowing out behind him.

217

Meg patches up Adam Gamble's leg as best she can. She has wrapped a tight bit of cloth around the top of his thigh to stop any bleeding. The wound will need to be cleaned because dog bites are nasty. They do not speak, either of them. Meg has resolved to carry the boy to North Burton, piggyback. It will take perhaps less than an hour. The dog yelps intermittently. Meg is glad it is still in its cage.

She sees movement below them on the horizon. Two horses ride up from the direction of North Burton. There's a flash of red to Captain Salter's tunic and the other rider is tall, she can see blonde hair coming out from under his black three-cornered hat, it is the coachman and constable, Danny Reed.

This is far from over.

They stop some distance off at The Captain's order and dismount. Danny Reed removes his musket from the brown bay and The Captain's own pistol is tucked into a clean leather holster at his side. They both have a look of disdain and confusion as they approach.

"Sit down on the cart there, Meg, go on, sit down next to Adam, nice and easy," it's the voice of Danny Reed, his musket in both hands, ready but not threatening.

"We're looking for Carrick. How did you get here?" asks The Captain.

"I stole a horse, I stole one of Farmer Thorne's bays, Jamie.

"You rode him?" asks Danny Reed with a note of incredulity.

"Aye."

"Well, where is he now?"

"He bolted," answers Meg.

"And what's happened here?" Captain Salter surveys the wreckage of the cart, the broken axle, the dog in the cage, growling as it looks up at him. He sees the body of Carrick laid on his back and the electricity of fear runs up his legs. "Mr Reed!" he calls to the constable.

They examine the body. The Captain pokes at Carrick's crumpled face with his fingers in black leather gloves. He sees the marks on the Rector's neck.

"Can you explain this?" he calls to Meg. There's no reason to lie.

"I killed him," she says. Danny Reed grimaces.

"You killed Carrick?" he asks.

"Yes. He would have killed me had I not. He would have fed us both to his beast." Danny Reed cannot understand this for a moment. Then he remembers Carrick threatening the boy with his dog against the church walls, thinks back to the comments Mr Pennyman made about The Rector as well.

"Is it true, Adam?"

"Yes," says the boy. "She throttled him." There is a faraway quality to Adam Gamble's voice as he sits there with one of the legs in his britches rolled up over his knee.

"Those men he killed," says Meg. "They were looking for him, perhaps like you are, Captain." Meg finds the lie comes easily. She wants this to be over and she will bend the truth to suit her, and to help all of them in North Burton.

"I guess we'll never know if he's the man you were looking for," says Danny Reed to Captain Salter.

"We will," replies the red-faced man. "He'll be carrying it."

"Carrying what?"

"The thing he stole." The Captain walks over and looks down at the dead figure of Carrick. He begins to check the pockets. He pats the outside ones and undoes the buttons on the dead man's tunic to reveal his hairy chest. The smell is foul and he puts the back of his hand to his nose in disgust. There, on a long chain around Carrick's neck is a ring. It is a silver circle with a black topaz in the middle. The Captain straightens up.

"It's the ring I'm looking for," he says.

"I didn't know there was a ring," says Danny Reed.

"Oh yes, there was a ring. I didn't say anything about it,

but now I see that, plainly, this is the man who I was looking for." Danny Reed gives a weak smile. Meg and Adam Gamble watch as The Captain walks over to them. They can see, all of them, that this man is making it all up as he goes along. Captain Salter looks down on Meg with a mixture of disgust and pity.

"You killed him, you say?"

"Yes, Sir."

"How?"

"I strangled him."

"Really?

"Yes, Sir. Then I smashed his face in with a rock." Meg does not need to mention the robber's pistol.

"Nobody will believe that," says Captain Salter. He removes his pistol from the holster on his belt and holds it pointing upwards.

"Now just a minute," calls Danny Reed. "If Meg has done wrong then she'll face the court and a trial. We'll do this right, Captain." There's steel in the young man's voice.

Captain Salter huffs through his nose as he looks down at Meg and his eyes are narrow in hatred, he isn't going to hurt her. The little man walks to the body of Carrick once more and stands at his feet, looking at the big man. He points the gun down, aims for a moment, and then pulls the trigger. The body shudders with the impact of the bullet and Meg turns away so she doesn't see what he's done. The Captain looks up at Danny Reed and then to Meg and Adam Gamble. He begins his lie that will soon be the only truth.

"I shot him in his face," he says. "Can you believe it? I mean, he had taken off in flight when he knew I was onto him. He'd thought to leave when there was a celebration up at The Pennyman Estate. You and I, Mr Reed, we followed him and found him, with his cart with a broken wheel. When I informed him that I knew his identity, and that he was to come with me, he refused and took this poor wretch girl to his chest, threatened to kill her if we didn't let him go." The Captain beams and his teeth are an off-yellow colour under the red well-groomed moustache. "So I shot him, over her shoulder, I shot him in the face. I agree with you, Mr Reed, it was one of the finest examples of marksmanship you have ever seen, so quick and accurate and so very right. He was a man who deserved to die, very much. The Duke of Marlborough himself will be delighted with the news."

"That did not happen," says Danny Reed. He looks across at Meg and she shakes her head as if he should not have said it. Black can be green or water can be milk if you are told it is. The little Captain approaches Danny Reed.

"You have a long way to go, Mr Reed. I like you, I can see why Mr Pennyman likes you. You have a sense of right and wrong and you have a duty to the people you serve, we can see that. However, this is a matter of national interest and indeed the King's interest. Let's get his body loaded up onto the cart horse here. You, girl, come on and help Mr Reed, you've had enough time sitting on your arse already while we've been doing the work. If it weren't for me, this Carrick fellow would have strangled you." Meg stands up and moves towards the body. It's that easy. The Captain just has to believe it has happened, and it is true.

"What's wrong with you lad?" asks the Captain to Adam Gamble.

"The dog bit me, Sir," he answers. There's a little of himself in this response.

"Can you walk?"

"A little, Sir."

"Well then, help them load the body onto the horse, will you?"

Carrick's body is heavy. They put him stomach down over the cart horse's back and tie it on with the long reins. Adam Gamble can hardly put any weight on his left leg but he tries. Meg and Danny Reed do the hard work. All the while the dog

barks in its cage, at points it whines, but mostly it yelps at
Carrick's dead body. Maybe it knows. Dogs aren't bad, this
Bear isn't bad, it's been broken with the way it's been treated,
that's all.

The Captain watches them work and reloads his pistol. He
is clumsy, awkward even. Black powder spills from the
package he rips open with his teeth. He uses the ramrod a little
too hard, almost like he has not loaded a gun many times
before.

When Carrick is on the horse proper with his big hands
hanging over one side and his legs the other, The Captain steps
over to the hulking dog in the cage. He points his pistol down
at the creature and it looks up at him, the lips curl back in fear
showing yellow, sharp teeth. He grins and aims, narrows one
of his eyes and pulls the trigger. There's the smoke and boom
and then a yelp. The little man wanders back to his horse and
puts his pistol back into his belt, it takes him a couple of
attempts to fit the nuzzle into the holster.

Captain Salter mounts up. Danny Reed is already in place
and leading the cart horse with Carrick's body on it. The
Captain looks down at Meg.

"You'll have to walk," he says. She looks up at him and
then down to her feet in servitude, and nods. "The lad will be
fine, just try to keep your weight off your bad leg, son."

Meg and Adam Gamble watch the three horses go down
the hill towards North Burton. They can hear the dog whining
from its cage behind. She will have to carry Adam Gamble
back down into the village after all. It's not so far.

At the cage, the dog, Bear has not been shot enough to kill
it. The bullet went through its shoulder and shattered one of
its front legs but it is still very much alive. The orange eyes
watch Meg as she finds a broken spoke from the cartwheel.
She picks off the bits so that the end is sharp and gently pushes
it through the bars to the dog's neck. She waits for a few

moments until the dog calms then jams it down with force. It's not a pleasant job but better than leave the animal to die a slow death.

The sun is getting low and it's cold. Adam Gamble is not dressed to be out in the snow and neither is Meg. She manages to get him onto her back and he wraps his hands around her neck and chest. It's a good job he's so thin.

"Thank you," he says.

"It's what we do, people round here, we help each other. It's what you did for me back there, Adam Gamble." These could be Nana's words.

"Who was that man?" asks the boy.

"Which man?"

"The one with the pistol. The one who would not take you with him."

"Nobody," answers Meg. "You never saw him and he was never here."

CHAPTER EIGHTEEN

It's just getting dark when Meg arrives back to the cottage in North Burton. She is grey with fatigue. Adam Gamble is not heavy for a few yards, but for a mile he is a dead weight. She sets him down at her front door, she will have to see to his bite tomorrow morning when there is enough light.

"Can you make it home?" she asks. He nods. "You're a brave lad, Adam Gamble," she adds.

"I love you, Meg," he says. The words are true. They hug, and then he limps the few yards to his own front door.

Inside Nana has made the fire and she sits in her chair. She has that daft look on her face which means she's drunk. Richie runs to Meg and she bends to pick him up as she sits down on the bench with him on her knee.

"What's gone on?" asks Nana. "We heard talk of Carrick dead, The Captain shot him in the face and that you and Adam Gamble were taken prisoner by him. Are you hurt?"

"No," says Meg. "We're both ok and Adam is back home also. He was bit by that horrible dog."

"Oh lass, sit yourself down, you look in a terrible state."

"What about the feast?"

"One of the kitchen lasses saw Carrick taking young Adam Gamble away in his cart, and when Danny Reed heard about it, he went after him with The Captain. After they got back and we saw Carrick's body and listened to what had happened, it was all over, but we had a good fill before that. I didn't know if I'd see you again," Nana is drunk but not profoundly so, she still has sense to her. "What about your Robber? I thought you might have gone off with him." Meg looks down on Richie, she does not like to admit this with him here.

"He wouldn't have me, Nana and I begged him."

The old woman looks down into the fire and her eyes mist over with sadness.

"You'd have ended up a whore somewhere, Meg. Just a drunk whore in Leeds or York, there'd be a good few years with him before that though, and it might have been worth it. You'll never know. Have you given up on my John?"

"He's not coming back, Nana. You know that."

"That Robber nabbed his ring."

"What?"

"While we were out the bastard went through my chair and everything that was inside. He pinched my best brooch and the wedding ring that John left here when he went to fight. The bastard. We should have let him die."

"He lied to me," says Meg.

"That's what men do." Nana leans over and picks up a cloth bag from beside her chair. She pulls out a bottle of something that Granddad Blackwood pilfered from the celebration at the barn. She passes the bottle to Meg.

"I've got two of these big sugar buns for you, Meg, as well. There were plenty of them. Archer Farthing ate so many he was sick." Meg looks at the bottle.

"I don't want it, Nana. I don't want anything."

"Have some lass, I promise it will take the edge off. It'll loosen you up as well and help you talk. You don't talk enough as it is."

"Talking is for fools."

"Aye, and which one of us is not a fool?" Sometimes Nana is the best Nana in the whole world. Meg takes out the cork and it makes a hollow pop. She feels shame. Shame that she would have left Nana and Richie alone, shame that The Robber did not want her and probably, that no one will want her. Why would they? She is the lowest of all the creatures in North Burton. She takes a swig and the liquid burns her mouth and throat so she coughs. She fights it down.

"What's there to talk about, Nana? What have I got to tell anyone? I did wrong. I did wrong and it blew back in my face and now I'm here. I'm sorry, Nana and I'm sorry only because it didn't work out for me." She takes another gulp.

"That's it, lass," says Nana. "Drink it up. Take comfort in it. You deserve it. You don't need to apologize to me, you do what you have to do to get by and you get your love where you can, and you grab it with both hands too. I would have done no different. Being perfect and good and rich, being happy, that's for Miss Charlotte and Mr Pennyman, not for working folk like us. We live right now, and so long as there's enough to fill our bellies and there's a warm arm to go round us, then there's no wiping the smile off our faces."

"Don't you wish for more, Nana? Don't you get sick of it? Don't you get tired of North Burton?"

"Aye, but you start thinking like that, then they've won, the Pennymans and that horrible Captain."

Meg takes another pull. It is warming her up.

"He was a terrible bastard that Robber," says Meg.

"That's it, lass," says Nana. "He was a bastard and he nicked your husband's ring as well."

The brandy made Meg sleep for an hour or so, but she is awake before it is light. Her face stings from where Carrick struck her, her neck is bruised. Richie wriggles on her lap, her throat is dry and her legs burn with pain. She killed a man yesterday. She sees the red face of Carrick as she strangles him and she does not feel anything at all. It was like pulling a weed out of the garden or twisting the head off one of her sick hens who will not make it through the night. Mr Pennyman and the good folk in the big houses up at Beverley would not understand this, but that is what had to happen to Carrick – he was poison and if nobody else was going to stop him, Meg was. Bad jobs have to be done.

The sky outside turns grey, but it is not so cold. The fire is dead in the hearth and Meg's face wears no emotion. The Robber did not want her and she can feel her heart hardening and freezing in her chest, like it hardened for her own mother,

226

like it hardened for Nana and maybe all the folk of North Burton, and all the folk of the world when they become old enough. It is the realisation that you are ugly and worthless, and there is no getting away from it because it will not change, and there will be no one to love you, ever; and all that stretches before you is a lifetime of work and duty. There is no need to be saddened by this, it's the truth, and anyone who thinks it is any other way is a child, or a fool, or so rich that they have other people to help them get dressed.

There are two dull thumps at the door. Meg looks up with a frown. Then two more thumps. If it were anyone friendly, they would knock. Two more thumps sound. She peels Richie off her knee.

"Who in God's name is that?" calls Nana in the half-darkness. The thumps come again.

Meg stands and opens the door, outside, in the grey morning with his face dark is Danny Reed. His three-cornered hat is low over his eyes and he looks down on her with flared nostrils.

"I'm sorry, Meg," he says. "You and Nana, you'll have to leave the house. Mr Pennyman is having you evicted." She looks past the tall man and, a hundred yards away, dressed in a thick cloak is the frowning face of Mr Pennyman. Next to him is Captain Salter with his red coat done up to his neck.

"On what grounds?" asks Meg.

"There's no man in the house. These aren't my rules, you understand. These are the laws of the land. My hands are forced on this." Danny looks sorry. This will not be his doing. It will probably not even be Pennyman's doing. It will be the little Captain Salter, eager to have things done as they should be. "So, you'll have to leave," adds Danny Reed.

"Now?"

"You've got ten minutes to get your things."

"Where are we to go?"

"What in God's name is this!" calls Nana. She has struggled

227

to the front door and appears next to Meg with her jowly, angry face. She shouts as loud as she can to wake as many of the other folk in the street.

"You're being evicted, woman," calls The Captain. "There's no man in your house and therefore Mr Pennyman has the right to take back his property."

"I'm a widow," she bellows, "and I have rights to this house till I die. My husband worked all his life for the Pennyman family, worked hard he did as well. This is my house by right, till I die," she repeats. Nana has sense. Along the street, Granddad Blackwood steps out of his house into the cold as he rubs sleep from his eyes. Hannah Farthing's door opens also and Mr Farthing comes to see what the shouting is about behind her.

"What's going on?" he asks.

"Nana is to be evicted, Mr Farthing, Pennyman's orders," calls Danny Reed. "With no man in the house, she has no legal right to live in it. This is the law." Pennyman himself looks on with a frown.

"It's the middle of winter," says Granddad Blackwood. "You can't throw her out the house, where will she go? She's an old woman." The Captain calls back:

"You watch your mouth, old man. Mr Pennyman owns all these houses and this whole village. One word from him and you'll be out as well."

"Who'll farm his land if we're sleeping in the woods?" Hannah Farthing cannot stop herself from shouting this. Meg steps out into the street. There's no point in speaking to Danny Reed. This is not his decision, he is just the mouthpiece. She addresses Mr Pennyman.

"I'm married, Sir. My husband is away fighting for King and country. What is to become of him if he returns and his home is gone?" Mr Pennyman does not answer.

"It has been more than four years, Meg," Danny Reed speaks with reason. "He'll not return. Not after all this time."

228

Meg looks over her shoulder at Nana behind her. The old woman returns her stare. There is an understanding between these two women. They will survive this. The world has already broken them, so many times that there is nothing that can be of any surprise, not now.

"Drag them out into the street, Mr Reed," calls The Captain. "If they can't hurry up." It has only been five minutes since this started, but the folk of North Burton are watching. All the Farthings are outside, Miles Blackwood too, even Adam Gamble stands in the street listening to this unfold. "I said drag them out, Mr Reed, drag her out by her hair. These people have had it too easy, they've taken advantage of the good nature of Mr Pennyman for far too long."

Danny Reed looks at Captain Salter with his red face and red moustache. He does not want to do this and he is caught between his duty and his humanity. The Captain steps forward and bellows like he is commanding troops, his hand goes to the pistol on his belt as if he is to draw it. "For God's sake, Mr Reed, do your bloody duty, or do I have to do everything myself?"

Richie catches sight of a lone figure standing up the street fifty yards away, he points. The man has a musket raised to his eyes. He's tall. Six foot two. On his head is a black tricorn hat and he wears a grubby red jacket. The red of the English army. His eyes are steel blue in the cold of the morning.

"Hold," he yells. The Captain turns to see this thin and tall man with the morning sun shining behind him.

"Who are you to point a gun at me?" he spits.

"This is my property," calls the man.

"You better put that musket down, soldier. I'm an officer."

"I will, just as soon as you step away from my wife."

This is new.

Meg steps back. She and Nana gawp at the figure, gallant with his musket trained on the little Captain. He looks like he can shoot it too. There's a silver pistol at his belt.

It is The Robber.

It could never be John.

The Robber is a foot taller. He's more handsome. He has black hair where John's hair was brown. There is a gravity to this one, with a commanding stare looking down the barrel of the musket, someone who may well put a lead ball through Captain Salter. John was shrinking, shy and quiet. You could forget he was there. This is not John. Anyone who knew him would tell you so, right away.

There is what is real and then there is what is true.

Richie is not Nana's son. She took him in when one of the servant girls at the house died while having him, but, the real truth is, that he is her son. This is North Burton. You have to take your love and your chance where you can find it, you have to grab it with both hands and clutch it to your breast – this is what is true. The old woman knows what is real and what is not. In a split second, her wise face grasps what needs to be done.

"Oh, John," she cries. "You've come back." The Captain turns.

"Who is this man?"

"It's my boy, John," says Nana. She must make this seem convincing as she struggles to walk, one of her hips dipping as she hobbles towards the figure. A few feet away she stops. The Robber lowers his musket and looks down at her.

"Mother," he says with a smile. Meg steps forward also and looks up at him. She cannot quite believe it. "My Meg," he whispers, his face is earnest. "I still have your ring." He shows his left hand and on the middle finger is the wedding band that the evening previous, The Robber stole from Nana's chair. She does not know how, but Meg's feet carry her forward and The Robber lowers the musket to one hand. They embrace and she grips him tight as he holds her, their cheeks pressed together. It is strong and real so Meg does not have to make it look convincing, and a tear rolls down her muddy cheek.

The faces of North Burton watch as the two embrace. They look good together. Hannah Farthing puts her hand over her mouth as if she might cry. Adam Gamble smiles wide for the first time in three days. Danny Reed takes off his hat and grins. Granddad Blackwood, like his son Miles both know that this cannot be John, but it might as well be if Nana wishes it. Farmer Thorne arrives from up the street after this stranger returned his horse, Jamie, and it makes sense now that the man seemed to know who he was.

Mr Pennyman walks to the couple and Meg peels herself from The Robber, her face is red and ashamed, guilty even.

"I'll expect you back at work tomorrow, John," says Mr Pennyman. "Just the same. Spend the day with your family, today."

"Thank you, Mr Pennyman, Sir."

"I can see that the years have changed you, considerably."

"Aye Sir, I'm more of a man than I used to be. That's what battle does."

Pennyman nods, though he would not know if this is true.

Inside the house, with the door closed, the air is cold. Nana struggles to her chair next to the fire and Meg stands behind her. Richie goes to her side and The Robber, now John, stands with his back to the door. He takes off his hat. From the rafters, Dutchy looks down with her deaf ears pricked up and green eyes wide.

"What did you come back for?" asks Nana. He removes a saddle bag from his shoulder and tosses it on the floor. There's the clink of coins from within the leather as it hits the ground.

"The silver I promised," he answers.

"You're not a very good robber, are you?" says Nana. "I'd have been off, me, off like a good one with all this silver."

"I was an exceptionally good robber, Nana. I was one of the best. They called me a pearlman because I could sense what was worth something and what was not."

231

"What did you come back here for, then?" asks Nana again.

"I came back for her," he says as he nods towards Meg. He struggles with the words that are not lies, not lies for the first time in so long that is difficult for him to get them out. "She's worth something, she's valuable."

"My Meg?"

"My Meg, now, Nana. If she'll have it."

"You want to be John? You want to live this life with us in this little house?" Nana's voice is incredulous.

"I want to be an honest man, a working man, a husband. I want to live in peace."

"You'll be off at the first chance you get."

"Be quiet, Nana." It's Meg. Her fists are clenched and her fingernails dig into her palms. She does not dare to believe that it is true. Her mother told her, love was close and that she had to reach out and be brave enough to take it, and that it was the time to speak and not to listen.

"Could you not have told me you would return, Robber?" she asks. His face is stern:

"In truth, I did not know I would. I found my silver where it was hidden, and I found Dandy Jim's camp in the woods too and I spent the night. At first light, I saw Carlos's coat, the one I wear now. He would never have parted with it. That and the ring, and it was my chance to return. If you had come with me, you know you would have been dead in a few years, perhaps sooner. It was out of kindness that I left you, that life is no life at all."

"Well, you can't stay here," blurts out Nana. "There's not enough room." She hopes her voice will block out the electricity between these two, but Meg's eyes already blaze at the man who is now John. He stares down at her in the same way. Nana feels the skin on her arms and back shiver with passion, and for a few moments, the room smoulders.

Later, Nana will tell what a pain it is to have him back in the house, and how he and Meg are like new lovebirds fresh